JAMES RAYBURN

THE TRUTH ITSELF

BLACK
STONE
PUBLISHING

Copyright © 2018 by James Rayburn
Published in 2018 by Blackstone Publishing
Cover and book design by Kathryn Galloway English

Printed in the United States of America

First edition: 2018
ISBN 978-1-5385-0748-3
Fiction / Thrillers / Espionage

1 3 5 7 9 10 8 6 4 2

CIP data for this book is available
from the Library of Congress

Blackstone Publishing
31 Mistletoe Rd.
Ashland, OR 97520

www.BlackstonePublishing.com

In memory of Clive Sacke

Grow your tree of falsehood from a small grain of truth...
Let your lie be even more logical than the truth itself.
—CZESLAW MILOSZ

Political language...is designed to make lies sound truthful and murder respectable, and to give an appearance of solidity to pure wind.
—GEORGE ORWELL

ONE

When Kate Swift, sitting at the wheel of her old Jeep, saw the two young men break the line of winter-stripped birches on the perimeter of the elementary school, she knew it was over. As she watched them trudge through the fresh snow toward the squat brick building, the tails of their identical black trench coats flapping in the raw wind that knifed down from Canada, she knew that the artfully spun weaving of half truths and carefully calibrated lies that had been her life story these last two years was about to be blown away like gossamer.

"It's here," she said to herself. "It's here, Kate."

As she spoke her name—her *real* name, not the one she had been hiding under in this tiny northern Vermont town—she whip-panned from the youths to the knot of first graders hurtling into the school, glimpsing her daughter's long dark hair and pink Hello Kitty backpack disappearing through the open glass doors.

It was here, but it hadn't come the way she'd always feared: a policeman's midnight knock at her door or a sniper's bullet fired from the woods. No, watching the advancing boys, she felt the cold breath of karma on the back of her neck.

A familiar rush of adrenaline charged Kate's body, and she heard the thrum of blood in her ears as she reached for the door handle of the Jeep and stepped down, her leather boots sinking into the snow.

She choked back a yell, knowing her daughter wouldn't hear her but *they* would. The young men, who were now free of the snow, were marching in step like catwalk models down the narrow strip of asphalt that had been plowed clear to the school entrance, which was thick with kids eager to get out of the cold.

When Kate opened her eyes that morning, lying in the darkness of her bedroom under the heavy quilt, she'd done what she'd trained herself to do every day these past two years: she silently ran her story.

She was Holly Brenner. She was twenty-eight. She was the single parent of six-year-old Suzie.

She forced away the fear and the dread that was with her each day upon waking, the certainty that today was the day it would end.

The day she would be revealed.

The day that Lucien Benway would have his revenge.

Quelling her anxiety, she'd reached out a hand, the downy hairs on her forearm teased to standing by the dawn chill, her index finger landing on a rectangle of frigid plastic, and muted the alarm clock just as it clicked to 6:00 a.m.

She'd padded through the upstairs hall to her daughter's room and kissed her on the forehead.

"Morning, baby," she'd said.

The child had opened her eyes and smiled. "Morning, Mommy."

"Who are you, baby?" she'd asked, as she did every morning.

"I'm Suzie, Mommy."

"Suzie who?"

"Suzie Brenner."

When they'd gone underground two years ago, Kate decided the risk of keeping her daughter's first name—the name that Suzie, a late talker, had taken so long to say—was outweighed by the confusion of teaching her a new one.

She'd kissed her again. "Good girl. Get ready now."

She went downstairs and made them breakfast, doing her best not to show her irritation when Suzie had taken too long to dress and missed the school bus that had wheezed along their street in the wake of a snowplow.

And so she was sitting in her Jeep at the school, watching as fate blindsided her, tapping into the fear that haunted every parent in the wake of Sandy Hook.

Dismissing the superstitious notion that it was preordained, that she was *meant* to be here, Kate left the Jeep and hurried toward the two boys, who were closing in on the entrance manned by the school security guard, Pops, in his rent-a-cop uniform. White hair flapping in the wind, he raised a friendly hand, and his greeting, "Hiya fellas, where ya headed?" was blown toward her.

As the youths kept on walking, she saw them exchange smiles.

They closed in on Pops, who took a step back and said, "Now, hold on, what's your business here?"

She hoped her instincts were wrong, that the boys were mime artists or acrobats or parkour *traceurs* come to entertain the kids, and that the lines of their jackets were ruined by the hidden tools of whatever trendy trade they plied. But the blond boy swept his coat wide and, producing an AR-15 assault rifle, shot the guard twice, and the old man was dead before he hit the snow. As she got closer, Kate saw the other boy laugh and try to free his weapon, which had snagged on the torn lining of his coat.

The first boy fired a burst, the recoil sending the rounds just over the heads of a group of screaming kids. Adjusting his aim, his finger was about to squeeze the trigger again when Kate, shaking off the rust of years of inactivity, hit the boy from behind and sent him sprawling. As she grabbed the rifle, she kicked him in the face and heard the cartilage of his nose crack. She swung the barrel onto the other youth, who had finally freed his weapon and was lining it up at her. Firing, Kate threw herself sideways and his bullets stitched the brick over her head.

She was sure she'd hit him in the shoulder, but he took off and ran into the building as she lined up on him again. There were kids in the way and she couldn't take the shot and then he was gone into the classroom nearest the door—her daughter's classroom.

Kate heard a ratcheting sound and turned to the prone boy as he cocked a SIG Pro semiautomatic pistol. Too close to take a shot with the rifle, she hit him in the throat with the stock, took the SIG, and killed him.

She found another clip in the dead boy's coat and smacked it into the AR-15 as she sprinted for the classrooms at the side of the building.

She knew that the windows were triple glazed (she'd contributed to the fund-raiser to upgrade the insulation of the classrooms for the long winter months) and was already calculating what effect the tempered glass would have on a round she fired.

Kate stopped and took a quick look into the room.

The second boy was standing with his back to the locked door. His left arm hung limp and there was blood on his jacket and his neck.

With his right hand, he waved the assault rifle at the wailing kids. When the teacher, a young newlywed named Marie Benet, approached him with her hands raised, he fired at her and she fell. The recoil drove him backward against the door, and more rounds struck the ceiling, taking out the strip lights and sending down a shower of glass.

Louder screams. Kate searched the crouching children for Suzie. She couldn't see her.

She got closer to the window, knowing she would have to take the shot despite the deflection and loss of accuracy, when she saw her daughter's face close to the glass. Kate saw her small hand working the stiff catch and prayed as the cold, trembling little fingers battled the latch that suddenly gave. Kate grabbed the window, swinging it inward and raising the AR-15 in one movement, just as the boy looked her way. She shot him three times, twice in the chest and once in the head, blood and brains spattering red on the white door. His weapon hit the floor before he did.

She dropped the rifle and reached in for Suzie, hauling her out the window, and held her close as she sprinted through the snow, driving her legs, lifting her knees, feeling the burn of the cold in her lungs. Kate raced for her car, hearing the wail of the sirens bearing down on them, knowing she had no more than a minute to get to the Jeep and get away.

TWO

Kate went into the turn too fast and the tires found a patch of black ice and all at once the Jeep was like a runaway Zamboni doing donuts, trees and low pewter sky and cute little camera-ready houses spinning by and Suzie screaming a choked, juddering wail.

Kate's training kicked in and she turned into the skid, her feet riding the pedals, her right hand a blur on the gearshift, digging all the right moves out of her muscle memory. As the Jeep came to a halt (perilously close to a tree) she saw the sheriff's cruiser coming right at them, howling, the light bar doing disco, before turning toward the school and disappearing from view with nothing more than the hint of a fishtail—these Yankees knew how to drive in a blizzard.

Kate looked across at Suzie. The child was silent, but her face was red and tear-streaked, mouth open and wet with spittle, her big, dark eyes fixed on her mother.

Kate reached over and embraced her.

"Who were those men, Mommy?"

"I don't know, baby."

"They were killing people."

"Yes, they were."

"Because of us, Mommy?"

"No, baby, not because of us."

She kissed the girl on the forehead, put the Jeep into gear, and headed toward their house, driving fast but carefully, the seconds of freedom emptying like sand in a timer.

"Now, I need you to do something for me, Suze, something that's crazy hard, but you have to do it. Okay?"

The child nodded. "Okay."

"Baby, I'm sorry, but the thing I told you might happen someday, well, it's here."

"It's here?"

"Yes. Because of what happened back at the school, people are going to be coming after me."

"But you saved us, Mommy."

"It doesn't matter. They'll know who I am and they'll be coming. So we have to go, understand?"

"We have to leave town?"

"Yes," Kate said.

"I have to leave my friends?"

"Yes."

"Can I say goodbye?"

"No. I'm sorry."

Suzie choked back her sobs. "You were brave, Mommy."

"So were you."

"I'll be brave now."

"I know you will."

Kate stopped the Jeep in the driveway of a small white wooden cottage with a pitched roof and twin dormer windows, a place that had felt cloyingly cute when they'd moved in two years ago, but that she'd grown to love. She ran up the stairs to her bedroom, furnished in what she'd once called "High Hallmark"—lacy curtains and comforter, fluffy animals on the bed, antithetical to her own stripped-down, austere taste—and shoved the antique brass bed aside, pulled up a throw rug, and loosened three boards on the hardwood floor.

In the space beneath, she'd stowed a bag, packed for a day like today. A wad of cash. Anonymous clothes with all labels removed. Fake identities. A medical kit. Nothing to connect her and her daughter to who they had pretended to be these last years.

Or who they once had been.

Kate hefted the bag and ran out onto the landing calling for Suzie. The child appeared from her bedroom, carrying three of her favorite dolls.

Kate shook her head. "You can't take them, baby. I'm sorry."

The girl teared up again, then she sat the dolls on a table and she kissed each one goodbye. Kate took the bag and stowed it in the Jeep, then drove them through the neat streets toward the black woods that grew thick across the invisible line that marked the unprotected border between the US and Canada.

"Mommy?"

"Yeah?"

"When we get where we're going?"

"Yes?"

"Can I get a puppy?"

"Yes, baby, you can get a puppy."

What was one more lie?

THREE

Lucien Benway stood in the shadows of the windowless basement watching as his man-of-all-work, Dudley Morse, used the Jordanian yellow pages to beat the American reporter tied to the kitchen chair.

An incandescent bulb dangled from the stained ceiling directly above the chair, its cylindrical aluminum shade focusing a hard shaft of greenish light onto the bleeding journalist.

When Benway cleared his throat, Morse, a very tall and very pale man, lowered the telephone directory and stepped back, his breath coming in gusts, his white shirt patterned with sweat and blood.

Benway stared at the reporter, who sagged forward restrained by a nylon rope. In a deep voice that carried just a trace of swamp Texas, Benway said, "You think you look like George Clooney, don't you?"

And although the journalist, with his thick black hair shot with gray and his photogenic jawline, did resemble the Hollywood actor, he turned toward the invisible Benway and shook his head and said, "No, not particularly,"

"But you've been told you do? *Women* have told you this?"

"Maybe. Sometimes." He spat an incisor onto the cracked mosaic floor tiles.

"But you're not George Clooney. Are you hearing me?"

"Yes. I am not George Clooney."

"And this is not a movie. Nobody is going to yell 'cut.' You understand?"

"Yes, I understand."

"Yet you're still telling me nothing?"

"Because I have nothing to tell you."

"Nothing?"

"Only that I'm innocent."

"You're innocent?"

"Yes."

"How do you know you're innocent?"

"Because I've had no covert dealings with Islamic State, al-Qaeda, Khorasan, AQAP, al-Nusra, the Houthis, or any other faction."

"Is that what you think this is about?"

"Isn't it?"

"No."

"Then what? What is this about?"

Benway stepped out of the shadows, his hands in the pants pockets of his seersucker suit. He was barely five feet tall with the body of a prepubescent boy and a massive head covered by a downy fuzz of pale hair. The harsh light threw into relief the latticework of wrinkles that covered the papery skin of his face.

The reporter found a laugh. "I see."

"You do?"

"Yes."

"And do you still profess your innocence?"

"I didn't know who she was."

"You didn't?"

"Well, not until it was too late."

"I think you're confusing ignorance with innocence."

Benway took a soft pack of the Turkish Samsun cigarettes he favored from the pocket of his jacket, shook one loose and lit it with the Ronson lighter he'd taken from the body of the first man he'd ever killed, catching a whiff of butane and then the rich fume of tobacco.

"What are you going to do to me?" the reporter asked.

"Behead you and dump you across the Syrian border," Benway said, exhaling twin plumes of smoke through his nostrils.

The reporter shook his head and opened his one good eye as wide as he could and said, "Cunning."

Benway waved his cigarette at Morse. "Leave us."

The tall man hesitated.

"Go," Benway said.

Morse placed the yellow pages on the folding table that stood near the chair, then turned and opened a door onto a flight of narrow wooden stairs, allowing a burst of a muezzin's warbling call into the room. The door closed and the room was silent again.

Benway dropped his cigarette onto the tiles and ground it dead under the heel of his tiny loafer, handmade by a cordwainer in downtown Washington, DC, then he lifted a long-bladed knife from the table.

The journalist stared at the gleaming blade as Benway stepped into the circle of light.

"What? I don't even rate a fuckin video?"

And, as he flashed that Clooneyesque grin, Benway could see exactly what had made his wife want this man, why he alone among her legion of lovers had tempted her to leave her husband of twenty years.

Benway cut the reporter's throat, then took him by his thatch of hair and finished the business of decapitating him.

FOUR

Driving the Jeep along the Autoroute 55 through the snowy plains of southern Quebec with Suzie dozing at her side, Kate could almost convince herself that she was making one of her too-frequent road trips to Montreal. Each time she'd crossed the border, she'd known she was taking a risk, but she was a big-city girl and had needed the kind of stimulation not to be found in a tiny village in the Northeast Kingdom. When she'd taken Suzie to Montreal's Quartier Latin, they'd pigged out on sweet, wood-fired bagels followed by sugar pie and strolled the cobbled streets of the old city, the French in their ears causing Suzie to break out her Inspector Clouseau accent that had never failed to crack them both up. Kate had shopped in the chic little boutiques and specialty shops for a few trifles to put in her store back in Vermont, where she sold trinkets to the visitors that seldom came. The town never quite gained traction as a tourist destination—the reason why, along with its proximity to the border, she'd chosen it.

But on those days, she'd listened to old Leonard Cohen songs (all about him saying "so long" to Marianne, or Suzanne taking him down to the river and feeding him tea and oranges) that had transported her into another time and another place—not the breaking news on WDEV-FM out of Waterbury that was giving an update on the shooting at Suzie's school.

Details were sketchy: Minor injuries were reported among the kids. Two staff members had been killed along with the two gunmen who had not yet been identified. Kate didn't care who the twisted little fuckers were, she cared only that she had stopped them before they'd massacred the children who'd been their targets. There was nothing about her in the news report.

Yet.

But she knew her prints and her DNA—hair tweezered from the rug by her bed, invisible skin flakes harvested from the inside of the jeans in her laundry basket and the sneakers that lay in the bottom of her closet—were being analyzed and very soon people somewhere would know who she was and the heavy machinery of the intelligence community would start to roll. A wide net would be cast, ready to ensnare her. If she were trapped, the sunniest outcome would be a show trial and life in prison, with Suzie left to find her way through foster homes and institutions, branded for life as "that traitor bitch's daughter."

That is, if Lucien Benway and his creature, Morse, didn't get to them first and put bullets in the bases of their skulls and dump their bodies in unmarked graves.

Kate shut down these thoughts and concentrated on the road, staying just within the speed limit, watching the mirrors for the white Taurus Interceptors favored by Quebec's highway patrol.

She'd stopped for a minute in the deep woods to remove the Vermont license plates, which she had frisbeed into the trees, and replace them with Quebec plates, with their fleur-de-lis and *Je me souviens* motto.

They allowed her to blend into the traffic but wouldn't hold up to a computer check, and neither would the Canadian driver's license in her wallet.

But the license, in the name of Mary McCloud, had enabled her to rent a self-storage unit on the outskirts of the small city of Magog two years before. The owner was a Quebecois who'd reluctantly conversed in English. Kate, raising her diphthongs a little before the consonants in a near-flawless impersonation of an Ontario native, told the guy that she'd moved from "Tronno" and needed some space for a while.

He'd been incurious but had managed a smile when she'd paid two years rental in cash.

She turned off at Magog, crossed the river, passed the dark brick textile plant that resembled a Dickensian poorhouse, and headed for the self-storage, a couple of rows of low buildings squatting in the gray snow. The facility was surrounded by a chain link fence topped with rusted barbed wire.

There were no workers on the premises. The owner ran the Shell gas station across the freeway and left the self-storage to pretty much take care of itself.

Kate stopped the Jeep outside the gate and was pleased to see that a snowplow had recently done its work on the roads leading to the storage units. She used the key she'd been given to unlock the gate, drove through, and locked it behind her, heading toward the second row of blocks. Kate stopped at the last unit, near the fence. A stretch of snow-covered ground lay between the fence and the freeway, the buzz of distant traffic reaching her.

She parked the Jeep and, leaving Suzie asleep, rolled up the door of the unit.

A five-year-old silver Hyundai with Quebec plates was parked inside. She'd bought the car from a dealer in Montreal, paid cash, and driven it here and stored it for just this day.

Before mothballing the car, Kate'd had the oil, antifreeze, and power steering, transmission, and brake fluids changed. She'd filled the gas tank and added PRI-G to stabilize it and slow down fuel deterioration, and disconnected the terminals of the brand-new battery.

The concrete of the unit was level enough for her to disengage the parking brake before storage so it wouldn't stick to the brake drum over time. She'd left the manual transmission in neutral.

These things were automatic.

These skills, like so many others, hammered into her by her trainers a lifetime ago.

She hadn't been here since she rented the unit, and there was a moment's anxiety when—after she'd lifted the hood and reconnected the battery—she sat behind the wheel and turned the key. The car whined and coughed then caught, the engine running smoothly.

While the car idled, she opened the trunk and unzipped the bag inside, revealing Canadian passports in the names of Janet and Brett Brewster. A bespectacled version of herself stared out from Janet's passport. Brett was a kid of four when the picture was taken, but if Kate cut Suzie's hair and dressed her in the boys' clothes she'd bought at H&M in Montreal, the girl would pass.

She did not relish the idea of getting Suzie to agree to the makeover.

Kate drove the car out and parked it, still idling, beyond the Jeep. Suzie was awake now, staring at her.

Kate opened the Jeep door and slid in beside her. "You okay?"

The girl nodded.

"You go wait for me in the other car, baby."

Suzie obeyed, and Kate drove the Jeep into the storage unit and removed their bags. She rolled down the door of the unit and locked it. After stowing the bags in the trunk of the Hyundai, she headed toward the exit.

"Where are we going, Mommy?"

"To do a few things."

"What things?"

"Oh, girlie things. Play dress up."

"Dress up?"

"Yeah."

"And then?"

"Then we're going to fly."

"Fly to where?"

"To find out about a man."

"What man?"

"A man who I think can help us."

"What's his name?"

"His name is Hook. Harry Hook."

"That's a funny name."

"Well, he's a funny man."

FIVE

The mother of all hangovers saved Harry Hook's life.

Despite the arctic air-conditioning in the lobby of the plush Bangkok Phuket Hospital, he was sweating profusely, a miasma of stale booze following him as he jogged into the elevator. He deliberately ignored a short, red-faced man in an expensive suit standing beside four bruisers. They encircled a striking bronze-skinned woman in traditional Muslim garb and a skinny boy of maybe eight in a knitted skullcap.

The woman's fine nose twitched and she whispered something to one of the big men, who kept the door open with a thick hand and said to Hook in an unplaceable accent, "Would you please take the next elevator, sir?"

It wasn't a question, and the stinking Hook retreated as the doors closed. This left him standing beside a plump Thai man in a tuxedo perched on a little dais playing "I Will Always Love You" on an electric violin. The song, a reminder of the event that had ended Hook's career and very nearly his life, brought with it a terrible foreboding that almost sent him bolting for the exit, but the lure of money had his finger repeatedly stabbing at the elevator call button.

When the next elevator arrived, Hook, fighting dizziness, rode up to the sixth floor alone, pleased there were no mirrors, although the jolly posters advertising discounted colorectal examinations in Thai and English made him queasy. He swiped toxic sweat from his forehead and waited for the doors to open.

Until the night before, Hook had been on the wagon for six years.

He'd chosen a different path from that of the many aging expatriates who, like remittance men of old, washed up on the beneficent shores of Thailand and went magnificently to ruin. They would spend their days pickling their organs in booze and party drugs, their aging skins becoming lizardy and their sagging tackle shored up by jolts of Viagra that wreaked havoc with their blood pressure and sent many, still semitumescent, to the ERs of hospitals such as this, where their exhausted hearts gave out.

The disgraced Hook had spent his first few years in Thailand behaving like them, snorting cocaine off the bud-like breasts of teenage bar girls, washing down handfuls of little blue bombs with tequila to combat the coke dick and enable him to continue on his toboggan course of F/F/M threesomes.

Somewhere in the midst of his booze-fueled orgy years, he'd surprised himself and decided he wanted to live, even though that meant that each sober day, he had to face the reality that twenty-two people had died on his watch.

Died when he'd made the wrong decision.

The fallout from that decision had prompted his resignation from the CIA (accepting a handshake that was far from golden) and caused him to flee to Bangkok, intending to end it all in a glorious blur of chemicals and cunt.

After he'd gone clean and sober, he withdrew to the jungles of southern Thailand, living in isolation with only his ghosts for company.

But despite his almost monastic lifestyle, his cash reserves were dwindling. They had taken a hit during his years of excess, and it was with an uneasy mind that he'd sat on the steps of his wooden shack in the jungle the morning before, attempting to forget his financial woes as he tried to capture in watercolor the pink light washing over the limestone cliffs shrouded in a soft mist that he'd feared was beyond his skills.

Maybe because he wasn't concentrating so hard the picture wasn't half bad. A keeper, even.

When his cell phone chirped, he wanted to ignore it, but old habits had him setting his brush in a glass of water and going inside—though he was tempted to retreat when he saw Johnny Martin's name on the caller ID.

Martin was a mouthy Brit who flitted around Thailand getting up to no good. Against his better instincts, Hook took the call.

"What's up, old sport?" Hook said in the vaguely patrician accent that was as fake as the last name he was currently living under: Henderson, from Bellow's *Henderson the Rain King*. Not really an alias. Just a way to distance himself from what and who he had been.

"Harry, I've got a little thing going. Over on Phuket," Martin said.

It was always a "little thing" with Johnny Martin.

"Yes?"

"Yeah, a little bodyguard gig."

"I'm not a bodyguard, Johnny."

"Well, of course you're not, Harry, but it's money for jam. I just need you as a floater."

"Isn't a floater an unflushable turd?"

Martin brayed a laugh. "Funny, Harry. Good one." He coughed and Hook could hear him lighting a cigarette and sucking on it. "You'll just be some guy in casual clothes, looking like a tourist, you know, keeping an eye on things from the fringes."

"Uh-huh."

"One of my crew got himself arrested last night. Some trouble in a bar. A girl. The usual. You know?"

"Yeah." He'd had a few of those skirmishes in his time.

"So I'm a chap short and I thought of you."

Hook knew he should end the call but he said, "What are you paying?"

"A thousand."

"US?"

"Yes."

"What's it involve?"

"You get the ferry across to Phuket today. I put you up in a hotel for the night and tomorrow at oh-nine-hundred you wait in the lobby of the Bangkok Phuket Hospital. You know it?"

"Yes."

"Me and my chaps will collect the clients from the airport and drive them to the hospital."

"Who are they?"

"My clients?"

"Yes."

"A woman and a kid. She's bringing him to the hospital for tests."

"Where are they from?"

"Burma."

"Why do they need bodyguards?"

"They're rich."

"Then why don't they bring their own?"

"A problem with travel documents. You know?"

Hook heard himself say, "Okay. I'll do it for two thousand."

"A grand and a half."

"Done."

Martin said, "You don't know me tomorrow when you see me, okay? You hang out in the lobby, then when we arrive, you drift along with us like an innocent party."

"I am an innocent party."

"Of course you are, Harry. Just a figure of speech." He laughed and Hook could almost see his ruddy face and yellow teeth. "You spot anything dodgy, you call me on my mobile, yeah?"

"Is there something you're not telling me, Johnny?"

"No, no. Not a thing, Harry. Scout's honor."

Hook hung up and wandered back outside and looked at the painting he'd never finish. He left it on the deck to dry and went in and started packing a small bag, uneasy in the certainty that there was more to this than Johnny Martin was revealing, that he was wandering into something dangerous and messy that was way outside his wheelhouse.

Hook had never been one for the dirty work, being more of a schemer, a plotter, a gambit man, attracted to intelligence work not for the blood and the guts but for the platform it afforded him to outsmart the opposition—for the *intelligence*, goddammit.

But the money would keep him going for a while.

Filled with misgivings, he took the boat from the mainland to the island of Phuket and, at sunset, checked into a cheap hotel near the hospital. The room was claustrophobic and the rattling air conditioner coughed warm, fetid air. Hook forced open the window and allowed in the snarl of the traffic and the cooking smells from the stalls in the street below. Martin had contrived to find a hotel in the shadow of one of the few mosques in the overwhelmingly Buddhist Phuket, and when the blare of a muezzin filled the room (and filled the jumpy Hook's head with old memories) he found himself walking the narrow, clotted streets, his nostrils thick with the scent of perfumed flowers, spiced food, exhaust emissions, and sewer gas.

Far from the girlie bars and massage parlors of Patong, this wasn't tourist Phuket, and he saw no other *farang*. Thirsty, he sat down at a sidewalk eatery and ordered a Coke. At the table beside him, six men were playing *pok deng*, a card game in which players win by beating the banker's hand.

They were drinking Laotian whiskey with a dead cobra coiled inside the bottle. One of them saw him watching and, smiling a gap-toothed grin, the man filled a shot glass and pushed it over to Hook who thought of refusing but didn't. He joined in the game and remembered buying another bottle of snake whiskey for his new best friends and then remembered little else until the bleat of his cell phone alarm that morning had dragged him retching and stinking from his sleep.

He'd puked, showered, and puked again. Dressed in khaki shorts and a patterned shirt, looking like just another aging tourist, he'd headed for the hospital, arriving late and almost missing Martin and his crew, who were already ushering the woman and the boy into the elevator.

Following them up in the next car, keen to get this done and get his hands on the cash, Hook watched the display hit six. As the doors slid open, he heard the unmistakable cough of suppressed weapons and looked into the hospital corridor as Martin and his men were ambushed by a group of men dressed as porters. They were left for dead on the polished floor as the shooters grabbed the kid and the woman and dragged them toward the stairs.

Hook gave no thought to intervention, and as weapons swung his way, he put up his hands, stepped back into the elevator, and hit the LOBBY and DOOR CLOSE buttons simultaneously. The doors took forever to shut, and just as they were about to kiss, a brown hand holding an automatic surged forward, but to no avail. Hook was moving down, bile in his throat.

He had a bad moment when the car stopped on the third floor, but it was only to admit an Australian couple who bid him "g'day," the woman as bruised as a prizefighter, her face bearing the signs of the cosmetic surgery the hospital was famous for.

Hook rode down with them and scuttled past the violinist and the little nurses in their lilac outfits, out the side exit by the mini-mart, and down the ramp into the heavy heat to where taxi drivers lounged, smoking in the shade of a jackfruit tree.

Then he was in a taxi and away, setting course for Phuket Old Town with its clogged streets and Chinese buildings, to the jetty where he found a ferry about to depart. He was sitting in the bow watching the land recede when the shakes hit him. He sat shivering and grinding his teeth for the next hour until the boat docked and he hurried to where he'd parked the old Yamaha dirt bike he'd bought off an indigent Ukrainian and kicked it to life. There was only one thing to do: buy a bottle and go home and drink it until he was unconscious.

SIX

A motel rose from the soiled snow along the A-10 to Montreal, the neon sign gamely jerking and jittering against a sky the color of a bruise. It was only early afternoon, but car headlights were on and darkness was ready to pounce beyond the low gray hills.

Kate clicked on the blinker and drove into the motel, parking close to the office.

"Stay here, Suze," she said and left the car, the windows of the Hyundai sufficiently misted to hide her daughter.

The office was so overheated that she could taste the sweat of the fat man in a yellow T-shirt who sat behind the counter watching sports on CNN. He glanced at Kate and then his eyes were back on the tube.

"Can I have a room, please?" she asked in her "Tronno" accent.

He grunted and slid a broken-backed registration book across to her. "Fifty dollars."

Kate paid with Canadian bills and used her Mary McCloud license to register. The man barely glanced at her ID and handed her a key with a smudged and crumpled paper tag tied to it.

"Room ten," he said, his eyes already back on the screen by the time she walked out.

Kate parked the Hyundai outside number ten, took their bags from the trunk, and hurried Suzie into a room that smelled of mold and mothballs.

She clicked on the TV and surfed past a couple of Canadian channels until she found CNN, which was still doing its sport roundup.

"Sit, Suze," she said, indicating the bed.

The child sat.

Kate unzipped a bag, removed the Brett Brewster passport and laid it open on the begrimed bedspread.

"You see that kid?" she said, tapping the photograph.

"Yes, I see him."

"You're not going to like this."

"I'm not going to like what?"

Then Suzie, a quick study, shook her head and raised her hands to her long black hair.

"No."

Kate shrugged. "I'm sorry."

"If I had a dollar for every time you said that today," Suzie said, sounding ancient.

"Yeah, I know."

"Why?" Suzie asked, staring at the passport.

"They'll be searching for a woman and a girl. Not a woman and a boy."

"You think I look like a boy?"

"No. But at airports they don't really look too hard at kids, you know?"

"Mommy …"

"Suze, please."

All at once the girl was crying, and Kate knew it wasn't about the hair she was about to lose.

It was about all she had lost already.

Kate hugged her. "Suzie."

At last her daughter hugged her back and said, "Do it, Mommy." Kate kissed the top of Suzie's head, then went to one of the bags and removed a comb and a pair of scissors. She brought a towel from the bathroom, spread it on the floor, and started to cut the child's dark bangs, exposing the planes of her cheekbones. As the girl's hair fell away, she saw the face of Suzie's dead father—the face of her dead husband—and it took all her strength to blink away the tears and hold herself together enough to finish the job.

"Take your clothes off, Suze," she said as she folded the child's hair into the towel and shoved it into her bag.

Suzie stripped to her panties.

"Everything," Kate said, feeling like a prison guard.

The child obeyed and Kate dressed her in tighty-whities, jeans, and a shirt, dropping a pair of clumpy sneakers at her feet.

"Put those on, Brett."

"Brett?"

"That's who you are now. Get used to it."

"For how long?"

"Not long. A couple of days."

As the girl pulled on the shoes, self-important music announced the top of the hour and CNN's breaking news.

A report about the school shooting opened the bulletin, the camera showing blood in the snow and scared-looking kids being led from the building by police. The principal, a pretty redhead, her face hollowed by shock, said that a local woman, Holly Brenner, had disarmed the two gunmen and killed them both, saving the lives of "countless children."

A blurred photograph of Kate filled the screen. It had been grabbed at the school's Christmas pantomime. Kate had instinctively turned away from a snap-happy first-grade teacher wielding her iPhone like a paparazzo, but apparently not fast enough.

There were shots of her house and store being searched by sheriff's deputies and blank-faced men in suits while the on-camera reporter said that Holly Brenner had disappeared.

The reporter, posed in front of the school, gazed earnestly into the lens and said, "The people of this small Vermont town may not know exactly who Holly Brenner is, but there is no doubt in their minds about *what* she is: she's a hero."

As Kate clicked off the TV, the phone in the room rang. She ignored it and it fell silent as she packed Suzie's discarded clothes into a bag.

Then it rang again.

Kate crossed to the phone and lifted it. "Yes?"

"It's you, isn't it?" the desk clerk said.

"What are you talking about?"

"On the news. This woman. It's you."

"You're crazy."

"Am I? Maybe I call the police."

"Why don't I come over and talk to you? We'll straighten this out."

"Okay. Come now. I am waiting."

The line went dead.

"What's wrong, Mommy?"

"It's the man at the desk. He wants more money."

Suzie stared at her, not buying this.

Kate pulled on her coat and gloves and slipped the scissors into the pocket of her jeans.

"You stay here, baby, okay? I'm just going to see this guy."

Kate stepped out into a fresh fall of snow and, hunched against the cold, hurried across to the office, which glowed yellow in the gloom. The fat man stood at the window, staring out at her.

He opened the door and let her step inside. His stink was like a dead thing in the room.

"What do you want?" she said. "Money?"

He smiled at her, showing bad dental work, and shrugged, his man-boobs jiggling beneath his T-shirt. "Maybe."

He locked the door and panted his way to the counter and lifted the flap.

"Come," he said, wagging a pink hand, and she followed him into a small living room crowded with threadbare furniture and stuffed animal heads.

She couldn't help but think of Norman Bates in *Psycho*.

The clerk lifted a smeared bottle of Canadian Club from the table and waved it at her. "You want?"

Kate shook her head and he drank from it, wiping his mouth on the back of his hand.

"You're pretty," he said and rubbed a paw over the zipper of his jeans and she knew what it was that he wanted.

She smiled at him and said, "You have a bedroom?"

"You catch on fast."

She stepped toward him, angling her body so that he couldn't see her free the scissors from her pocket.

"Why waste time?" she said.

He smiled and set the bottle down and grunted as he put a heavy hand on her back, saying, "Whyn't you take your clothes off?"

She allowed him to pull her close, almost gagging on his stink—sweat, stale urine, and something darker and more disgusting. When she was right in under him, she plunged the blades of the scissors into his chest, severing the aorta where it branched off from his heart.

He stared at her, his eyes glassing over, and she stepped back in time to watch him fall like an imploding building onto the table, upending it and sending the whiskey bottle shattering to the floor.

Kate kneeled and pulled the scissors from his ribcage, the blades making a sucking sound when she yanked them free. She wiped the blades clean on his T-shirt, pocketed the scissors, and went through to the front office, where she opened the cash register with her gloved fingers and took a thin pile of cash, leaving the empty tray jutting out like a tongue.

Kate quit the office, shutting the door behind her, hearing the lock click. She hurried across to their room. Suzie sat on the bed, looking pale and vulnerable with her cropped hair.

"We have to go, Suzie."

"Brett."

"Yeah, *Brett.*"

"Go where?"

"The airport. In Montreal."

Kate cleaned the room of any sign of their presence, and they went out to the car and drove into the dusk.

"Are we ever going home?" Suzie said, huddled down in her seat, her face hidden in the shadow of a baseball cap.

"Yes, we're going home, just not right now."

"And where is that?"

"Where's home?"

"Yes."

"I don't know. Not yet. But it's out there, waiting for us."

"Promise?"

"Yes, I promise."

SEVEN

Lucien Benway stood at the window of Amman's Kempinski Hotel eating pitted dates from Saudi Arabia as he watched the cars far below scuttle by like scarab beetles.

He was freshly showered and dressed in a pair of lightweight slacks and a silk shirt that his wife, Nadja, had had made for him in Paris.

Benway wondered what she was doing at that moment. Was she in bed with a man, or had her relationship with the reporter heralded an era of unprecedented sexual exclusivity?

He'd been made aware of the seriousness of the affair when Morse alerted him that Nadja was using a disposable cell phone. How Morse had known this, Benway neither knew nor cared.

Two nights ago, when his wife was taking one of her very long baths, soaking herself in unguents and lotions, a Dvořák piano concerto playing on her docked iPod, Benway had found the burner phone in the Chanel bag in her bedroom and discovered a text-message exchange that had left him stunned:

I'm boarding now for Amman. What's your answer?

I'll tell you when you return.

Leave him, Nadja. Leave the poison dwarf.

She had not replied, and the reporter had sent another, a minute later:

I love you.

Her reply was like a blade through Benway's heart:

I love you too.

In the twenty-one years they had been together, she had never once said those words to him.

Absurdly, standing at the window of the Jordanian hotel room, he felt the sting of tears in his eyes as the stream of cars below in Abdul Hamid Shouman Street blurred.

Benway placed the bowl of dates on a table, wiped his eyes with a monogrammed handkerchief, turned from the window, and crossed to the minibar that was concealed in a cabinet beneath the mute TV. He knelt, reaching into the freezer for a couple of ice cubes, and felt the familiar twinge in his spine where a fragment of a Druze mortar (a memento of an ambush in Moukhtara during the Lebanese Civil War when Benway was supplying weapons to the Maronite Phalangists) was embedded against his twelfth thoracic vertebra. It was a constant source of agony and often triggered metal detectors, but the surgeons had refused to remove it, deeming the risk of paralysis too great.

Benway stood and uncapped the liter of Cutty Sark he'd had sent up. His erstwhile mentor, Mrs. Danvers (who'd taught Benway most of the dirty tricks of the trade he now plied with such relish) had introduced him to the pleasures of the whiskey.

There were far superior scotches, but there was something about pouring a Cutty that had taken on the weight of ritual, and the habit had endured.

The ice hissed and crackled as the liquid kissed it, and Benway returned to the window and sipped his drink slowly, staring out at the desert that stretched far from the city.

A rap on the door and he turned, depositing the drink on the desk beneath the mirror as he crossed the room.

He opened the door to reveal Morse, who wore clean clothes and smelled of carbolic soap.

Benway had to quell an irrational spike of annoyance that the man had taken the time to freshen up before reporting to him.

"Come in," he said, stepping back.

Morse nodded and entered the room, standing beside the bed at parade rest with his feet spread and his hands clasped behind his back, ever the Marine, though he'd last worn the uniform a quarter of a century before.

"Sit," Benway said, indicating the red armchair by the window.

"That's okay, sir," Morse said.

Morse had long refused to call Benway by his given name and his use of the honorific was polite but not obsequious. He could—when the mood took him—make it sound condescending in the manner of an English butler paying mock deference to his supposed betters in one of the TV shows Nadja binge-watched while washing down Godiva chocolates with Russian vodka before disappearing on one of her trysts.

"I insist," Benway said and Morse moved to comply, inclining his head and sitting with his hands on his knees.

As Benway topped up his drink, he observed Morse, all bony limbs and impassive, pale face, in the mirror.

On first being introduced to the man many years ago, Benway's wife had shaken his hand and deadpanned, "A pleasure, Mr. Morose" in her husky Balkan voice, and the name had become a private joke between them, so apt that Benway still had to work hard not to say it to the cadaverous man's face.

"Scotch?" he asked, although in all their years together, he'd never seen Morse drink alcohol.

"No thank you, sir."

Benway perched on the edge of the bed, the toes of his shoes not quite scraping the blue carpet.

"So," he said. "How did it go?"

"Smoothly. I got our associates to dump him across the Syrian border and some splinter group'll claim responsibility."

Benway, these last two years a pariah who'd had to endure the very public severing of all links to Langley, the Pentagon, and the White House, now worked as an independent contractor with a very questionable client list, mining the fissures in the facade of radical Islam where allegiances shifted like sand. Dollars, weapons, and promises of everything from drone strikes to blond women bought both dubious loyalty and easy betrayal.

"I feel I should apologize," Benway said.

"For what?"

"That thing earlier was personal. I shouldn't have involved you."

"He was a leftist scumbag, sir. He won't be missed."

"Still."

"And not even a real journalist. A *blogger*."

As Benway laughed at Morse's unexpected snobbery, his cell phone rang and he reached across to where it lay blinking and whirring on the bed.

"Yes?" he said. He listened for a moment as he took another sip of the whiskey. "Jesus Christ." He stood and killed the call.

The atypical blasphemy had been enough to get Morse staring at him.

Benway reached for the TV remote and thumbed the buttons until he had CNN on the screen.

He was looking at a photograph of Kate Swift. The picture was blurred and her hair was long and dyed blond. But it was her.

"The FBI will sit on Swift's identity for a few more hours," he said, turning to Morse, his desire for vengeance driving all thoughts of his wife and her treachery from his mind. "But the window is closing. I want eyes on Mrs. Danvers. Immediately."

EIGHT

At seventy-seven years old, Philip Danvers—who had spent his entire adult life scrotum-deep in the mire of human iniquity, frailty, treachery, turpitude, and just plain vileness—had lost all capacity for surprise.

So whenas he stood in the raw cold before the plinth-mounted head of the Nazi eagle outside Berlin's decommissioned Tempelhof Airport, he saw his granddaughter appear through the mist holding the hand of a child, he barely missed a beat in his vivid description of the Berlin blockade. He was holding forth in his still-powerful Brahmin bray to an entranced group of American gray-hairs who had escaped their retirement homes and parted with good money to tramp around Berlin and Vienna with him on his tour of Cold War hot spots, lapping up the insider's view that came with years spent spinning webs of deceit in US intelligence.

Of course, she wasn't *really* his granddaughter; his carefully hidden sexual proclivities had exempted men of his generation from parenting, unlike the same-sex couples of today who merrily adopted and used surrogates, but in his dotage he had secretly come to see himself as the patriarch of a uniquely dysfunctional family.

And if, in this family of his geriatric imagination, Kate Swift was his granddaughter, then Harry Hook was his beloved if wayward son and Lucien Benway his deeply regretted bad seed.

It was Benway—the mean little jockey had always had an unerring instinct for the lowest blow—who'd started calling him "Mrs. Danvers," after the shrewish housekeeper in du Maurier's book and Hitchcock's film *Rebecca*, and the name had stuck.

But if surprise was no longer on the menu, self-doubt was the dish du jour. Without pausing his schmaltzy but crowd-pleasing vignette about the candy bombers—the US pilots who'd parachuted Hershey bars to the ragged little *kinder* who'd lined the fence of Tempelhof, gazing up in awe at the Skymasters thundering overhead—Danvers glanced beyond his flock at the woman. She was taking in the sweeping facade of the airport, and he saw that the child whose mittened hand she clutched was a boy. He silently berated himself for allowing his imagination free rein.

Mother and son walked away, and Danvers, on autopilot, understood that the news reports he'd caught in his hotel room about that business at the school in Vermont—he'd been certain that the blurred photograph of the woman who'd prevented another Sandy Hook was his once-upon-a-time protégé, Kate—had fueled his aging imagination.

But he still felt in his water (the water that dripped and spattered from him in weak and stuttering piddles during his many bathroom breaks, dammed by a malignant prostate that was busy killing him) that it *was* Kate and that she would reach out to him.

He dismissed the thought and smiled and nodded at the young German tour guide, signaling her that he was about done, before he again addressed his audience.

"So, my friends, it's back to the coach. Enjoy your last night in Berlin. I'll see you tomorrow in Vienna, where I trust you shall all be wearing trench coats and whistling the 'Harry Lime Theme.'"

Shrugging off a few questions with resolute politeness, Danvers walked south toward the Tempelhof U-Bahn station, his characteristic long-legged stride hobbled by his illness.

He didn't ride with the others in the coach at the end of the day, savoring what would almost certainly be his last visit to Berlin, a city he had once loved for its claustrophobia and intrigue.

He'd been unable to quell a tinge of regret when he'd watched the razing of the Wall on TV in a hotel room in Islamabad with Harry Hook, whom he'd been mother-henning through one of his earlier escapades.

Hook had scripted a magnificently Machiavellian plot to co-opt an Iranian physicist as an asset in Pakistan to acquire P-1 centrifuges from the A. Q. Khan rogue nuclear supply network, which pivoted on the scientist ending up in a three-way with a pneumatic ghazel singer and a polysexual former cricketer. Nobody except Harry had believed it would work, but it had—brilliantly—yielding video that if it reached the eyes of the Ayatollahs, would surely have resulted in the physicist's death-by-stoning for this *zina* crime, leaving Danvers looking like an oracle for having recruited the wunderkind Hook.

Walking carefully along the icy sidewalk, he couldn't shake the feeling he was being followed. He glanced behind as he passed a city toilet cubicle and was sure that he saw the woman and the boy standing by a railing amidst a clump of chained bicycles, shooting a photograph on a cell phone.

Danvers took the stairs down to the U-Bahn station, reaching the platform just as the yellow train hissed to a halt. He validated his Berlin City Tour Card at the ticket-stamping machine and boarded the crowded train, standing near the door.

As the train took off, he felt a presence at his side, and the blond woman and her child squeezed in beside him.

So, his aged urine had been right.

"Do you know where he is?" Kate asked, staring out at the dark tunnel.

"And hello to you too, Kate."

"Do you?"

"Who?"

"Philip, please."

He looked at her and saw the strain on her face and had to quell an impulse to embrace her.

The child gazed up him, silent. A girl, he saw, wearing the haircut and clothes of a boy.

So this was the spawn of Kate and the Palestinian. There was something of the father's languid Levantine beauty (Danvers had once harbored a secret and quite ridiculous lust for the sleepy-eyed Yusuf) in the face that peered up at him.

"Not exactly."

"But you can find out?"

"Yes, I can find out."

The train halted at Paradestrasse, and even though his stop was farther along at Stadtmitte, near the Regent Hotel where he was staying, he stepped out, saying, "Meet me at the Holocaust Memorial in two hours."

Danvers, left alone on the platform, buffeted by the hot wind of the departing train, wished he were home listening to Chopin and sipping the single Cutty Sark that he allowed himself each evening. As he hauled his dying body up the stairs using the handrail, he felt very, very old and very, very tired.

NINE

Benway flew home on Emirates, a two-hour hop from Amman to Dubai and then direct to Washington. First class, with the private cubicles he preferred, had been fully booked, but at least Emirates had lie-flat seats in business class. Anyway, for Benway, legroom was never a problem.

Morse had gone ahead, hitching a ride on an unmarked 747 with Special Forces cronies of his who were returning to Fort Bragg after some black flag operation in Yemen. Even with his connecting flight, he'd be in Washington ahead of Benway, who was in no hurry.

The enforced inertia of fourteen hours in the air was what he needed to process the emotions that the reappearance of Kate Swift had stirred up, for she had been the instrument of his downfall. She was the reason that he'd been disowned by the CIA and the administration (narrowly avoiding criminal charges) and now had to live in the shadow of an ongoing Justice Department investigation into his international contract work for contraventions of the Foreign Corrupt Practices Act.

The heat of that investigation had seen the majority of his clients, shy as roloway monkeys, withdraw from him, and his stunted list now comprised only the outlaw governments of pariah states who continued to prize the insights of an American of his stripe and cared not a fig for international condemnation.

A humiliation for a man who'd had the ears of four successive American presidents.

He sighed and signaled the stewardess for another Cutty Sark, and she brought him a little green-and-gold miniature that he uncapped and poured into a glass over ice.

As he sipped the drink he thought of Philip Danvers and realized, to his shame, that he wished his relationship with the old man was still intact, that when he landed he could turn to him for succor.

An absurd notion, since it had been Benway who'd engineered the palace coup that had seen Danvers forced into early retirement.

When Danvers had quashed Benway's initiative to go private, to take their shadowy, unnamed unit off the books and leave them far beyond the reach of intelligence oversight committees on the Hill, he'd gone over his mentor's head, lobbying his allies in the DOD, and the executive and intelligence communities who were tired of having their wings clipped. He'd won the day, ousting the old man and, in effect, creating his own little fiefdom, reporting directly to the White House.

The unofficial nature of this relationship (his standing bon mot when being briefed by station chiefs, generals, and presidential aides had been "and for whom am I *not* working today?") had made for great freedom, but his hubris had led to his downfall.

He'd inherited Kate Swift, who'd remained too much Mrs. Danvers' little pet for his liking, and he'd been distrustful of her marriage to Yusuf Hourani. An American, yes, born in Chicago, but the son of Palestinians who'd once supported Arafat, his mother reputedly one of the Black September band, along with Leila Khaled, who on August 29, 1969, hijacked TWA Flight 840 on its way from Rome to Athens, diverted the Boeing 707 to Damascus, and blew up the aircraft after the hostages had disembarked. Though when Benway had searched for proof, he'd found only rumor and innuendo.

The elder Houranis had put that behind them and become academics, and their son, it seemed, was a patriotic American until 9/11. After the invasion of Iraq, he'd flirted with radical Islam and it was Kate Swift who'd seduced him and made him her agent, infiltrating him into al-Qaeda.

His intelligence had enabled Swift to assassinate an al-Qaeda leader high on the administrations kill list. This had purified Hourani's heathen soul and she'd married him and borne him a child.

This hadn't mollified Benway, who'd been convinced that Hourani remained loyal to al-Qaeda, that the death of the leader was merely a matter of housekeeping, and opined pithily, "That boy has a missile in his future."

How else, Benway had maintained, could Hourani, after a spell as a stay-at-home dad to their mixed-blood daughter, suddenly reactivate himself and travel with Swift to Pakistan to reconnect with an al-Qaeda cell hidden deep in the mountains on the Afghanistan border? He'd dismissed Kate Swift's contention that after she'd left Hourani in Lahore and returned home, he had, at great personal risk, gone to South Waziristan to help transport two of his erstwhile assets and their families to safety.

Benway had made a convincing case to the White House that Hourani was caucusing with al-Qaeda heavy hitters and advocated kinetic action. A drone strike had been authorized, and Benway, in a moment of gloating grandiosity, had sent the link to the Predator's camera feed to Kate Swift so she could see her husband being erased half the world away.

Benway and Morse had watched the strike in their Washington office, Benway smoking Samsuns and drinking Cutty, Morse standing easy. When the screen had flared pleasingly, Benway had exhaled a plume of smoke at the acoustic-tiled ceiling, raised his glass, and said, "*Allahu Akbar!*"

Kate Swift had responded by going public and exposing the chain of command in the attack on her husband (the leftist media anointing Hourani as an American hero) that led straight to the White House, resulting in the resignation of the president's chief counterterrorism advisor and the sacrifice of Benway, who'd been squeezed like a suppurating boil from the corpus of US intelligence.

Swift, meanwhile, had taken her daughter and gone dark. Benway, fighting for his life, had leaked fabricated reports that she'd done a Snowden and gone to Russia, the only country that would have her, and that she'd been sighted in the company of one-time Russian mole, Anna

Chapman, a.k.a. Anna Vasil'yevna Kushchyenko, having her nails done in a Moscow beauty parlor.

The administration had made it clear that if she ever set foot in the US again, she'd be tried for treason.

Benway had suspected that she'd never left America and had used his increasingly meager resources to find her, without success.

But she *had* been there all the time.

Hiding in plain sight.

The irony that Swift had been flushed out not by the machinery of the state, nor by her own ineptitude, but by the mindless actions of a pair of the mutants who incubated with such monotonous regularity in America's psychic butt crack, was not lost on Benway.

No matter. She was on the run and this was his chance to find her. And find her he would.

Benway wagged a finger at the stewardess for another Cutty Sark and as he sipped his drink, the rumble of the jet beneath his feet, the little plane on the seat-back display taking him ever closer to home, he felt sufficiently anesthetized to think about the other woman who awaited his vengeance: his treacherous wife.

TEN

Nadja Benway, as Lucien was wont to announce over cognac and cigars at their increasingly infrequent dinner parties, had had more cocks in her than the First Street Tunnel had had trains, but this time it was different.

She really *was* going to leave her husband for another man.

This certainty came to her as she sat smoking her breakfast cigarette at the kitchen table of the Q Street town house, oblivious to CNN chattering away on the small TV on the counter, and it gave her pause, her elbow propped up on the tabletop, the ash growing like a centipede on the tip of the Marlboro Menthol held in the fork of her fingers.

Nadja was chic in the European way. She would wander through Union Market dressed in a slightly grubby cashmere sweater, jeans and sneakers, her strikingly beautiful face free of makeup, her long black hair still tousled from a recent encounter with one of her roster of paramours and render the overdressed, nipped and tucked Georgetown matrons invisible. She drew the eye of every man there, leaving him with a faint hint of musk and Guerlain Samsara in his nostrils and the gnawing certainty that his life would be incomplete for never having known her.

So cocks had been abundant and there had been more than a few offers for her to ditch the gnomish Benway, offers she had always scoffed at.

But during these last weeks some strange and hitherto unknown emotion had sprouted inside Nadja, as if it had been fertilized by the commingled fluids of her and her latest lover.

At first she'd believed that she was ill and had moderated her consumption of cigarettes and vodka and the Belgian chocolates she consumed in such massive quantity with no effect at all upon her figure.

Then she'd understood that she *was* sick.

Lovesick.

Good god, how adolescent.

No matter.

There it was.

She was in love and through the roseate lens of love she saw her marriage for the tawdry business that it was.

When she'd sent her lover off to his latest little war wearing the leather bomber jacket she'd bought him at Dr. K's Vintage Shop on U Street, a shit-eating grin, and a mantle of boyish bravado—the last had left her unimpressed, for one thing Nadja knew about was war—she'd promised him an answer on his return.

She'd expected her ardor to cool in his absence but if anything it had grown stronger, and, as she stared out at the snowbanks on the sidewalk, she knew she was going to elope with him.

He'd been offered a job in Paris—a city she'd always found agreeable—with some desperately soigné online current affairs, culture, and politics magazine, and she'd decided, just now, to go with him.

And Lucien be damned.

As she laughed and finished her cigarette and stared out the window at the flurries of falling snow, not really listening to the shrill American voices of the news anchors—the usual Barbie and Ken duo, all porcelain veneers and spray tans—she realized that, for the first time in many years, she was happy.

And when she turned and saw Michael Emerson's face on the TV screen, she thought she was allowing the stuff of her daydreams to bleed through into the real world. But it *was* Michael, smiling *that* smile in a photograph taken the night he'd won a Pulitzer for his reports on the rise of ISIS, and she heard Barbie telling of the discovery of his beheaded body in Raqqa, Syria, another American journalist fallen victim to the lunatic jihadists.

Nadja reached for the TV remote and, with hands that betrayed not the slightest tremor, killed the newscast.

Her eyes traveled from the dead gray tube to the small drawing that hung beside the refrigerator. The charcoal was of a Balkan peasant girl from the middle of the last century wearing a little hat, a waistcoat, and an embroidered blouse, smiling shyly. It was the only thing Nadja had retrieved from the casino villa that, during the siege of Sarajevo, had been the headquarters of a brigade of Bosnian Serb forces and where, as a pubescent, she'd been held captive for more than a year by a Serb colonel.

The drawing—only later, in America, had she discovered it was the work of the portraitist Ismet Mujezinović and was quite valuable—had hung over the colonel's bed and she'd stared at it during the many hours he raped her before handing her around to his men while mortar rounds whistled overhead.

In the last days of the war, the casino was surrounded by a ragged band of Bosnian Muslims who killed most of the Serbs in a protracted firefight. The colonel, wounded in the shoulder, walked out waving a craps stick with a white shirt tied to it.

The Bosniaks shot him where he stood and were inclined to consider Nadja a collaborator when a troll of a man, barely five feet tall with a huge head, stepped forward. His American accent and mysterious authority cleared a path through the ragged militia, and the next thing she knew she was in an old Mercedes being driven to a UN hospital and then it was on to America, Lucien Benway using his contacts to secure her refugee status.

She was fifteen. Lucien was thirty-one. He never laid a finger on her. When she turned sixteen, he proposed and she accepted and they had been married for twenty years. A marriage that had never been consummated.

Lucien Benway had rescued her, or that's how he would tell the tale. Truth was, he'd enslaved her, digging at the scabs on her psychological and spiritual wounds to keep them festering, goading her into a roundelay of meaningless sexual encounters with strangers that left her loathing herself, the idea of living without him unthinkable.

Until she'd met Michael Emerson, the love of her life, who had been left lying headless in the sand, like some fucking joke Ozymandias.

Nadja crossed to the refrigerator and opened the freezer, reaching in for the bottle of Stolichnaya that lay on its side, glass milky with ice.

She took a tumbler from the cabinet above the sink and sat down at the table, hearing the crack of the cap as she unscrewed it, and poured the chilled liquor into the glass.

She drank herself insensible.

ELEVEN

Kate Swift held tightly onto Suzie's gloved hand as they walked along Ebertstrasse not far from the Brandenburg Gate, heading toward Berlin's Holocaust Memorial.

The Wall had tumbled when she was a child, but she knew that it had run along most of the length of this street, bisecting the city that she'd always considered Philip Danvers' spiritual home.

It had been, in its schizoid state, the perfect metaphor for all of them—for all spies, everywhere.

No sooner had she thought of him than she saw Mrs. Danvers— Lucien Benway's bitchy handle had been adopted by even those who loved Philip, or *had* loved him—crossing the street, a second's uncertainty just as he gained the sidewalk hinting at his age.

He paused a moment beneath a denuded linden tree, taking in the 2,711 gray coffin-like concrete slabs arranged in a precise rectilinear array, before he walked into one of the narrow alleys between them, his silly little green Tyrolean hat with its jaunty feather disappearing as the ground plunged.

Kate followed, towing Suzie with her, scanning the street for pursuers. She saw nothing suspicious. Which meant nothing.

"Is that the old man from the subway, Mommy?" Suzie asked.

"Yes."

"Who is he?"

"Just a man I used to know."

"Is he your friend?"

"Yes, he's my friend," Kate said with more conviction than she felt as she led the child deeper into the narrow alley, the uneven cobbles slick with melting snow.

As they were dwarfed by higher and higher slabs, the city views reduced to slices from a gun turret, claustrophobia oppressing her.

This stone maze was the perfect venue for an ambush.

Kate was about to turn on her heel and flee with the child when Danvers appeared from behind a slab, his breath a plume as he spoke.

"Kate."

"Philip."

"I won't say that you look good."

"And neither will I."

Danvers coughed a laugh. "Why did you risk exposure, Kate? By coming to me?"

"Are you going to expose me?"

"God knows I should."

"Then why don't you?"

"Call it the caprice of a sentimental old man."

He looked at her with eyes faded to the color of dust and she could see the veins beneath the thin skin stretched across the bones of his face. He'd missed a spot shaving that morning, a trio of white hairs rising like antennae from a dewlap in his wizened neck.

"Why did you stay in America after you did what you did?" he asked.

"It's my country. It's her country." She nodded at Suzie, who was playing a solitary game of hide and seek.

"The country you betrayed?

"Philip, that's hopelessly one dimensional and you know it. We no longer live in simple times."

He raised his fine patrician nose and looked down its full length at her. "Oh, don't you dare to presume, Kate. I'm ancient enough to have seen it all, remember? In the sixties you would have been Jane Fonda. In the seventies, Patty Hearst. You're just another cliché."

"I was widowed, Philip. My child was left without a father. That's not a cliché."

"It's what you signed on for, Kate. And so did Yusuf."

"So I was meant to keep my mouth shut and grieve in private?"

"It's what we do."

"Maybe it's what *you* do. The noble warrior."

"Definitely not noble. Not now. I'm just an old man watching the parade from the porch of his retirement home."

He pinched the bridge of his nose between his fingers and closed his eyes for a second. Then he stared at her.

"Why do you want to connect with him, Kate?"

"Have you found out where he is?" Kate asked.

"Yes."

"Where?"

"First I need to ask you something."

"What?"

"What are your intentions?"

She laughed. "My *intentions*?"

"Yes. Forgive me if I feel protective toward him, but he was always the most fragile of us."

"How would I know? I've never met him."

"Don't be disingenuous, Katie. Are your demands going to be emotional?"

"No."

"No?"

"I need his help, Philip."

He cocked his head. "Help with what?"

"I want my daughter to grow up safely. To have a normal life. I want this over. I want to be invited back to the table."

"That's a big ask."

"Yes, it is."

"So you want a happy ending?"

"Yes. And if there's anyone who can script it, it's Harry Hook."

TWELVE

Hook, holed up in his wooden shack, a chorus of cicadas heralding the coming night, had been drinking without stopping since the previous afternoon—drinking away the memories that the mess at the hospital had stirred up, drinking to try and drown the guilt he carried like rocks in his pockets—and had reached a kind of plateau of inebriation where he seemed unable to become any drunker.

"How about another scotch, sport?" Hook said to himself, wagging the bottle of Cutty Sark in the thick air.

"Don't mind if I do," he replied and as the bartender freshened his drink to the strains of "I Will Always Love You" he was no longer Harry Hook, he was Marvin Murray—always a sucker for the alliterative nom de guerre—and it was over a decade ago, in the living room of the American consul's house on a tiny Asian island. Back when he was in his handsome midforties, tanned and smiling, and the drink in his hand was not the symptom of a problem or, god forbid, a disease, rather a social lubricant, a prop, all part of his cover as every needy foreigner's favorite sort of Yank: rich, philanthropic, and just a tad misty-eyed and naive.

This little shindig didn't merit a band, just as this island caliphate, a flyspeck on the ass of Indonesia, didn't merit an ambassador, merely a newly appointed consul—who looked as if he were still in his teens— working under Jakarta's umbrella.

The American evening, the brainchild of the consul's wife (a pretty little strawberry blond who held Hook's eyes for just a beat too long as her husband trundled her around the dance floor to the strains of

Whitney Houston from the stereo) was attended by the small expatriate community: the usual lizard-like older parties who needed the sun to keep their blood from congealing, here for the free booze in this dry land; a few sensibly shod do-gooders of a vaguely Christian stripe who were given short shrift in this Islamic enclave; and the ubiquitous "businessmen" who sniffed around these climes dispensing bribes in exchange for oil, cell phone, and resort concessions.

Hook felt a hand on his sleeve—the consul's wife.

"Mrs. Partridge," he said, "what a lively gathering."

"Call me Sally, please," she said. "Oh, it's a frightful bore." She plumped her lower lip in a toddleresque moue that made Hook want to bite her until she bled. "We were in Paris, you know, before this? And then Donald …" She wagged a freckled hand. "Well, let's not go into *that*."

Hook made a mental note to find out exactly what Donald Partridge had done to earn this hardship post.

Then Sally was in his arms, and he swung her out onto the floor, her tight little aerobicized belly pleasantly abrading his cock as Whitney warbled on: "Ahhhhhhhhh-yee-yiiiiiiiiiiii willa always lurve yeeeeeeewwwwww."

The shots that killed the two Marines at the gate seemed to be heard only by Hook, his ears, perhaps, attuned to a darker frequency.

Instinctively he stepped away from Sally Partridge and her succulent lower lip and moved toward the door just as eight men armed with AK-47s burst in, swinging the barrels like hoses, forcing the guests to stand with their hands up.

Somebody yanked the power cord, silencing Whitney. The leader of the group (who were all from Jihadist central casting) stepped forward, unwound his kaffiyeh and said, "Everybody, please stay calm," in mellifluous Oxbridge tones.

Hook knew him.

Knew Arsen Bujang, the charismatic British-educated leader of a little band of rebels who opposed the filthy-rich royal family that had leeched the blood of the poor islanders for centuries.

In fact, it had been Hook's, or rather Murray's, mission to befriend him, to seduce him with promises of American patronage via his entirely fictitious Global Peace Foundation—Hook at his showrunner best, creating websites and videos and setting up telephone lines that were answered by women with musical voices who spoke fulsomely about the foundation and the worthiness of Marvin Murray's deeds.

And he had, in his estimation, done this perfectly. Had turned Bujang into a believer, and had recommended to Washington that they back the rebels in their efforts to overthrow the royal family and thereby gain a foothold in this increasingly fundamentalist part of the world.

Hook stepped forward, showing his clammy palms when the gun barrels locked on him. "Tuan Bujang," he said, "what is this?"

"It's what the media will soon call a hostage situation, Mr. Murray." Bujang smiled through his beard. "Please, let's not turn it into a hostage *crisis.*"

The consul appeared, his voice shaking. "You're on the sovereign soil of the United States of America. I must demand that you withdraw immediately."

Bujang swiped him with the stock of his weapon and the man went down on one knee, bleeding from the nose.

"Mrs. Partridge, please tend to your husband," Bujang said.

Sally Partridge was moving toward the consul when another three men appeared from within the house, dragging with them a local woman and two strawberry-blond children, a boy and a girl, both under five. The children ran to their mother and gripped her legs and the Muslim woman stood wringing her hands and said something that earned her a back-handed slap from one of the gunmen. She folded in on herself and wept.

Bujang jerked his head at Hook. "Come with me."

Hook followed him into the kitchen where Bujang leaned against the counter, his weapon dangling casually from his shoulder.

"Okay, Harry Hook, you're rumbled, old son."

"I don't know what you're talking about. I'm Marvin Murray."

"You think I'm a bloody fool?"

"No."

"You're CIA." He saw the look on Hook's face, "Or one of its nameless bloody offshoots. Let's not split hairs. You're in the very belly of the imperialist beast." He flashed an ironic smile.

"Maybe so, but I've recommended that the administration give you its backing."

"Very white of you, Harry."

"Isn't that what you want?"

"A few crumbs from Mr. Bush in exchange for my soul? No, I think not."

"Then what? What *do* you want?"

"I want the attention of a world that is blissfully ignorant of our little nation and its egregious ills."

"Well, you'll get it. But you'll also get reamed by the platoon of Special Forces that'll be heading this way."

"It'll take a while for them to get their boots on the ground. Enough time for the global media to home in on our little bit of theater."

"What about the local militia?"

"Those Keystone Cops? They're trained to collect hush money for the regime and not much else. Anyway, they'll kowtow to your lot."

Hook knew he was right.

"And the hostages?"

"Oh, they'll be fine. As soon as we've had our bit of time in the media sun we'll free them."

"You killed the Marines."

"They were soldiers, Harry. An occupational hazard. But that ragtag bunch of civilians ..." He flapped a long-fingered hand in a dismissive gesture.

"You'll release them?"

"Pinky promise." Bujang grinned. He had very good teeth.

"And what about you and your men?"

"Martyrdom awaits, Harry. A glorious death."

Hook squinted at him. "Surely you don't really believe that horseshit?"

"Don't let my posh accent fool you, Harry. I'm as bloody fanatical as you'll get." He pushed away from the counter. "Come on, let's go and mingle."

The night passed with little incident. The rebels allowed food and water to be served and supervised bathroom breaks.

Hook was delegated as the voice to the outside world and he spoke first to the ambassador in Jakarta, who had been briefed on his mission and said, "Damned lucky to have a man like you on the inside, Harry."

When pressed for the rebels' demands, Hook had said they were still being formulated and all outside elements should stay in a holding pattern.

The media jetted in. The stringers from Jakarta, Singapore, and Manila arrived first. Then the Aussies. And finally the big guns: the American contingent and a handful of Europeans. Satellite dishes mushroomed outside the house, and a low wasp's buzz of assembled media drifted through the predawn air, only to be swamped by the call of the muezzin.

At sunrise, Hook spoke on the phone to the Special Forces colonel who had laid siege, ready to storm the gates.

"No action is required, Colonel," Hook said. "I have Bujang's word that all the hostages will be released."

"And you believe him?"

"Yes."

"Then you're either a goddamn fool or a goddamn seer."

Finally Bujang made his first, and only, demand.

An American TV reporter and camera crew were to be allowed in to record a statement.

How it was decided who would have the honor Hook never found out, but a brittle beauty with shellacked hair and the face of a starved greyhound, her toned body squeezed into fetching khaki pants and a flak jacket, came in with a cameraman who had the decency to look nervous.

The correspondent was all business, dismissing Hook and getting up close to Bujang.

Klieg lights were positioned, and the camera loved Arsen Bujang, with his fine voice and his flashing teeth and his dark good looks.

He spoke eloquently about the suffering of his people. About the years of oppression. About the brutality of the corrupt regime. He demanded that the world take note and ended with the pledge that this was merely the first action of a coming struggle.

He asked all the hostages to group together to be filmed, the tallest at the rear, the children standing with their parents in front. The cameraman did his work then he and the woman correspondent were escorted out.

Hook said to Bujang, "So, that's it?"

"Yes, it's time."

"Will you release them now?" he said, nodding at the hostages who still stood in formation.

Bujang said something to his men in the local language and two of them grabbed Hook and held him while the leader and the other men fired at the hostages, killing them all. They executed the two children, standing screaming over the torn bodies of their parents, last.

The smoke-filled room stank of propellant and blood and shit.

Hook, struggling, crying, puking, was restrained by the gunmen.

Bujang spoke again and Hook was pushed out into the yard where the helmeted, body-armored Special Forces soldiers were advancing weapons first, and they threw him to the ground and yelled at him and he didn't care if they shot him but they didn't, just bundled him into the street and established his identity and took him to the medics where he sat on a camp chair, still deafened from the noise in the room, and heard the muffled pops of the firefight that killed all the rebels and two Special Forces soldiers.

Why Arsen Bujang spared him he never knew.

Perhaps he'd understood that leaving Hook alive was a greater punishment than killing him.

Not only was he blamed for a bad judgment call that cost twenty-two people their lives, he was tainted with the suspicion of collusion. Philip Danvers had championed Hook, ensuring no formal charges were brought and the old man had, at first, refused to accept the resignation Hook tendered via email after jetting across the Straits of Malacca to Bangkok.

But Hook, judging himself more harshly than any tribunal could, had begun his own sentence of self-imposed exile, wearing an albatross of guilt that he would never shake.

In his jungle house, attempting to pour another drink, Hook knocked the glass from the table and it shattered. He lacked the inclination and the coordination to fetch a replacement and drank straight from the bottle.

Drank long and drank hard in a quest for oblivion.

THIRTEEN

Close to midnight, Kate, fighting sleep, sat staring out the window of the speeding train at the German countryside flying by—an old church hidden in the shadows of bare trees; a row of sodium lights staining the snow orange; a lone, tiny car panting at a level crossing.

Suzie sat across the table from her, hands in the pockets of the bulky jacket, wearing the baseball cap pulled low. Kate couldn't see her eyes and hoped she was asleep, but then Suzie looked up and said, "Where are we, Mommy?"

"I don't know. Not exactly. Somewhere between Berlin and Hamburg."

The girl flipped open the comic book she'd bought at Zoo Station, smudging a finger over the manga characters, then fixed Kate with a look that was heartbreakingly like her father's.

"That old man today, he called you Katie."

"Yes."

"Why?"

"Because that used to be my name."

"Before you were Holly Brenner?"

"Yes."

"What was my name, before?"

"Suzie. Susan. It's always been the same."

"No. My last name."

"Can't you remember?"

"No, you made me forget it."

"Yes, I did. I'm sorry. It was Hourani. Susan Hourani."

"Hourani?"

"Yes."

"Was that Daddy's name?"

"Yes."

"But not yours?"

"No, I was Kate Swift."

"But you were married?"

"Yes, but I kept my name."

"Why?"

"I just did."

"I like Suzie Hourani."

"So do I."

"Will I ever be her again?"

"Yes, I hope so."

The child went back to the comic book and Kate closed her eyes for a moment and the rocking motion of the train lulled her dangerously close to sleep.

She stood. "Come."

"Where?"

"I need coffee."

Leaving their bags stowed in the overhead racks they walked down the carriage. They passed the toilets, and the glass doors to the dining car sprang apart to allow them through.

Kate scanned the car. A uniformed attendant stood behind the counter checking his cell phone, a middle-aged couple sat at a table in hunched silence and a young blond woman was seated alone, reading a paperback copy of *The Looking Glass War*.

Kate showed Suzie to a table and approached the counter, ordering an espresso and a Coke from the attendant.

She usually forbade Suzie sugary soda drinks, but they had a long night ahead—a flight from Hamburg to Copenhagen where they would get their plane to Bangkok—and she didn't want the child wilting on her.

The doors opened and a man in his thirties wearing blue jeans and a checked shirt entered and slumped down at a table, staring out at the night.

Kate took the Coke can and the small paper cup of espresso to where Suzie sat. The man looked up at her for just a moment before his gaze shifted out the window again, but she knew, just as she'd known at the school, that it was on.

Kate sat and opened the can for Suzie before taking a hit of espresso even though she no longer needed it—a jolt of raw adrenalin had smashed away any sluggishness.

She stole a glance at the man.

He was sandy-haired and fair-skinned. They wouldn't send a swarthy man, not even one who could be just another Turkish *Gastarbeiter*. This guy looked German, looked like he drank beer and yelled at the TV when Hamburger SV scored in the Bundesliga. He was probably a Slavic Muslim, a Chechen, or maybe a Bosniak.

Who had sent him?

She didn't know.

The face-to-face with Mrs. Danvers had brought its risks, and Kate was still on hit lists that spanned the Middle East, despite her betrayal of the hated America.

The man who had come to kill her was just a grain of sand in the shifting landscape of fundamentalist Islam. Sunni, Shiite, Wahhabi, Palestinian, Zaidi—in her years in intelligence, recruited by Philip Danvers after 9/11, Kate had used them all. Lied to them all. Fucked some of them. Blackmailed some of them. Killed some of them.

Married one and watched him die.

And Lucien Benway, like some contemporary Lawrence of Arabia, had a roster of Muslims of every breed on his payroll.

Kate took another unwanted sip of her coffee and leaned in toward Suzie.

"I need to go to the bathroom." She leaned in closer. "What's the time?"

Suzie consulted her boyish wristwatch. "Eleven fifty-two."

"If I'm not back in five minutes you go to that woman over there reading the book and you ask her to help you. You don't speak to anybody else. You get her to take you to the police and you tell them who you are. Who you *really* are. Okay?"

Suzie was staring at her in fear. "Mommy …"

"Do you hear me?"

"Yes. I hear you."

"It's okay, I'll be back."

Kate stood and didn't look at the man as she headed toward the exit, the doors opening and guillotining closed behind her.

She stepped into the toilet, keeping the door open a crack. After a few seconds she heard the hiss and suck as the doors of the dining car opened, followed by the scuff of a footstep. She came out fast and hit the sandy-haired man in the throat with the blade of her hand.

She was off her game—a few years ago the blow would have killed him, but she missed the hyoid and he merely grunted and buckled, so she dragged him into the toilet, kicking the door closed behind her.

Kate felt the shape of a pistol at his hip. She freed a Beretta 92FS sporting a YHM Wraith silencer from his jeans and was tempted to use it, but even the muffled report would be dangerously loud in this confined space, so she dropped it into the stainless steel sink.

The man threw his weight back and her skull smashed against the bulkhead. He tried to turn but she rabbit-punched him in the kidneys and he whinnied and sank. Still shaking off the blow to the head, she didn't follow up fast enough and he sent back an elbow to her solar plexus and she felt the air leave her. He managed to spin and punch her in the ribs and caught her with a right to the jaw that was hard enough to dim the lights.

She was on her back and he dropped onto her with one knee, pinning her to the floor, simultaneously reaching into the sink to retrieve the gun.

As she saw the black snout of the silencer pointing at her she drove a knee into his groin and lashed out with her fist, knocking the weapon from his hand. She reached up and jammed a thumb into his eye socket and crushed his eyeball.

He screamed almost soundlessly.

She forced him to his knees, got above him, took his head in her hands and broke his neck.

Kate stood, gripping the sink, and vomited, then rinsed her mouth and her face and finger-combed her hair in the mirror. She left the toilet, pulling the door closed behind her, and went back into the dining car where Suzie sat staring at her with a look of terror on her face.

The train's PA was announcing their arrival at somewhere called Büchen. Kate took Suzie's hand and said, "Come, quickly."

She walked her through to their carriage and grabbed their bags and joined the few people waiting at the doors.

The train stopped and Kate took the child's hand again and they hurried into the night to find a taxi to take them to Hamburg.

As they passed beneath a streetlight, Suzie said, "You've got blood on you. On your sleeve."

Kate looked down and saw it was true. She folded the sleeve back. "It's okay," she said, "it's not mine."

FOURTEEN

As the old elevator sighed and creaked upward with painful slowness, its winding drum moaning ominously, Lucien Benway stood staring through the scissor gate at the passing floors, trying to ignore the smell of urine and worse.

There had been a terse message from Morse on Benway's cell when he'd fired it up after landing at Dulles, his head thick with scotch and travel fatigue. He'd returned the call, expecting news of Kate Swift, but Morse had summoned him here, to this fleabag hotel.

At last the cage lurched to a halt and Benway shoved aside the folding gate and stepped out. Only one of the overhead lights worked, and it fizzed and strobed, illuminating the passageway in hard green bursts.

Morse, standing in front of a closed door, his feet planted wide apart, his hands behind his back, came to semiattention as Benway approached him.

"Sir."

Morse pushed the door open and stepped aside, allowing Benway a view of as sorry a hotel room as he had ever seen.

His wife lay supine on the roiled bed, a greasy sheet covered her nakedness. Benway flashed on Morse, like the undertaker he so resembled, drawing the sheet over Nadja.

But his wife wasn't dead.

Just dead drunk.

The room stank of puke and sex. An empty bottle of vodka and two smeared shot glasses on the bedside table told the story. A coiled condom—a slug trail of semen dribbling out onto the filthy carpet that sucked at the soles of Benway's shoes—was the punch line.

Benway sniffed the air like a terrier, smelling his wife (Samsara, musk, her juices) mixed with the stink of an unwashed male.

"The man?" Benway asked.

"I got rid of him," Morse said, unconsciously flexing his right hand and sending it behind his back, but not before Benway saw the abrasion on one knuckle, a small scab already forming.

The man would remember more than Nadja's pale thighs when he reminisced on this night.

"Who was he?"

"Just a drunk." Morse sucked his teeth.

Benway sighed as he looked down at his wife. She'd wanted to punish herself tonight, to take herself to a low and dirty place.

"I called the facility," Morse said. "They'll be here shortly."

A very discreet and very expensive detox clinic in leafy Maryland. They knew Nadja well.

"How did you find her?"

"A beat cop saw her coming in here. He recognized her from the DUI a few years back and called me."

"Did you compensate him?"

"It's taken care of, sir."

"Thank you, Morse." Benway caught a glimpse of his lined face in the peeling mirror and looked away.

The tall man stood even straighter.

"Sir, the other business."

"Yes?"

"Kate Swift made contact with Danvers in Berlin and then caught a train to Hamburg."

"And?"

"She killed our man on the train."

Benway winced and squeezed his temples between thumb and forefinger. "His orders were to watch her? Nothing more?"

"Exactly, but he clearly underestimated her."

"Yes, I made that mistake myself." He sighed and busied himself with lighting a cigarette, the Ronson clicking and flaring. "Any idea of her destination?"

"No. I'm checking all the flights out of Hamburg."

"Go. Make that your priority. I'll take this from here."

Morse nodded and left the room, closing the door quietly.

Benway stood over the bed, smoking, and as he studied his insensible wife's face he saw the girl he'd rescued from the rubble of Sarajevo twenty years before. She'd come so far and yet she hadn't moved at all.

FIFTEEN

Maybe it was jet lag, sleep deprivation, or stress, but as Kate stepped from the air-conditioned taxi into the molten heat thick with gasoline fumes she was no longer in Bangkok. She was in Lahore and it wasn't Suzie's hand she clutched, but Yusuf's, his blood hot and sticky as it spilled down the sleeve of his *kameez* onto her fingers.

She'd rushed him from a car, the driver already accelerating away, across a sidewalk of street vendors and into an alley, sitting him down on the filthy asphalt. Yusuf reached up and, shifting the scarf she wore over her hair, touched her face, smiling at her through his beard. His white teeth flashing as he said, "I'm okay, Katie. I'm okay. It's just a flesh wound."

And it was.

That day he'd been lucky. So had she. The car bomb on the Empress Road that had left scores dead had flung them to the ground, but only Yusuf had been injured, taking a small twist of metal to the upper arm.

Kate should have forced Yusuf to drive with her to the airport, should never have left Pakistan without him.

But he'd insisted that the bombing was a coincidence. That he still needed to rendezvous with the man who would take him to his erstwhile assets in South Waziristan. That the lives of two families depended on it.

Looking at his face, thinking of their daughter back home, in the care of Yusuf's parents, had caused her to nod and drive alone to the airport.

She had never seen her husband alive again.

"Mommy! Mommy?"

Suzie, tugging at her sleeve, brought her back into Bangkok, the air thick with rotting trash, spiced food, and the stench of the canals and the river.

She paid the taxi driver and took Suzie into a street market, a garish sprawl of clothing, electronic gadgets, Buddhist trinkets, deaf people selling Viagra and imitation Patek watches, and strange food cooked in the open on woks, the fragrant smoke clinging to their clothes and hair. Kate, even though she'd shed her coat and boots, sweltered under her winter clothes.

She shopped quickly, knowing that the press of people around her and Suzie hid them but would also obscure anyone tailing them.

She bought boys' T-shirts and shorts for Suzie, despite her daughter's protests and the beeline the girl had made for the stalls selling knock-off Roxy beachwear for girls. She bought them both flip-flops. She bought lightweight shirts for herself and a pair of linen drawstring pants.

Walking in search of a taxi, they came upon a looming hotel with a doorman dressed like an extra from *The King and I*. He ushered them into the cool interior with its soothing rattan décor, and she took the child into the bathroom and they changed into their tropical gear.

Suzie, in her T-shirt, boardshorts, and cap looked even more like a boy. A miserable boy.

Kate looked like just another pallid Westerner in Thailand for the sun.

She left the suitcase containing their winter clothes in the bathroom and, toting the bags filled with the beach gear, led Suzie across the lobby into the street, where she flagged down a taxi to take them back to Suvarnabhumi Airport, to get their flight to the south and Harry Hook.

SIXTEEN

"Nadja? Nadja, can you hear me?" Michael asked.

But when Nadja Benway opened her eyes and her pupils slowly adjusted to the light and found focus on the face hovering near hers, it wasn't her dead lover's, it was her wrinkled husband's, and she felt a dread so profound that she could do nothing but shut them again.

After what felt like hours she allowed her right eyelid to lift just a fraction.

Lucien was still there and—in his typically flagrant disregard of other peoples' rules—drew on a cigarette, exhaling smoke through flared nostrils.

"Welcome back." Lucien smiled at her. "You're in the clinic. You've experienced some kind of a … breakdown."

"You did it, didn't you?"

"Did what?"

"Killed Michael."

Lucien shook his head. "I don't know any Michael."

"Liar!"

Nadja tried to lunge forward, wanting to tear out his deceitful tongue, but she found she couldn't move her arms and legs.

Tilting her head, a task almost beyond her, Nadja saw her limbs were harnessed to the metal bed frame by cloth straps.

She screamed and Lucien smiled down at her complacently.

A white-clad figure hurried in and fiddled with the drip dangling over her. The room, and Lucien with it, were consumed by a spiral of darkness.

SEVENTEEN

Hook awoke to the grind of an engine struggling up to his house. Unwashed, fogged, and shaking, he dragged himself from his bed and crept to the window. He saw it was nearly sunset, the lurid sky too bright for his torn eyes.

He snagged his tortoiseshell Wayfarers from the table and peered out the fly-screened window. When he spotted a little bile-green van jolting up the track—whoever sat in the taxi's covered flatbed getting shaken like shucked peas—he relaxed a little.

He knew this particular *tuk-tuk*. The Thai driver, Ton, did him the odd favor in exchange for cash.

The tuk-tuk clattered and gasped to a halt and threatened to roll back before the emergency brake held.

Ton—small, dark, and wiry—slid from behind the wheel as a young woman and a boy stepped down from the rear, flapping their hands at the cloud of red dust.

Hook pulled on a befouled T-shirt, stepped out his door, and stood at the top of the steps leading down to the dirt.

"*Sawadee kap*, Harry."

"*Sawadee kap*, Ton."

"*Sabaidee mai?*"

"I'm good, Ton. Who are you bringing here?"

Before he could answer, the driver's cell phone rang and he started a loud conversation in Thai. The kid stayed by the taxi, but the woman headed toward the stairs.

Hook held up a hand like a cigar-store Indian. "Whoa, lady, I think you're lost."

"Can I come up?"

"What for?"

"I need your help."

"I'm not in the tourist business."

"I know that. It's you I'm here to see."

"Clearly you're confusing me with somebody else."

She shook her blond head and his old spy's eyes saw the fingers of black creeping in at the roots. "No, you're Harry Hook," she said.

When she spoke his real name, Hook lurched down the steps, his head throbbing.

"Who the fuck are you?"

"My name's Kate Swift."

Weighed down by days of drinking, it took a while for the dots to connect but when they did, he gaped.

"Yes," she said, "the traitor."

"I was going to say whistle-blower."

"I'm not a soccer referee." She tried a smile but her tense jaw muscles made it more of a grimace.

"What are you doing here?" Hook asked.

"As I said, I need your help."

"How did you find me?"

"Mrs. Danvers."

"Christ, he must be getting soft in his declining years."

"Or compassionate." When Hook snorted, she said, "You know what's happened? With me?"

"Hell, yes. Two years ago you got on everybody's shit list."

"No, not two years ago. Two *days* ago."

He shook his head. "No. Why would I know that?"

"It's been all over the news."

"I don't get time to watch the news. I've been busy."

Kate looked at his stubble and his soiled clothes and said, "Yeah, I can see that." She moved a strand of hair from her face. "Two days ago my cover was blown and I'm on the run. We are. Me and my daughter."

He looked over at the kid standing by the taxi, watching them from under a cap.

"I thought it was a boy."

"That's the idea."

"And you came to me? Why?"

"I know your reputation. I know that you have a way of making things happen."

"Had."

"Huh?"

"Had. Past tense. Whoever I once was, I am no longer."

"Please."

"No. I can't help you. Now you get the hell out of here. Let the taxi take you to the airport. Pronto."

"You're turning us away?"

"Lady, I can't even fix my own problems. I wouldn't know where the hell to start with yours." He called across to the driver. "Ton, get them to the airport, okay?"

Kate Swift looked like she was about to speak, then her mouth closed and she turned and walked back to the taxi, took the kid's hand, and they climbed into the back.

Ton started the *tuk-tuk*, giving Hook one of those blank Buddhist looks that warn of bad luck ahead.

"Fuck you," Hook said to the dust of the retreating taxi, "and the karma you rode in on."

***

As they bumped back down the track, Kate leaned forward and spoke to the driver. "Is there still a flight out?"

"One last plane to Bangkok," Ton said. "It leave seven o'clock."

"Take us, please." She sat back.

"Was that him, Mommy?" Suzie said.

"Yes, that was him."

"Then why are we going?"

"Because he's just a story, baby."

"A story?"

"Yeah, a story he made up a long time ago that your mommy was dumb enough to believe."

She looked at the limestone cliffs that reared out of the dense green jungle, creased rocks glowing red in the late light. The stuff of postcards. The taxi slowed for a pothole in the road and they crept past a pile of torn black trash bags, a stray dog feeding on the ripe garbage that rotted in the sun.

"Where are we going now?" Suzie asked.

"To get another plane."

"Another plane where?"

"To someplace better, baby."

EIGHTEEN

Hook sat staring at the liter of Cutty Sark that stood atop his elderly Sony Trinitron, the vibrations from the soundtrack of the subtitled Stallone action movie that was reaching its wild and bloody climax causing the golden liquid to undulate slightly in a way that was almost sexually seductive.

It was night, and the only light came from the TV. Hook sat before the tube dressed in a pair of shorts, his bare torso covered in a thin sheen of sweat.

A mosquito had breached the net on the window and whined around his head, Hook too entranced by the dance of the whiskey to do more than wag a limp hand in defense.

He wanted to drink.

Jesus, he *needed* to drink. He knew that sleep would elude him unless he uncorked that bottle and swallowed its contents and let the amber liquid lead him into the arms of Mr. Sandman.

Then why was he resisting?

The answer to that question was the push he needed and he sat forward on the cane chair, the damp flesh of his back separating from the woven rattan with an audible smooch, and reached across for the bottle.

His hand stopped midair.

The Stallone movie had given way to breaking news: a live feed of the crash site of a passenger jet that had fallen en route to Bangkok— burning jungle, cops, soldiers and firefighters, and hurtling emergency vehicles.

Hook couldn't understand Thai—the complex tonal language was beyond his grasp—but he knew exactly what he was seeing, and he sat rapt, his hands gripping his knees, watching the images of horror and devastation, the Cutty Sark invisible to him now.

NINETEEN

Benyamin Klein, stinging sweat running from under the *kippah* pinned to the thinning hair on his crown down into the furrows on his thick neck, sideburn ringlets and long beard as wet as if he'd stepped from a shower, black suit pants and white shirt clinging to his flesh beneath the plastic coveralls, carried a body bag across a scorched and smoldering clearing the size of a city block. The dense green foliage of the jungle had been incinerated when the Airbus A320 hurtled from fifteen thousand meters and exploded on impact the night before, the nearly full fuel load igniting in a huge fireball that had been seen fifty kilometers away, or so the Thais said.

The body bag, which lay across his extended forearms like an offering and drooped on either side, appeared weightless.

The aircraft had been almost completely destroyed, with none of the fuselage remaining. The only recognizable components were the forward landing gear (a pair of huge wheels that lay upside down near the canopy of singed trees marking the perimeter of the crash site) and half of the tail section, the garish yellow-and-red logo of the low-cost Asian airline still visible. Such was the devastation that the first responders had found none of the 171 souls aboard intact—just hands, arms, legs, and heads hanging like strange fruit from the palms.

Klein and his four colleagues—members of a Haredi voluntary community emergency response organization—and three secular Jews from the Magen David Adom emergency medical services had arrived late in the morning and the larger chunks of remains had already been removed and carried to a makeshift morgue in a nearby Buddhist temple, its garish heathen pagodas grinning over the thick green bush. They'd brought DNA samples, fingerprints, and dental records on the eleven-hour flight from Jerusalem and were now charged with identifying and collecting the body parts of the sixteen teenage Israeli gymnasts and their three coaches who had been aboard the doomed flight.

Once the larger pieces of flesh, which were too burned for visual identification, were collected, Klein and his team set about fine-tooth-combing the wreckage for smaller body parts. This they were uniquely equipped to do. Attending the aftermath of intifada suicide bombings over the last twenty years, he'd seen an average of thirty bodies a week.

It was his calling to do this. His sacred task to recover every part of the bodies for a Jewish burial.

As Klein walked, smoke still rising from the blackened earth, his feet crunching on metal and glass, he blinked away sweat.

He was used to heat, yes, coming from Jerusalem. But it was the humidity that stunned him, and this place—with its palm trees, coconuts, monkeys, and small brown people who worshipped idols—was a spiritual wasteland for him.

It was not his first visit to Thailand.

He had been here over a decade ago, in the aftermath of the tsunami in Phuket, searching for the bodies of Israelis. He and his colleagues had become known as "the team that sleeps with the dead" because they'd toiled nearly twenty-four hours a day to identify victims, the disinfectant the Thais sprayed over the mounds of corpses doing nothing to mask the stench of decomposition.

A bad time.

A hell on earth.

Klein came to a halt, getting back his breath, resting his bad knee, the plastic of the black body bag hot to his skin.

His wife, Batsheva, had tried to stop him from volunteering yesterday when he'd gotten the call at their small apartment in Mea She'arim, Jerusalem's ultra-Orthodox enclave.

"You are old now, Benyamin," she'd said. "Let the young men go."

"No," he'd said, "it is my duty. They need a man of my experience."

"But your knee is very bad."

He'd shrugged off her protests, even though Thailand was the last place on God's earth he wanted to go and his knee burned as if the flames of Gehenna were licking at it.

Thirty years ago, full of faith and fire, Klein had refused to sit beside a woman on a bus in Jerusalem and had demanded that she move. Another woman, young, in the uniform of a soldier, had sworn at him, saying he was a parasite and a coward for refusing to fight in Israel's wars, and told the woman to stay seated.

When he'd called the soldier a whore, she'd punched him in the face like a man, kicked him in his private parts with her heavy boot, and thrown him from the moving bus. He'd fallen to the roadway, shattering his knee, left bloody and weeping in the filth of the gutter.

He'd limped ever since and, as he'd become heavier with the years and Batsheva's cooking, so had the discomfort increased.

One of Klein's colleagues, prodding at a twist of buckled metal with a stick, spoke to him in Yiddish, asking him if he was unwell.

"*Es geyt gut, a dank*," Klein said and limped on.

A tent had been set up beside the crash site, guarded by Thai police and military who kept back the media and a horde of chattering onlookers. Inside, poring over the remains culled by Klein and his fellow volunteers, were the secular Jews: a DNA expert, a dentist, and a fingerprint man.

One of them looked up at Klein and nodded.

"What do you have?" he asked in Hebrew.

Klein deposited the body bag on the floor and the man unzipped it beneath the light of bright lamp, revealing a chunk of blackened flesh, possibly the meat of an upper thigh; a boy's sneaker, one of those garish American ones with all the colors and the straps and buckles, with a foot still inside, the bone and flesh sheared off at the ankle; and a finger, severed just below the knuckle that, judging from the size and the well-manicured cuticle, appeared to be a woman's fifth digit.

The flesh was charred and blackened, but when the man's gloved hands turned the pinkie over, the intact whorl of the fingerprint was thrown into relief by the glare of the lamp.

TWENTY

The black SUV growled up the freshly plowed driveway of a nondescript tract house in the Washington suburbs and came to a halt alongside its twin in a double garage, the motorized door clattering and thumping as it rolled down and obliterated the cold and dismal night.

The driver, a youngish man in a suit, had a vivid swoosh of shaving rash on his neck and the blank face that spoke of blind obedience and an almost sexual penchant for self-abnegation—in other words, he was exactly the type that Philip Danvers had *never* recruited for his surrogate family.

Danvers stepped down from the car that was as hot and stifling as an East Village bathhouse back in the day and shivered in the unheated garage. The other SUV still pinged and creaked and Danvers felt its warmth as he brushed its gleaming flank on the way to the wooden door that was being held open by the driver.

The house, something thrown together in the sixties—stucco with a pitched roof—was remarkable only for its lack of furniture.

The driver led Danvers along a corridor with beige carpets, passing dark, empty, echoing rooms with bare walls. He stopped at a closed door at the end of the corridor, rapped on the wood, and swept it open.

This room was furnished with a steel desk and two chairs. A gray-haired man in a black suit sat behind the desk in the pooled light of a lamp.

"Thank you for coming in, Philip."

Danvers walked into the room and stood with his hands on the back of the empty chair.

"Why have I been summoned here?" he asked, although he had a very good idea why he'd received the call an hour earlier that, though it had been polite, had hardly been a request.

"Philip, please sit," the gray-haired man said.

He was powerful—and accomplished—enough to have occupied a niche interfacing between four successive administrations and the less-than-savory apparatchiks of the intelligence community. He'd long been known as the Plumber, and Danvers had forgotten his real name, if indeed he had ever known it.

Danvers stayed standing, drumming his fingers on the chairback's unpleasant synthetic fabric, his fingertips itching at the touch.

"Philip, please," the Plumber said, extending a scrubbed, blunt-fingered hand.

Danvers sat, hitching up his pressed trousers and crossing his legs at the knee, the jiggling of his highly polished but magnificently creased leather brogan a barometer of his choler.

"We're here tonight to discuss the recent developments in the Kate Swift fiasco," the Plumber said, and Danvers felt a slight reflex retraction of his ancient scrotum.

Was that a trickle of warm urine he felt escaping into his underpants?

Dear God, had the hour of the adult diaper finally come?

"Let's start with an irrefutable fact. For two years, until she single-handedly stopped that school massacre three days ago, Kate Swift lived in New Devon, Vermont, as Holly Brenner. DNA harvested from her home has proved this."

The Plumber placed a plastic ziplock bag containing a blackened, severed finger on the table. "The second irrefutable fact." He looked at Danvers. "This is the little finger of Kate Swift's left hand. It was recovered from the crash site of a domestic flight in Thailand."

Danvers was racked by a bout of nausea so powerful that he was certain he was going to spew his dinner onto the desktop. He gulped for breath, the Plumber watching him without expression.

Danvers, fighting for control, said, "How did you acquire the finger?"

The Plumber shrugged. "We back-channeled it." He stared at Danvers. "Let's now venture into the area where educated guessing meets speculation. We believe that Kate Swift made contact with you in Berlin two days ago. Is this true?"

Danvers sat a while, shaken, bereft, then said, "Yes. She did."

"And you didn't think to inform us?"

"I felt she had been sufficiently betrayed."

"Interesting. Some would say that *she* was the betrayer."

"I was one of those, yes."

"And yet?"

Danvers shrugged. "And yet …"

"What was the substance of your conversation?"

"She wanted me to tell her the whereabouts of Harry Hook."

"Did you?"

"Yes."

"And where is Hook?"

"In southern Thailand."

"What did she want with Hook?"

"She thought he could broker some sort of rapprochement between her and your masters. She knew of his formidable strategic skills."

The Plumber stared down at the blackened finger, then he looked up at Danvers. "Have you had communication with Lucien Benway about any of this?"

"Lucien and I have not spoken in years. Why?"

"The plane's black box hasn't yet been recovered, so this is pure speculation …" The Plumber paused. A pause so pregnant it was practically panting on all fours.

"Surely you don't believe Lucien downed that plane?"

The Plumber shrugged. "We're not ruling it out."

"Not even Lucien would do that."

"No? Benway is Benway …"

"Dear God, yes."

"So we have decided to make no announcement about Kate Swift's presumed death. Or that of her child. Not until we have more clarity."

Danvers nodded. "Obviously. I understand."

The Plumber stood. "Thank you for your time, Philip."

Danvers stayed seated, staring at the ziplock. "May I take that finger?"

"Why?"

"Call me sentimental, but I think Kate deserves some kind of burial. Even a symbolic one."

The Plumber hesitated before he pushed the bag across to Danvers, who lifted it, doing his best not to look at its contents as he slipped it into his pocket.

"I'm counting on your discretion, Philip."

"Of course."

Danvers stood, lightheaded, and steadied himself on the back of the ugly chair.

He left the room, and as he followed the young man back to the garage, he thought about his own imminent death and felt the weight of a long lifetime of sins upon his narrow shoulders.

TWENTY-ONE

Maybe she *had* died. Died and gone to heaven.

Kate drifted out of sleep, lying in the shade of a beach umbrella, the cloth beneath her hot from the sand. The incoming tide, the sea warm as tea, lapping at her toes woke her.

She heard laughter and looked across the sprawl of pristine white beach to where Suzie played at the water's edge with the Frenchman, Jean-Philippe, he of the teak-colored tan, the sun-bronzed hair and the ridiculously ripped abdomen.

JP grabbed the girl and lifted her, beads of water from her maypoling hair catching the low sun that lay like golden ink upon the impossibly blue ocean, and ran with her into the placid waves, the two of them laughing and shouting with nobody but Kate to hear them on this island, a tiny fleck of paradise lost somewhere in the Andaman Sea.

Kate got as far as shifting her sandy hair from her face, fully intending to raise herself from the cloth and join her daughter and the Frenchman, but she closed her eyes instead. And the twinge of pain from her left hand, the stump of her little finger bandaged and wrapped in plastic to protect it, was not enough to drag her back from the sleep that took her deep and far away.

***

When hands shook her awake, Kate's first impulse was to fight, to protect herself and her daughter who slept beside her. She lashed out with the blade of her hand and heard an oath.

"Fuck, it's me," Harry Hook said.

Kate pulled the punch that she was about to throw and sat up, panting, enough gray dawn light bleeding in through the window to see Hook rubbing his face as he stood over her, a blurred shape through the mosquito net anchored to the ceiling, covering them like a shroud.

"I need to talk to you," Hook said and retreated.

She could smell him—sweat, old booze, and a sour whiff of fear, like an ashen ghost flitting through a charnel house.

He closed the door to the single bedroom in his house, the room that he'd surrendered to her and Suzie the evening before.

Kate, still dressed but shoeless, sat up and cursed herself for her lack of vigilance, for allowing herself to sleep.

She stood and felt the press of her bladder. She needed to pee. Badly. Which meant going out there and facing that man. Her woefully inept would-be savior.

Yesterday, after she and Suzie had rattled away in the *tuk-tuk*, they were almost at the junction of the gravel track and the blacktop when an old dirt bike, belching exhaust smoke, headed them off. Hook had dismounted and walked to the rear of the van.

"Okay," he said.

"Okay, what?" Kate said.

"Okay, come back to my house."

"Why?"

"At least rest up and maybe we can figure something out."

"Why the sudden change of heart?"

"We're both alumni of Mrs. Danvers' finishing school. That has to count for something." He smiled and she glimpsed a flash of threadbare charm hiding under the sweat and the stubble.

She wanted to tell him to fuck off but sheer desperation and the knowledge of who he was—or, rather, of who he had been in his salad days—had her nodding her agreement. He spoke to the taxi driver who turned the vehicle and they went back up through the dense jungle, so green it hurt her eyes.

Hook sped by them in a cloud of dust and by the time they reached his house he was standing at the bottom of the steps, waving them up. He grabbed the bags from her and took them into the only bedroom.

The place was squalid. Rank.

He saw her face and shrugged.

"I'm not going to apologize," he said. "I'm not big on company."

He pushed open a door to reveal a toilet and an uncurtained shower, just a spigot and a hole in the wooden floor.

"You can wash up if you like."

Suzie looked around and grinned and said, "Cool."

Hook winked and crossed to the refrigerator, found a can of soda and tossed it at her.

He wagged a bottle of Chang beer at Kate, his eyebrows raised. She nodded and took it. She wasn't a beer drinker, but the cold, bitter liquid tasted good.

He cracked a can of Coke, drank, and belched softly. "You hungry?"

"I am," Suzie said.

"Okay, why don't you two freshen up and I'll go down to town and get us some supper." He saw Kate's face. "It's okay. You're safe here." He shrugged. "I'll stay if it makes you feel better."

"No, go."

Kate heard him kicking the bike to life—it took a while, and he encouraged it with a string of oaths—then it roared and clattered and he was gone.

She got them showered, tepid brown water spluttering, and the waft of a fetid smell from the septic tank mingling with the heady fragrance of flowers in bloom outside the bathroom window.

They were dressed and sitting at the table when Hook returned with an array of small bags tied at the top with rubber bands: rice, chicken curry, and grilled pork. He'd also brought coffee from Starbucks and Popsicles for Suzie.

He spread out the feast and took paper plates from a drawer and set them on the table and they dove in with their fingers. The spicy food was delicious and Kate amazed herself at how much she ate.

By the end of the meal Suzie was wilting. Kate lifted her and carried her through to the bedroom and gently laid her on the bed. The linen smelled like it hadn't seen a laundry in a long while.

Kate went back and joined Hook at the table. A bottle of Cutty Sark stood unopened on the counter, but he sipped from another Coke can.

"Drink if you want," she said.

"I kicked it years ago," he said. "Until two days back. Fell off the wagon."

She said nothing, watching as he toyed with the can and drew on the surface of the table with some of the spilled liquid.

He looked up at her. "Did you see Mrs. Danvers?"

"Yes. Yesterday, in Berlin."

"How is he?"

"Old."

He took a pack of unopened Camels from his pocket and showed them to her. "Do you mind?"

"It's your house."

He shook out a cigarette and lit it with a disposable plastic lighter. "I kicked these too."

"Yeah?"

"I only smoke when I'm nervous."

"Relax, we'll be out of your hair soon. You can get back to your busy schedule."

He laughed smoke and then sat back and stared at her. "What do you want, exactly? From me?"

"I want my daughter to grow up in America. I want to live there without threat."

He shook his head. "That's not possible."

"It must be."

"And for some reason you think I can do this? Why?"

"Philip made all us young wannabes study your methods. You were like some guru who'd wandered off to live in a cave. A legend."

He exhaled at the ceiling. "That's me. The drunken master."

"You were, and I'm quoting Mrs. Danvers here, 'able to conjure connections, opportunities, and unexpected victories out of the ether.'"

"Yeah, I was a regular fucking magician, wasn't I?"

"I thought so."

"Then I made twenty-two hostages disappear. Poof. Just like that." He snapped his fingers.

"That wasn't your fault."

"No?"

"No."

"But it happened on my watch."

"Look, let's not sit here and rehash our old sins."

"No, let's not." He drank the Coke, but his eyes lingered like a lecher's on the whiskey bottle. He turned to Kate. "This is rough on your kid."

"Yes. She's been through hell."

"Yeah. Well. What you chose to do …"

"I didn't have a *choice*."

"We always have choices, Kate. You knew what would happen if you did what you did."

"What would you have done?"

"I'm too much of a coward to have taken the stand you did."

She rose. "We'll go in the morning."

He shrugged and stared at the bottle, smoke rising from his cigarette. "Okay," he said, shrugging again.

She'd gone into the bedroom intending to sit vigil, but she'd slept and now it was dawn and she needed to pee.

Kate went out and Hook was standing in the doorway of the front room, wearing only frayed khaki shorts, watching the first sun paint itself across the cliffs.

He nodded. She said nothing, crossed to the bathroom, and

emptied her bladder then brushed her teeth and ran her fingers through her hair.

When she went back into the room, he was standing by the old TV. The Cutty Sark was still balanced on its top. Unopened.

"There's something I want you to see," he said, clicking on the local news.

She saw people yakking in Thai, like chickens clucking, and then scenes of an air disaster in the jungle.

"It crashed shortly after takeoff last night. Killing everyone on board. We're talking blown to pieces here."

"So?"

"What if you and Suzie were on that plane?"

She stared at him. "But we weren't."

He shrugged. "Who's to say?"

"Are you drunk?"

"No," he said. "I have an idea."

"Yeah?"

"You want a shot at wiping the slate clean?"

"Yes."

"Then let's kill you. And, just maybe, sometime later we can bring you back to life."

TWENTY-TWO

Riding on the back of the dirt bike, holding onto Suzie who was squeezed between her and Harry Hook, Kate's head was still spinning at the sheer audacity of his plan and the conviction with which he had sold it.

The almost metaphysical ability Hook possessed—once he'd believed, really *believed*, in what he was peddling—to beguile his asset, his colleague, his reluctant superior, his murderous enemy, or some woman in a cocktail bar he was intent on seducing, had been the stuff of myth long after his departure from their shadowy unit.

Philip Danvers himself had attested that there'd been no escape when Harry turned it on.

And an hour ago, in the gray light of his seedy front room, Kate had become a convert when Hook had sold her his idea with a zeal that had been irresistible.

He'd sketched how it would work, what was expected of her, and what she would have to sacrifice. His word: *sacrifice*.

Hook had made his pitch with an almost Biblical fervor, and Kate had seen that if he hadn't been drawn to the godless orthodoxies of espionage, how easily he could have become some kind of new age huckster, or—with a bit of spit and a polish—a smoothly grinning proselytizer of the rampant free market, selling futures or pork bellies or Ponzi schemes to suckers who couldn't part with their money fast enough.

Part grifter, part charlatan, part messiah.

His plan was mad. Wild. A bravura mix of tragic truth (the plane crash) and inspired fiction, and he, somehow, had conjured it up before her very eyes and made her a believer.

Now they rode through the near-deserted early morning streets of the beach town, ready to put it into action.

Hook swung the bike up a side road and past some ramshackle wooden houses and a stagnant pond, the surface thick with green scum. A rundown resort and a derelict apartment building, stained and peeling and surrendering to the jungle, smeared by as Hook bumped the bike up a track carved into the bush, the rear wheel spinning on gravel and threatening to lose its traction. Kate grabbed onto Suzie, sure they were all going end up in a bloody heap on the road, but Hook, kicking at the gear shifter with his flip-flop like a demented flamenco dancer, had them out of trouble and roaring on up to a small brick house that seemed ready to be consumed by the undergrowth.

A pair of old scooters stood out front, one with a flat tire. A chicken pecked at the dirt and fled at their noisy arrival. An aged dog, surely blind and deaf, scratched at its molting coat and ignored them.

Hook brought the bike to a halt and deployed the kickstand. He lifted Suzie off and dumped her on the sand.

She was smiling and Hook grinned back at her, then he looked at Kate and the smile faded. "Are you ready for this?"

"Yes," Kate said. "I'm ready."

"You're sure?"

"Yes. Let's do it."

Hook went to the front door and pounded on it and carried on pounding until somebody coughed and cursed within.

"Lars! Lars, it's Harry."

More pounding and finally the door was flung open to reveal an ancient, emaciated man dressed only in tighty-whities, his sagging skin hanging like saddlebags from his scrawny body.

"Good God, Harry, what is it?" he said in accented English.

"There's an emergency," Hook said.

"Is one of them hurt?" Lars squinted at Kate and Suzie.

"No, but the woman needs surgery."

The old man said, "Come back at ten," and started to close the door.

Hook leaned on the door and dug in the pocket of his shorts and came out with a fistful of banknotes.

Lars sighed and flapped a hand, waving them inside.

***

From where he stood in the doorway of the bedroom, Hook couldn't see Kate's face, just the swell of her body under the sheet as she lay anesthetized, right arm white as milk on top of the cover, a drip disappearing into a yellow bruise below the elbow.

The rancid old Dane, Lars Johansen, scuttled into view, wearing a none-too-clean T-shirt and shorts under a green plastic bib. He waved a palsied hand.

"Come, Harry. Help me now."

Hook, hands sweating in surgical gloves, closed the door and stepped into the room, which, despite the rattling air conditioner that dripped water onto the tiled floor, was feverishly hot.

Kate's eyes were half-open, scummy, seeing nothing.

She lay on a makeshift operating table, a door resting on two wooden trestles. Johansen lifted her left hand and placed it inside a chrome kidney bowl.

"I need you to secure the hand, please."

Hook hesitated.

"Now, Harry. Now."

Johansen—an esteemed surgeon in his native Denmark years ago until a family tragedy and the subsequent plunge into alcoholism had his license yanked and sent him seeking refuge out here in the tropics— was usually assisted in these off-the-book procedures (abortions, digging bullets out of drug dealers, stitching up foreigners whose dubious legality made it impossible for them to enter the Thai medical system) by the local woman who lived with him, a crone as wrinkled and silent as one of the limestone cliffs that ringed the town.

The woman was away, where and for how long Hook did not know, so it fell to him to aid the Danish drunk in the amputation.

He felt panic now that what he had scripted was about to become reality, and he was overwhelmed by the moment: he heard the drip of the air conditioner, the babble of the cartoons the child was watching in the other room, the call of a bird out in the jungle, and he saw sweat fall from beneath the mask of the Danish alcoholic and land on the blade of the scalpel that he held in his shaking hand.

The preoperative consultation had been mercifully short. Once Hook had explained their requirements the decrepit man had turned to Kate and said, "You want this?"

"Yes."

"You are sure?"

"Yes."

"It'll save her life," Hook had said.

"Ah, if Harry Henderson says it is so, then I must believe it," Johansen had said. "It is a good thing I am no longer bound by the Hippocratic oath."

Kate had taken Suzie into a corner for a whispered consultation, and the girl had nodded and sat down in front of the tube, hugging her knees, eyes on the cartoons but shooting worried glances at the room her mother had disappeared into.

"Harry!" the Dane barked at him, bringing the scalpel closer to Kate's small finger.

Hook stepped forward and gripped Kate's wrist with his left hand, using his right to separate her other fingers from the fifth digit.

"We begin, yes?"

"Yes," Hook said.

By some miracle, as soon as the blade of the scalpel touched Kate's finger, Johansen's tremors ceased and he set about paring the flesh, crimson blood spilling profusely from the hand into the kidney bowl.

Hook looked away, staring out the window, catching his reflection in the glass—hunched and soft-edged, like a melting snowman. An iridescent blue bird swept over the roof of the house and landed on the faded red satellite dish mounted outside the window. Hook imagined painting the scene, wondering if he'd ever be able to reproduce the almost electric hue of the bird's plumage.

An unpleasant cracking sound startled him from his reverie and Hook saw the aged doctor, a miasma of boozy sweat around him, grasping the bare bone that protruded from Kate's fifth knuckle in the jaws of an instrument that resembled a nutcracker—the name *rongeur* drifted to the surface of his memory, although he had no idea how he knew this.

The Dane grunted with the exertion and the cracking sound was followed by a sharp ping as the amputated finger landed on the chrome surface of the bowl.

Johansen wielded a rasp, no different from one he would use on wood, and shaved away at the bone jutting from the nub, then he set about closing the wound with sutures.

"Do you still need me?" Hook asked.

The grizzled old man shook his head, bent over his work.

Hook dug a ziplock bag from the pocket of his shorts and lifted the severed finger, dropping it into the container and sealing the top.

Still wearing the surgical gloves, he left the room, tucking the bag in his pocket and removing the mask as he went through to the front room where Suzie watched frenzied Thai cartoons.

"Is Mommy okay?" she asked.

"Yes."

"Can I see her?"

"In a while."

He headed for the front door.

"Where are you going?"

"You stay there, kiddo, okay?"

Hook closed the door and stood on the steps, breathing in the muggy air, then he walked down to his bike and retrieved the liter bottle of gasoline he had stowed under the saddle that morning. Carrying the bottle he went around the back of the house, where a sealed forty-gallon drum stood rusting.

He took the ziplock from his pocket, shook the finger onto the drum and doused the upper end and the knuckle in gasoline. He kept the nail and fingertip clean.

Taking a moment to compose himself, he found his lighter and applied the flame to the finger, watching it flare and blaze, the sweetish smell of burning human flesh in his nostrils.

Using a twist of wire he turned the finger to make sure it was evenly singed—shoving away nauseating childhood memories of backyard barbecues—before he knocked the still-flaming digit to the ground and stood on it, pressing it into the dirt and killing the flames.

He kneeled down and touched the tip of one of the gloves to the amputated digit.

It was cool enough for him to lift and inspect. The pinkie was blackened and filthy, but the fingerprint was intact.

Satisfied with his efforts, he dropped the finger into the ziplock bag and secured the top.

As Hook stood and turned toward the house, he saw the child standing at the kitchen window, watching him.

TWENTY-THREE

Benyamin Klein believed the heat was going to fell him, send him to the tiled floor of the hotel room like a sacrifice to Moloch.

The room was hot, yes, with no air-conditioning and just a ceiling fan that did nothing more than lazily stir the thick, humid air, but it was an inner heat that bedeviled him, that filled his mind with all that was forbidden.

From the moment the plane from Jerusalem had touched down an hour ago and he and his colleagues had stepped out into the searing light, into the air thick with fragrance and stink and lust, he had not been able to free himself of thoughts that were carnal and forbidden.

The small yellow-brown women walking around in skimpy dresses and shorts cut high enough to expose the cheeks of their backsides inflamed him, just as they had more than ten years ago.

Sweating, Klein grabbed a bottle of water from the refrigerator and chugged it down in one gulp, moisture patterning his beard. He wiped his mouth with the back of his hand and brought his mind to his wife Batsheva, her broad face framed by the heavy wig she wore over her shaven head.

In the nearly forty years they had been married he had never seen her naked. Sex had been transacted in the dark, both of them wearing rolled-up flannel nightgowns. There was no touching, it was over quickly, and it always left him with a sense of being unclean and ashamed.

As they had aged, after their two children were born, these furtive gropes had ceased altogether and Klein had settled into a life of study of the Torah.

Until the tsunami over a decade ago.

The carnage on that jungle island teeming with the rotting dead—the monstrous stench, the sheer scale of it—had left Klein unhinged, and the night before he flew back to Israel, in a filthy hotel room, he had committed an unspeakable sin.

Standing in *this* hotel room, in a very different town, Klein forced that memory away.

God knew he had atoned. He had fasted and spent more than ten years in study and prayer to erase the stain of the sin from his soul.

And pray he must now, for the strength to do his duty to the Israeli dead from the fallen airplane without succumbing to the darkness within himself.

As he stared down at the tefillin—the two small black leather boxes containing scrolls of parchment inscribed with verses from the Torah—that lay on the bed, he rolled up the left sleeve of his white shirt.

He reached for the arm tefillin and placed the black box against his exposed biceps, adjusting it so it rested against his heart and recited the blessing, "*lehani'ach tefillin.*"

Then he fastened the strap, winding two coils over the leather box and making another seven coils around his forearm. The rest of the strap he wound around his palm.

He took the head tefillin and placed it so that the box sat above his forehead, and the knot just above his neck. He unwound the strap from his palm in order to make three coils on the middle finger. The remainder of the strap he wound around his palm again and he intoned, "*Baruch Shem Kevod.*"

There was a knock at the door and he assumed it was one of his team, getting ready to move to the crash site.

He unwound the tefillin and stowed them in his bag. He donned his black jacket and as he limped across the room he heard louder, more impatient knocking.

When he opened the door, he knew he would need more than prayer to save himself.

***

Harry Hook, the kid at his side, looked at the Haredi Jew and said, "Benyamin, it's time to settle your debt."

The man stared at him, then down at the child, his face settling into an expression of infinite weariness.

Klein had aged since their last meeting. His hair was sparser and whiter, his long beard more gray than brown, and his dark eyes were almost lost in a crosshatching of wrinkles. When he stepped back and retreated into the seedy hotel room, his limp was more pronounced, his left foot dragging with an audible scuff.

Hook ushered Suzie into the room and closed the door. Klein stood at the window, silhouetted against the glaring light, keeping his back to them as if he could wish them away. A TV set, nearly as old as Hook's, was mounted on a bracket on the wall. Hook crossed to the dresser and thumbed the remote, hearing the crackle as the tube came to life, and when garish cartoon figures gamboled across the screen, he turned the volume up loud, filling the room with shrill Thai.

"You watch that, while I talk to this man, okay?" Hook said to Suzie.

She nodded and sat on the bed, staring up at the TV but shooting glances over her shoulder as Hook edged the Haredi back toward the door, putting as much distance between them and the girl as he could.

When he'd last seen the Israeli, Hook had still been operational in Thailand on the trail of a group of Tamil Tigers who'd been based in Phuket, selling heroin to fund the purchase of weapons to wage their separatist war in Sri Lanka. Hook was undercover as an arms dealer, claiming to have access to a shitload of ordnance from the wars in the Gulf, his mission to develop one of the Tamils as an asset, the White House growing uneasy about their cozy relationship with North Korea.

The Tigers were billeted at a dump of a resort high on one of the hills flanking Patong Beach, far from the ocean. The hotel was strictly low-rent, attracting Thai working men and the poorer class of Asian sex tourist, drawn to the brothel that operated in sordid rooms on the lower floors. There was no way an American could believably check into the hotel, so Hook had struck up a mutually beneficial relationship with the brothel madam, a skull-faced refugee from the poverty-stricken rice paddies of the northeast, and she had made it known that he was a *farang* whose tastes ran to the cheap and the nasty, that he liked quantity rather than quality, sometimes shelling out for half a dozen girls at one time.

In reality Hook had done nothing more than part with wads of dollars and sit in a moldy room, chain smoking to kill the smell of stale sex on the bedclothes, drinking scotch, and waiting to find a way to get close enough to one of the Tigers to weave his spell.

He'd been unable to make contact—the Tamils were as elusive as their feline namesakes—and was ready to admit defeat (a rarity for him) when the big wave had come and destroyed the low-lying areas of the island. Hook and a bevy of half-dressed harlots had stood on the hotel terrace watching the devastation far below.

Phuket was shut down and he couldn't leave. The air was thick with death and raw sewage. There was no water or power. A hellhole. But his Tamils were marooned too, and circumstances had thrown them together—Hook, believably now, seeking shelter at the resort. He had used the situation to his advantage and by the time the airport had reopened, he'd made one of the Tigers—codenamed, naturally, Tigger—his very own.

Standing close to Klein he caught the same sour smell of sweat that had filled his nose all those years ago when the madam of the brothel had come to Hook's room to beg for his help. He'd been sitting, drinking and reading Graham Greene by the light of a candle, dressed only in skivvies, the cramped room as hot as a sweat lodge. Pulling on a pair of shorts, he'd followed the woman into another room where he was confronted with a sight that would have given Diane Arbus pause.

The bearded, ringleted, Haredi Jew, wearing his yarmulke and nothing else, stood over a naked, lifeless bargirl.

The girl wasn't dead, just badly beaten, the Haredi panicking postcoitus and deciding that the way to expunge his sin was to kill the vessel that still held his seed.

Hook, acting purely on instinct, had shot photographs of the bizarre tableau on his cell phone and then extracted what little cash he could from the Israeli, supplementing it with some funds of his own (or rather his employer's), and after he'd smoothed things over with the women, the Haredi had been allowed to depart for home and hearth.

Benyamin Klein hadn't crossed Hook's mind in years until the night before, when he'd seen on the news that Israeli gymnasts were among the casualties on the plane, and it had taken him two phone calls and one email to erstwhile connections in Jerusalem to establish that his old friend was heading to Thailand with the volunteer rescue team.

Hook, sitting in front of the TV in his wooden house, his cell phone still warm in his hand, watching the devastation in the jungle and listening to the light snores of his female guests, had felt a sense of inevitability at the almost occult way wheels had turned, components had clicked together, and elements had aligned into a beautifully audacious plan.

He checked that Suzie was glued to the tube and leaned in close to the sweating Israeli. "Benyamin, I still have those photographs."

"Yes," the man said in his guttural accent, "but of course you do. What do you want?"

Hook removed the ziplock bag from his pocket, using his body to shield the severed finger from the girl as he showed it to Klein.

"You're going to find this at the crash site. You're going to make sure it gets identified. Yes?"

The man looked at him, closed his eyes, sweat tobogganing along the ridges and grooves of his weathered face.

He opened his eyes and said, "Yes, this I can do if I must. And in return?"

"When I am satisfied that you have done what I ask, I will destroy the photographs."

"How can I trust you?"

"Believe me, I'll have no further use for you after this."

Klein said something in Yiddish then nodded and took Kate Swift's finger and stashed it in the pocket of his black suit pants.

TWENTY-FOUR

What was it about trouble, Kate wondered, that it found her like a compass needle found true north?

Lying naked in the dark in the bedroom of the beach hut beside her sleeping child, she heard the creak of the hammock on the balcony and the scratch of a matchstick as Jean-Philippe fired up a joint.

JP was discreet. He never smoked grass in front of Suzie, always walked off down the beach and returned smiling a little wider, just the faintest whiff of weed hanging in his blondish curls.

A good man.

A man who, even though he must know who she was, had never asked any questions, just done as he'd promised, paying off some unspecified debt of honor (his words) to Harry Hook, or "'Arry 'Enderson" as JP called him.

And she'd gone all soft and dreamy and girlie. Stopped being tough and vigilant even though her life and the life of her daughter depended on it, and allowed him to be humiliated.

Letting the heat and the balmy ocean lull her into a lazy stupor—her body drinking the sun like it was an elixir after all the months of snow—not even the dull ache in her hand could ruin her mood.

The drunken old Dane had given her painkillers, but she'd refused to take them, not wanting to lose her edge and slow herself down. But the sun and the sea had done it anyway.

And so had the fallout from a kind of battle fatigue, the realization that too many years had been filled with stress and terror.

And grief and loss.

Jesus.

As loath as she was to admit it, there was something about having no choice but to be becalmed on this speck of an island, at the mercy of Harry Hook and his crazy plan, that was soothing to her, almost like a balm to the soul.

Kate woke late in the morning. She lay in the sun and swam and hung out with her daughter, just talking silly, meaningless girl talk while JP caught small silver fish—glinting like shards of broken mirror when he pulled them from the ocean—that he cooked on a fire on the beach while she made salad in the kitchen.

And if, as she chopped peppers and shallots, he brushed against her on his way to get a beer from the fridge and she caught the pleasant scent of his clean sweat and felt a hunger for more than food, what of it?

Earlier that night she'd stood out on the balcony just after sunset, letting a hot little breeze fool with her hair. The breeze carried snatches of reggae from the neighboring island that lay a mile or so south—a bigger, touristy place, with bars and restaurants on the beach, their bobbing red lanterns visible from where she stood, reflecting in the flat ocean.

A burst of distant laughter reached her on the wind and she felt happier than she had in years. Dangerously happy.

"Hey, JP," she said.

The Frenchman came out of the house swigging a Heineken. "Yeah?"

"Let's go over there."

"To that beach?"

"Yeah."

He shook his curls. "You know what 'Arry said."

"'Arry, 'Arry, 'Arry." She laughed. "He won't know."

JP shook his head again and she wondered what it was that had made him beholden unto Harry Hook.

He'd told her he was a diver, taking tourists on day trips out to the reefs. What else had he done? Drugs? Contraband?

She didn't know enough about what went on in these parts to string together an educated guess, but JP wasn't a hard man, that much she knew. Not a fool either, but she had a sense of him diving headlong into something that'd gone way deeper than he thought it would go, and when he started to sink it was Harry Hook who'd been there to rescue him.

Harry Hook with his lazy smiles and his cool and his collection of IOUs.

"Please, JP," Suzie said, joining them on the balcony. "Just for a little while."

So, outgunned and maybe a little cabin-fevered himself, JP took them down to the Zodiac inflatable, yanked at the outboard's pull cord, and puttered them across the placid ocean. The moon was a fat orange fruit hanging low in the sky, the music and revelry getting louder and the smell of spicy food carrying across the water to them as they neared the bigger island.

JP cut the motor and lifted the propeller free of the water, and the inflatable coasted ashore, beaching itself.

They stepped off the boat onto powdery sand that was still warm to their bare feet and walked across to a place called Hippies Bar, a ramshackle structure of bamboo and wood built under an umbrella of palm fronds. A skinny Thai guy wearing only torn shorts, dreadlocks hanging to his ribs, juggled burning torches while a trio of Thai Rastas played guitars and slapped bongos, a gaggle of *farang* girls watching them. Thai men were different from Arabs and South Asians, who were all hungry eyes and grabbing hands when it came to foreign women. These guys were laid back and let the women do the running.

Suzie led them to a table and they ordered drinks and food, and when Kate's fingers touched JP's as they were both reaching for a slice of papaya she left her hand on the top of his long enough for him to understand and he grinned at her through the dancing flame of the candle.

The place was filling up with *farang*—Scandinavians, Australians, and three beefy Russians dressed in bad beachwear hassling the small, pretty Thai waitresses who smiled and zenned their way through it all.

The fire show ended and some kind of fast-paced ragga fusion blared out of the speakers and Suzie was up and dancing. When she tried to pull her mother out of her seat to join her, Kate resisted at first, but Suzie was relentless. Kate, a couple of rums inside her, found herself on her feet and letting her body go, enjoying the way JP was eyeing her, knowing she looked good, better than she had in years.

Tan and chilled and, hell yes, sexy, even.

One of the Russians said something when she and Suzie swayed past their table, and his friends laughed in a way that knocked the shine off things just a little. It reminded Kate that she wasn't on vacation, and she walked her daughter back to where JP sat and downed the last of her drink.

JP said, "Maybe we are going?"

"Yeah," she said.

By the time they paid their tab, the Russians were gone, and as they walked down onto the sand toward the Zodiac Kate was happy again, expectant, knowing that something was going to happen when they got back to their hideout.

Or, at least, hoping that it would.

As they passed a row of palms she heard men's voices. Two of the Russians were pissing against the trees, the one who had spoken standing so that he was exposed to them.

Kate took Suzie's hand, aware that JP was standing straighter.

The Russian called out, "Hey, don't go, baby, baby, baby." Doodling piss onto the sand, his friends laughing.

JP stopped and said, "There's a kid here, man." A *keed*.

"They're never too young," the Russian said, slowly tucking himself away, adjusting the hang of his balls.

JP hit him with a solid punch to the jaw and the Russian went down on one knee, lifting a hand to his mouth.

"Come on, JP," Kate said, putting her arm around Suzie, and they started walking on, but the other two men came after them, one of them grabbing JP's arms while the other slapped him.

The Russian kneeling in the sand stood and, smiling through a little trickle of blood from his lip, came over, leading with his heavy shoulders.

JP tried to fight himself loose but the two men held him tightly.

Kate pushed Suzie behind her, grabbed a length of driftwood from the sand and swung it at one of the men holding JP. It caught him on the temple and felled him. The other man turned toward her and she broke his jaw with the driftwood.

The biggest guy was on her now and she didn't have time to swing the wood and couldn't block with her wounded left hand, so she took a punch to ribs that were still tender from her brawl on the train. When JP lunged at the Russian, the big man hit him hard in the face and he went down.

Kate had lost the wood with the blow to her ribs and had to work quickly to find the space to send a roundhouse kick to the man's chin, dropping him. Instinct and adrenaline had her lining up a kick to his throat.

"Don't kill him," JP said, and she checked the kick.

He was right. She couldn't afford to leave a corpse lying on the sand.

JP stood and wiped his mouth, looked at the men and looked at her as she went to Suzie and comforted her. He said nothing as they went back to the Zodiac and he powered up the outboard. They crossed to their beach in silence, Kate sitting with her arm around Suzie's shoulders.

JP dragged the inflatable onto the shore beyond the tide line and went into the hut. Kate saw him in the bathroom washing his face.

She stood in the doorway and said, "You okay?"

"Yeah," he said and closed the door.

She took Suzie to bed and told her a story and calmed her down, and the child fell asleep.

Kate undressed and, lying beside Suzie in the dark, she heard JP smoking in the hammock and she knew she should stay where she was. She had done enough tonight.

But she wrapped a cloth around her nakedness and went out onto the balcony anyway, leaning against the rail, watching the firefly of the joint moving under the mosquito net.

"You Frenchies know what bogarting means?"

He said nothing, just held the spliff out to her. She took a hit. Just a small one, just as a way of finding purchase on the slippery slope that separated them.

"I'm sorry," she said. "I shouldn't have made you take us across there."

"I'm sorry, also. I wasn't much good at defending you and Suzie."

"You did fine."

"They would have kicked my ass if not for you."

"I dunno."

"I do." He laughed. "You can fight."

"For a girl?"

"For anybody. You are fucking *fierce*."

"I've had some training."

"That I can see."

"So, you gonna lie out here and lick your wounds?"

He shrugged. "What else is there to do?"

"Maybe I can lick them?"

"What is this? Sympathy?"

She moved the net aside and said, "No."

They kissed and it was the first time a man had touched her since Yusuf. And JP didn't touch her the way Yusuf had. This was different, and that's what she wanted.

She climbed up onto the hammock and straddled him and they kissed harder and she tasted his mouth and his skin and only when he went inside her did she know how much she had needed this.

TWENTY-FIVE

When Nadja Benway surfaced again, a dusky woman in a nurse's uniform sat at the foot of her bed watching a telenovela on the wall-mounted TV. Nadja, her hands still bound, tried to get up, but the nurse muted the audio and gestured for her to lie down.

"I need to piss," Nadja said.

The nurse produced a bedpan and slid its chilly metal surface beneath Nadja's buttocks.

After Nadja released a long, noisy stream of urine, the impassive nurse covered the bedpan with a cloth and disappeared into the bathroom, and Nadja heard flushing and the sound of running water.

The woman returned, taking up her station again.

"How long have I been here?" Nadja asked.

"Three days," the nurse said.

"God. And how did I get here?"

The nurse shrugged and consulted her watch before leaving without saying another word.

Nadja listlessly observed the antics of the swarthy cast of the telenovela, their lips moving soundlessly as they yelled, beseeched, and sobbed their way through garish living rooms and bedrooms until her mind drifted and she couldn't stop herself from thinking of the night she met Michael at a cocktail party.

They were the most beautiful people in the room, two suns around which the drab and the ordinary had orbited. They smiled at one another and within an hour were fucking in a suite at the Fairfax Hotel.

The sex had been less than stellar. As accomplished as they both were it was as if the one's magnificence had nullified the other's. They were used to feeding on blander food. It took a few days for them to find a rhythm and then it was good.

Great, even.

But after sex that first night something unprecedented had happened: she'd fallen asleep. Nadja, the queen of the speedy retreat, had drifted into a catlike slumber beside the softly snoring Michael, no overnighter himself.

When they awoke and stared at each other, she saw some softness in his eyes and was ready to despise him, just as she'd despised the endless string of nothings who had fallen for her in the past, men who had refused to understand the cold, hard terms of the transaction: you can have my cunt for a few hours, but you will never, ever have my heart.

But Michael had blinked the vulnerability away, flashed his trademark ironic smile, and dressed, and then they'd left.

They carried on seeing each other after that. Often. And he'd made a point of keeping things uncomplicated. Light. Amusing.

Until one day, as they sat in his bed eating the Szechuan takeout from the Pavilion on K Street that he'd sworn was proof of the existence of God, he'd looked at her over a forkful of moo shu pork and she saw something in his eyes and knew what was coming. She reached out her fingers, fingers that still smelled of their sex, and placed them on his lips and said, "No, Michael. No."

He laughed and said, "Hey, I just wanted to offer you some moo shu," and they'd both known he was lying as he kissed her and they'd started fucking again.

The Latina nurse reappeared with a tray of food and a cocktail of pills that, in their kaleidoscopic profusion, made Nadja feel like she'd fallen through a rip in time and landed in the *Valley of the Dolls*.

The woman loosened Nadja's hands and helped her to sit up.

She picked at the food—steamed fish and bland vegetables—and gobbled all the pills, praying they would take her back to limboland.

They did.

TWENTY-SIX

Lucien Benway sat behind the desk in his office, smoking and studying the photograph that Morse had placed before him. The only sign of his agitation was his swinging feet, the highly polished toe caps of his little chukka boots barely scraping the Bokhara rug.

Benway stood and walked across to the window and watched the snow falling onto the street outside the town house as he sucked the last life from his Samsun, a pall of Turkish tobacco smoke shrouding his huge head.

He had worked from home for the last two years.

One of the strictures that had come in the wake of Kate Swift's treason was that he could no longer hang out his shingle. No offices. No staff. Morse was on the books as his chauffeur.

Benway stubbed out the cigarette in an ashtray wrought from the hoof of an African forest elephant—a gift from a genocidal sultan who had long since rotted to death in a Mombasa prison—and returned to the desk to study the image of Kate Swift's finger.

He looked up at Morse. "What is the exact provenance of this photograph?"

"The forensic technician who ran the prints and the DNA shot it on a cell phone and sent it to me."

"Can he be trusted?"

"She."

"She?" Benway raised his eyebrows.

Morse shrugged. "Lying to me would not be in her best interests, sir. This intel is good."

"Who initiated the forensic work?"

"The trail is murky, but it points to the Plumber."

"Fascinating."

"Yes, sir."

"What are the odds, Morse, of a finger being recovered from a crash site? A little better than the proverbial needle being found in the haystack?"

"The Israelis found it."

Benway pondered this. "That Haredi crew?"

"Yes, out there to recover the remains of the gymnastic team."

"They're thorough."

"Yes, they are."

"Zealous, even."

"They believe it is their sacred duty to recover even the smallest part of a victim's body. They don't rest until they do."

"What does your technician say about the condition of the finger?"

"Consistent with having been traumatically severed and burned."

Benway steepled his own fingers, the tips yellow with nicotine. "Harry Hook is still in Thailand?"

"The last time we looked."

"What's he doing there?"

"Nothing, sir."

Benway tapped the photograph. "A coincidence?"

Morse shrugged. "Unlikely. My guess is that Danvers put Swift in touch with Hook."

"I'd tend to agree. But what would she want with Hook?"

"His help?"

"Yes, maybe. So she goes out there and dies in a plane crash?"

"Planes crash."

"They do, they do. Particularly Asian ones, it seems. Still ..." Benway turned to the window, watching snow swirling against the gray sky. "But the great mystery here, Morse, is why the White House is sitting on this little bombshell."

TWENTY-SEVEN

It was all too good.

Too tranquil and quiet.

Kate was too happy.

It made her nervous.

Stop, she told herself. Be in the moment. Enjoy this. You're just reacting to emotional bleed-through, to old stuff. Jumping at shadows.

So she worked hard at relaxing as she walked down from the hut onto the beach, wearing a bikini, carrying a beach cloth and a bag with water and lotion like a tourist who'd fled the cold and was out here in the steamy tropics to get some sun and get laid.

Both of which she'd done.

The feel of JP was still on her skin, the slight abrasion from his beard around her mouth. That sweet ache still in her core.

She laughed out loud at the memory of that swinging hammock.

What could have been awkward wasn't. Not at all.

Kate had left him last night and fallen into bed beside Suzie. She'd slept deeper than she had in years and woke to see him out in the Zodiac, fishing.

She thought he might be avoiding her, so she went into the kitchen to make Suzie a juice, but when he came in carrying a trio of little silver fish that still fluttered on the line, he gave her a smile that hinted at their secret, but kept cool, not pushing anything.

She'd liked him even more for that.

Kate swam and dozed and watched her daughter at play and the day was maybe the best she could remember since she'd given birth to Suzie, when she had taken a few months' unpaid leave (against the wishes of Lucien Benway, who had succeeded Philip by then).

Mrs. Danvers had cooed like a crone when she'd told him her news, but not Lucien. He'd said, "You're an operative. A warrior. You made a choice. Now you're coming off like some *girl* with screaming ovaries who got all broody and wants maternity leave."

But she *had* taken time out.

Time for Suzie to be born.

Time to nurse her.

And what made her ashamed now, as she lay on a beach in Thailand, listening to the whisper of the ocean and feeling her skin soaking up the sun, was that—as much as she'd loved her daughter, she'd grown restless. Bored. Longed for the rush that came with action and danger.

Dress it up. Call it patriotism if you will. And it had been ... at first. Some kind of idealism. But now she knew better.

She knew there would always be people like her, who did what they did not because they had to, but because they *wanted* to.

She'd found a nanny, and Yusuf was at home most of the time—no adrenaline junkie, he. A brave man, sure, but also a man who could lounge around the house in grungy sweats, rolling on a blanket with their baby, delighting in each coo and drool. He relayed everything in hyperrealist detail to her on their infrequent Skype sessions, only possible when she could safely surface for a few minutes. Kate, lying with her feet in the water, tried to push the thoughts away.

She'd spoken out, hadn't she?

Spoken out about how Washington used the Benways, the private contractors (who weren't private, just the administration sailing under false flags) to do everything that was filthy and debased. Meanwhile the men in Langley and the Pentagon and the Oval Office—and the women, too, they were part of it with their clicking heels and their power suits and their helmets of hair and the look in their eyes that said, *once we were oppressed and we fought the battle and we have fucking won the right to take names and kick ass and too fucking bad if the asses that are kicked are brown and black and poor and civilian and female and underage*—sat in their climate-controlled hush and did what they did, certain of their righteousness.

And Kate's speaking out, hadn't that been just a manifestation of *her* selfishness?

Her hurt.

Her pain.

Her grief.

Yes, she'd blown the whistle on the illegal operations and the civilian deaths and the lack of accountability, and a suit or two had been forced to resign. Benway had been sent into limbo, unfriended by the powerful cronies he'd admired so very much, gone from show dog to mongrel pariah in five seconds flat.

For this, he hated her enough to kill her.

But, really, wasn't she just saying, you murdered my husband, you bastards, and you *will* pay? *I* will make you pay.

I will do my patriotic duty and call you out on your transgressions. But I *will* have my pound of flesh.

She sighed, closing her eyes in the shade of the umbrella. With the hot breeze flapping the fabric and making a sound like a bird taking flight, she fell asleep, the day taking flight too, lazily winging its way toward the horizon with its streaks of cumulus and its oranges and reds and velvety blues.

TWENTY-EIGHT

Philip Danvers sat at the desk in his musty, book-lined study on the top floor of his old house. The dormer window offered a view over the frosty woods, the encroaching suburbs invisible from where he sat. If not for the laptop on the desk, he could have been in the rural Virginia of his canny grandfather who'd parceled off acres of farmland for development, making himself and his descendants obscenely wealthy.

But Danvers wasn't admiring the view. He sat staring at the finger in the ziplock bag that lay on the desk beside a dog-eared copy of Thomas Merton's *Conjectures of a Guilty Bystander*. As his days grew fewer, Danvers had come to find the reflections of the Trappist monk soothing.

Merton had also died in Thailand, in Bangkok, Danvers remembered—electrocuted by a faulty fan as he stepped from his bathtub. He'd been the victim of a CIA assassination (or so insiders like Danvers had come to learn) due to his criticism of the Vietnam War, which had made him no friend of LBJ's. The recollection added a synchronous zest to his musings.

Darkness came suddenly and Danvers clicked on the desk lamp, the bulb throwing the amputated finger into vivid relief.

He saw the nail, ragged and grime encrusted.

He saw the seared, blackened skin.

He saw the frayed flesh above the knuckle where the digit had been severed.

And when he saw Kate Swift and her daughter walking away from him at Berlin's Holocaust Monument, the memory so vivid he could feel the cold air on his skin, he felt a grief so absolute that he closed his eyes, sank his head into his hands, and allowed a moan of lamentation to escape his skinny old lips.

Then his keening turned to laughter as he saw through the foggy lens of memory Harry Hook—the Harry Hook of more than a decade ago, his good looks blurred only slightly by time and careless living—raising a glass of Cutty Sark, saying, "Cheers, sport!" And when Danvers opened his eyes and regarded the finger anew, he understood what he was seeing. The mangled finger was at once Kate's fifth digit (fingerprinting and DNA testing had made that indisputable) *and* evidence that Harry Hook was still out there, his brilliance undimmed.

Danvers stood, grunting at the jab of pain in his nether regions, and walked across to the window, staring out.

If Lucien Benway was the zealot, cloaking his sociopathy in Reagan- and Bush-era jingoism, and Kate the patriot—her allegiance to flag and country forged as a fourteen-year-old standing in her school uniform on a lower Manhattan sidewalk, watching the Towers fall, inhaling the dust of the dead—then Harry Hook was the visionary.

The seer.

The magus.

And this thing had all the hallmarks of his genius.

Yes, a plane had crashed.

Yes, Kate's finger had been recovered from the wreckage.

But had Kate and her daughter actually been on that plane?

The passenger manifest of the low-cost Asian airline was a mess: there was evidence that at least three of the deceased were traveling on stolen passports, many of the victims' names were misspelled and some didn't appear on the list at all. The authorities remained uncertain of exactly how many people had died.

But standing at the window, his breath condensing on the frosted pane, Danvers knew in his toxic old water that this was the work of Harry Hook.

And inspired by this insight, the dying man decided that he, too, was capable of one last act.

A swan song, if you will.

He found himself humming Tchaikovsky as he hurried down the creaking staircase, grabbing a coat and a hat as he went out to where his old Volvo waited. Still humming, he drove faster than he should have past the bare white oaks, out to a strip mall in one of the advancing suburbs in search of a pay phone.

TWENTY-NINE

David Burke—a great bear of a man, his soft white body covered in a pelt of black hair—sprawled naked in postcoital languor across the marital bed of his Foggy Bottom apartment, watching a CNN follow-up piece on Michael Emerson. It was a shameless bit of puffery, colleagues in the media waxing lyrical about what a talent he had been, how moral, how ethical, how fearless.

Jesus Christ, all they weren't saying was that he'd often taken strolls across the Dead Sea.

Burke's wife, also naked but physically his polar opposite—a tiny redhead with a Rockwellian spray of freckles across her elfin nose—came from the bathroom and caught him in the act, even though he quickly surfed to MTV, pretending to bop to an old Pearl Jam thing he hadn't heard since his Columbia days.

"So how are you adjusting to not having a bête noire?" Janey said, in that achy-breaky voice that could move effortlessly from gutter to cotillion.

"Come on, that's overstating things."

"You're telling me that when you heard Mike Emerson was dead there wasn't an element of schadenfreude?" she said, sliding in under the comforter.

"Schadenfreude?"

"Hey, everybody needs to hate somebody sometime."

"That's catchy."

"What did you hate most about him? That he won the Pulitzer or that he got so much strange?"

"Strange? *Strange?* What are you, a frat boy?"

"Oh, I'll be a frat boy if you want me to be," she said, dipping down and tonguing him and making him hard again.

Then, typical ADHD Janey, she sat up, taking a baggie of weed and cigarette papers from the bedside drawer, and started to roll a joint.

As he watched his wife's deft little fingers, Burke tried to keep his mind clear of his annoyance, no, *rage*—call it what it fucking was—that Michael Emerson had walked away from the *Washington Post* to take some fancy online gig in Paris on the very day that Burke was fired from the same newspaper. Fired for fighting too long and too loud with its executive editor, protesting his refusal to publish a piece on extra-judicial killing that his boss had called "nothing more than wish-fulfillment and fantasy held together by overwrought adverbs."

Burke had lifted a heavy spherical award from the editor's desk, gripped it in his palm, and pirouetted like the shot-putter he had been in college. He'd been convinced until the very last second that he had the orb securely in his grasp (his intention merely to intimidate), but the projectile flew from his sweaty hand and narrowly missed braining the cowering man on its way to shattering the window of his office.

Ten minutes later, Burke, his sorry belongings dumped in a box, had been escorted by security guards from the building, and he now found himself unemployable.

His wife lit the doob, took a good hit, and held it out to him as she leaked smoke from mouth and nose and made little *huh, huh, huh* sounds.

As he was about to take the spliff, the landline rang.

It was such a rarity—the instrument left unused in the hallway, neither of them getting it together to call Verizon and cancel—that Burke obeyed some Pavlovian impulse, leaving the bed and padding toward the front room and the quaintly ringing analog phone.

"Let it go, Dave," his wife said, coughing, "it'll just be a telemarketer."

But Burke shoved aside a pile of magazines and newspapers and lifted the receiver and said, "Yeah?"

He listened, said, "Yes. Yes, okay," and then was left with the purr of dial tone in his ear.

He walked back into the bedroom, scratching his right ass-cheek in a ruminative fashion.

"That was Philip Danvers," he said.

Janey squinted at him through the smoke. "Danvers, Danvers, Danvers …"

"The Gray Ghost."

"Jesus, yes! He called *you?*"

"He called me."

"C'mon, someone's messing with you."

"It was him. I swear."

"How did he have your number? *Our* fucking number."

"Exactly."

She shivered and hummed a few bars of the *X-Files* theme.

"He wants to meet me in a park," Burke said, stepping into a pair of boxers.

"A park?"

"Yeah, in Bethesda. Right now."

"That's so *The Spy Who Came in from the Cold.*"

"Uh-huh."

"What does he want?"

"I dunno. He hung up before I could ask."

"You're going?"

"Fucking straight, I'm going."

"What are you going to wear?"

"What am I going to *wear?*"

"You've got to look the part. You have to wear a trench coat."

He found his Levi's on the floor and pulled them on, along with a plaid shirt and a sweater and a pea jacket. He wound a scarf around his neck.

"I'll let you leave with this uplifting thought," Janey said.

"What?"

"Michael Emerson couldn't pull off that scarf right now."

"That's funny."

"No, it's not funny, it's true."

"It's funny *because* it's true."

"Whatever. Be careful, Dave." She hugged her knees under the comforter, her brow furrowed.

"Chill," he said, "this is DC, not Damascus."

"Exactly."

THIRTY

Sleep eluded Harry Hook.

He lay on his bed, sweating, listening to the scuffs and shuffles coming from the jungle, smelling the mingled scents of Kate Swift and her daughter still trapped in the folds of the linen. A clean, vanilla smell. Powdery. The smell of everything he'd never had in his life.

Hook sat up, threw aside the mosquito net, and walked through to his front room.

The TV set was on, sound muted, tuned to a Thai news channel, the only one he could receive without a satellite dish, just a twisted coat hanger dangling from a nail in the wall. A car bomb in the far south had replaced the ill-fated plane as the major news item.

He crossed to the table in the kitchen and flipped open his laptop, and while he listened to its aged drives churn and grumble, he eyed the bottle of Cutty Sark, still sealed, standing beside the sink.

Why didn't he throw it out?

Or drink it?

The screen of his computer lit up and he went online to surf all the major international news channels for information on AirStar Flight 2605.

On CNN there was an interview with a Spaniard—already back home in Seville—whose passport had been stolen in Pattaya a month ago and had been used by one of the passengers who died on the plane. "Look," he said, pointing at his face, "I am alive!"

The BBC offered up a press conference where a harried airline official, a wizened Asian man blinking behind truck-windshield glasses, tried to explain inaccuracies in the passenger manifest. "It is very complicated process. What we do is to assemble from many, many list, from manifest, from baggage list, from immigration list. We are checking all these. Check, check, check. But some peoples we are not finding. Yes, them we are still not finding."

Hook surfed on. SKY. Al-Jazeera. CNN again. He googled until his eyes blurred, but there was nothing about Kate Swift's finger.

Had Klein failed him?

A possibility, but somehow he doubted this. The man was too terrified of exposure.

Somebody was suppressing the information.

Hook saw Kate Swift lying unconscious, blood spraying as the drunken Dane took her pinkie.

He remembered the child watching him through the window as he set fire to the amputated finger.

"Well, I guess you overpromised, sport," he said out loud and this made him laugh a hollow laugh.

He stood and crossed to the sink, and this time got as far as laying a hand on the curve of the scotch bottle.

Then he turned and walked away and stood at the window, looking out into the dark jungle.

He didn't need a drink. He needed a miracle.

THIRTY-ONE

Philip Danvers lurked under a tree in Battery Lane Park in Bethesda, Maryland, close enough to the men's washroom to catch the tart whiff of urine and dung, reminded of times gone by when he'd risked far too much for hasty and furtive assignations in dank privies like this one.

He heard a car door slam and saw a bulky shape move into the orange light of the lamp that hovered over a bench.

The big man stood a while, his breath condensing, stamping his feet in the snow. He looked around, rubbing his gloved hands together, then sat, jiggling his knees.

As he watched David Burke, taking a few minutes to make sure that the man was alone, Danvers allowed himself to slip back in time to the dying days of the last century, back to a restaurant in Beirut eating tabbouleh, fattoush, and baba ghanoush and drinking arrack in the company of Harry Hook and a couple of new recruits who'd hung on Hook's every word. Hook pointedly ignoring the very young and very beautiful Bryn Mawr blond who would be in his bed within an hour.

Hook was delivering his Subterfuge 101, and even though Danvers had heard it in all its many evolving forms over the years, he was still held in its grip.

"The thing with any good lie," Hook had said, wiping oil from his lips with the back of his hand, "is how you propagate it. In this age of misinformation, the boundaries between truth and fiction, which have always been nebulous, have become increasingly porous. And cheers to that."

He threw back his arrack and one of the acolytes topped up his glass.

"There is a machine out there, boys and girls. An insatiable machine. Hungry for information. Eager to chew it up and spit it out. Bully for that, we say. Makes our job easier. But what's vital is how we feed that machine."

He stopped eating, all eyes on him.

"The vital component is this: find your nightingale. Then let it sing. Let it shout its song from the fucking rooftops."

Danvers shook himself free of the memory. The bulky shape on the bench looked more like a trussed turkey than a nightingale, but Danvers was sure he would have met even Harry Hook's exacting standards.

A self-styled crusader.

A believer in good.

A believer in the righteous power of the fourth estate.

The perfect songbird.

Danvers walked forward and the big man sprang to his feet, towering over him.

"Sit, please," Danvers said.

Burke sat.

Danvers, hitching up his trousers and lowering himself onto the bench, said, "Of course I will deny ever being here. You understand?"

"Yes."

He removed the ziplock bag from his coat pocket and held it up to the light. Burke recoiled a little, his mouth open, a flash of white teeth in his beard.

"What's that?"

"A finger."

"I can see it's a finger."

"It belonged to Kate Swift."

Burke stared at him.

"It was recovered from the wreckage of AirStar Flight 2605 that crashed in Thailand three days ago." The man stayed silent, listening. "The intelligence apparatus and, I believe, the White House, know about this. Know that Kate Swift and her daughter were on that plane."

"And yet they've said nothing?"

"Quite."

"Why?"

Danvers shrugged. "That is the question."

"Did we down that plane?"

"Define *we*."

The big man chuckled softly—the sound of a rasp on wood.

"As I'm sure you're aware," Danvers said, "within hours of the crash the usual suspects were all over Fox News and the internet, perceiving the work of the Islamic State, PLO, the Iranians, or Putin, or decrying yet another 'false flag' operation by the forces of the New World Order."

"And who was it?"

"I don't have a clue. There may have been no author. For all I know, it may have been pilot error or metal fatigue. Those Asian airlines are notoriously lax when it comes to crew training and aircraft maintenance." He stared at Burke. "What is indisputable is that the powers that be are staying silent. Curious, no?"

"Surely you're able to find out why?"

Danvers shook his head. "I'm no longer invited to the table, Mr. Burke. All I'm privy to are the crumbs that fall to the floor."

"Where did you get the finger?"

"It fell my way."

The man hesitated. "Why me?"

"Why did I choose you?"

"Yes. Why not some hotshot investigative reporter?"

"Because, Mr. Burke, you have something very rare in this sordid world."

"What?"

"Integrity."

Burke laughed and scratched his beard. "Okay, but there's a huge elephant in the room, man."

Danvers stared at Burke. "An elephant?"

"Yeah. Benway. Lucien Benway."

Danvers bit back a smile. "What's Benway got to do with this?"

"Exactly."

"I'm not sure I follow."

Burke shook his head. "Sure you do. Knocking a plane out of the sky to kill the woman who ruined him isn't beyond Benway."

"That's pure speculation."

"And it would be a mega-fucking-embarrassment for the White House. Their one-time dirty-tricks head honcho pulling a stunt like this."

"Well, that's an interesting theory."

Burke looked at him. "What do you want me to do with all this?"

"Only your job."

"I no longer have a job."

"Oh, come on, we aren't living in the time of Gutenberg. You know how you can get this out there." He dangled the ziplock. "Take it."

Burke shook his head, but he took the bag and put it into his coat pocket.

Danvers stood and walked away and didn't look back.

THIRTY-TWO

Benway left his office, and even though it was very late at night—or early in the morning, rather—and he was alone in the house, he locked the door after him. He walked past his bedroom, as monastic as a monk's cell, and entered the bedroom of his wife, clicking on the light.

The room was dominated by a neatly made double bed with an ornate brass headboard and footboard. On the black-lacquer wood vanity positioned against the wall, a bottle of Samsara, a tube of Chanel lipstick, and a pack of Marlboro Lights stood amidst an array of framed photographs.

Benway shut the door and approached the vanity. After inspecting the photographs (Nadja in Rome with the Fontana del Tritone in the background; Nadja, dressed in evening clothes, caught in the harsh glare of a flash bulb as she drank a vodka and smoked a cigarette at a Foggy Bottom cocktail party; Nadja on a Nantucket beach, fully dressed, her chinos rolled to her ankles, a breeze tugging at her hair) Benway uncapped the Chanel and twisted the tube, a peach-colored sheath rising from its interior.

He pictured Nadja's lips, parted on her very slight overbite.

He had never kissed his wife. Not even on the day they were married.

As Benway closed the lipstick with a little click, he noticed a slender string of pearls snaking from behind one of the picture frames. When he tugged at it, the necklace dragged in its wake Nadja's white-gold wedding band and diamond engagement ring. Benway rested the rings on the palm of his hand, the lamplight a starburst on the gemstone.

He returned the rings to the vanity and avoided his eyes in the mirror.

Lifting the lid of the pack of Marlboros, he drew out a filter-tipped cigarette and placed it between his lips. Benway clicked open his Ronson, catching the gassy whiff of lighter fuel. He flicked at the wheel, which at first produced nothing more than a spark, but then a bluish flame danced and he applied it to the cigarette, hearing the paper burn like a far-off brush fire.

He crossed to the plain wooden desk by the window where a Montblanc fountain pen and a Moleskine notebook lay, as if waiting for Nadja to sit down and write.

Surrendering to temptation, Benway opened the notebook and saw that it contained just one line in his wife's beautiful cursive handwriting: "There are mistakes too monstrous for remorse …"

The American cigarette was noxious to him and he stubbed it out in the ashtray on the desk where two other butts, stained with Nadja's lipstick, lay curled like dead silkworms.

Benway shut the notebook and sat on the bed, closing his eyes, inhaling the mingled scents in the air—the ever-present residue of tobacco smoke and the carnal whiff of tuberose, redolent of both jasmine and bloody meat, as if the mattress of the bed had been doused in perfume to disguise darker, more base odors: the stink of his wife's lust and betrayal.

Benway, suddenly short of breath, rose from the bed and left the room, closing the door behind him. He unlocked his office and sat behind the desk, staring at the photograph of Kate Swift's severed finger, using it to focus his thoughts, to shut down his emotions, to take himself to a place that was cold and dry and clean.

And safe.

THIRTY-THREE

"Mrs. Benway?"

"Yes."

"Why don't I call you Nadja? Are you comfortable with that?"

Nadja shrugged the shoulders of her white hospital gown, staring out the window at the stripped trees silhouetted against a taupe sky.

"Please, sit down," the psychiatrist—Nadja hadn't allowed his name to become fixed in her memory—gestured toward the chair that faced his.

He was the only person she'd seen aside from the Latina nurse; Lucien had never reappeared after that one occasion, and she was still uncertain if she'd imagined that or not. The doctor had visited her each day, taking her pulse, checking her blood pressure and laying his cool, pink fingers on her abdomen, gently palpating her flesh as if selecting fresh produce at a market, all the while quietly humming a tune Nadja almost recognized.

Nadja turned from the window of the cramped office and walked to the chair, feeling as if she were wading through water, her movements made sluggish by the medication that dimmed her brain.

As Nadja sat, he said, "Are you feeling calm today?"

"Yes." Nadja felt nothing.

"Good. Then perhaps we can review the events that brought you here?"

Nadja nodded, the room blurring and lagging with the movement of her head, leaving the pale, bespectacled quack in the rumpled white coat as formless as a wraith.

This was the first time Nadja had been allowed out of the ward—a huge brown orderly whistling Motown tunes had sped her along endless, fluorescent-lit corridors in a wheelchair, tires screaming on the polished floors.

"How long have I been here?" Nadja asked in a dead voice.

"Five days," the doctor said.

Nadja blinked. "Five days?"

He nodded. "Yes."

Her eyes were drawn again to the light from the window, her thoughts as difficult to contain as a tumbling waterfall.

"Nadja," the doctor said, and she slowly focused on him, seeing her twin reflections in his glasses. "Do you have any recollection of how you came to be here?"

Nadja scratched at her arm, trying to conjure up some memory. Nothing.

"No," she said.

Her last memory was drinking in some downtown bar. Drinking to cauterize the Michael wound.

"What is it? What have you remembered?" the quack asked.

Nadja shook her head. "Nothing. Nothing at all." He stared at her before he consulted the clipboard on his lap.

As if he had read her mind, he said, "Who is Michael?"

Nadja intuited that any mention of Michael had to be suppressed. She had to pretend that he had never existed. All she could do was try to assemble a little raft of sanity and stay perched atop it, riding the roiling waters of grief and madness that were doing their best to capsize her.

"I don't know anyone named Michael."

The doctor shuffled the pages of his clipboard and hummed that tune again. "You spoke his name on occasion. In your sleep."

He stared at her, tapping his pen on the clipboard. Nadja wanted to seize it from him and stab him in the eye.

The doctor pursed his lips and said, "Would you like to go home, Nadja?"

It was the last thing Nadja wanted: she desperately wanted to be away from here, but not to return to another prison, the prison of

Lucien's house, but she knew agreeing to it would be her only escape.

"Yes," Nadja said, "I want to go home."

"I see no profit in you staying here. I don't believe you are a danger to yourself any longer. If you agree to keep taking your medication and stay clear of alcohol and return for weekly consultations, I will release you immediately."

Nadja fabricated a smile. "Thank you."

He stood.

"You have your husband to thank. Mr. Benway called earlier and petitioned me to allow you to go home. He can be very persuasive."

Even in her addled state, Nadja divined the truth: Lucien had dispensed largesse and controlled the terms of her sojourn at the clinic. If it had pleased him, Nadja would have languished here for months, but for some reason he had decided he wanted her free.

"Yes," Nadja said as she floated toward the door like an untethered balloon, "my husband is a singular man."

THIRTY-FOUR

The heat had a heft. A weight. It leaned down on Hook, almost felling him as he threaded his way through the sidewalk stalls that sold cheap trinkets and gaudy beachwear to the tourists with their hot brown flesh, sportive as seals as they avidly lived la dolce-goddamn-vita.

Sweating, he dodged the skinny Nepalese barkers who called him "mate" and tried to corral him into their restaurants for watery curry and overpriced beer, then ran the gauntlet of *tuk-tuks* and snarling bikes. As he jogged across the bubbling blacktop of the main road to the beach he was almost flattened by a truck festooned with banners of Thai girls in provocative poses, its speakers blaring a looped message about a newly-opened titty bar

Hook stood a moment in the shade of a dusty palm, catching his breath. Suddenly dizzy, he reached out a hand and held onto the trunk, the bark rough and unpleasantly fleshy to his touch. In a blink, a column of black ants—a Morse-code stipple—had advanced from the bole onto his hand, bites like hot needles in his flesh.

Hook cursed, pulled his fingers away from the tree, and smacked at his hand, battling to open the bottle of tepid water he carried in the pocket of his swimming trunks, pouring the warm liquid over his skin, washing off the ants.

Sweat pooled under his jaw and his hair was stuck to his forehead and he wondered just what the hell he was doing out here.

He shook off the thought and the weakness and walked down the ten stone steps to the sand, stepping over prone foreigners basting them-selves in the sun, making his way toward the waiting flotilla of long-tail boats that bobbed at anchor, greeting one of the boatmen who gathered passengers for a trip.

The man's wooden boat was typical of the area, with a frayed Thai flag, colored sashes, and a garland of sun-frazzled flowers tied around the long prow. Hook kicked off his flip-flops and waded up to his knees into the warm water, then hauled himself onto the long-tail, his weight causing it to rock and splash.

He found a seat under the canopy and ignored the tourists around him who were chatting in a babel of Norse, Italian, Mandarin, and Russian.

More and more Russian.

The boatman, agile as an acrobat, hopped up and took his station at the rear of the craft, balanced on bandy sea legs as he fired up the old car engine mounted on an inboard turret-like pole, the propeller seated directly on the driveshaft.

The engine roared to life, belching a cloud of black smoke that hung like a stain against the lemon sky and then dispersed slowly as a breeze unraveled it and the boat took off across the electric blue ocean, the roseate cliffs pressed against the horizon, a spray of water raining onto Hook's face and chest, though not enough to cool him.

Hook made this trip once a week to play chess with an American expatriate, Bob Carnahan, a retired dam builder from New York who lived with his wife on a narrow peninsula that was accessible only by long-tail.

The boat ride took fifteen minutes and the view was spectacular once the tawdry tourist town was lost to sight. Even after six years Hook hadn't tired of it, had never grown bored with the play of light on the water and the majesty of the rock towers, bearded with jungle vegetation, that rose from the ocean, always restored somehow by the sheer splendor of it all.

But today he was fatigued and his mouth tasted as if he'd been sucking on pennies.

He regretted coming, but he knew he would have been worse off at home neurotically surfing the internet, his eyes caressing the bottle of Cutty.

The boat found the beach and Hook disembarked, wading out onto the sand that burned the soles of his bare feet, quickly stepping into his flip-flops.

He trudged past rows of sundrunk bathers and entered the private gates of the Beach Club—a dozen large wooden houses built at the base of a cliff, thick foliage giving them privacy from the oceanfront and one another.

Wealthy expatriates lived here, some of them renting the houses out when they went home to Chicago or Rome or Paris or Copenhagen.

Hook made his way along a stone pathway and arrived at a two-story house with a well-tended garden and a gurgling Buddha water feature trickling into a koi pond.

Betty Carnahan sat in the shade in a bamboo recliner reading a book. She smiled when she saw him.

"Harry."

"Betty."

"How are you?"

"Good."

Betty was maybe sixty, still beautiful. She'd spared herself from the harsh sunlight, and her skin was fine and just a little melba-colored. Her salt-and-pepper hair wasn't dyed, and her face had not been stretched and tweaked and Botoxed at one of the many clinics that offered these services dirt cheap in this part of heaven.

She flapped the book at him. *Play It as It Lays* by Joan Didion.

"Ever read this, Harry?"

"No," he said.

"It must be my fifth time. Do you think it's a sin?"

"What?"

"Rereading a book so many times when there are so many new books out there?"

"I think that novelty is overrated, Betty. There's a lot to be said for the familiar."

"Spoken like a true fogey."

"Yeah. Well."

Bob Carnahan appeared from inside the house. He was a craggy guy with a shock of white hair and a bandito mustache, shirtless, still muscular, wearing Bermuda shorts. He handed Betty a drink and their hands touched and they smiled at one another with their eyes and Hook wondered about all the things he had missed in his life.

He followed Carnahan into the living room and the American poured him a Coke and prepared the chess board.

The room was beautiful, furnished in pale wooden furniture and prayer rugs and what Hook was certain was an original Rothko hung on one wall amidst a constellation of framed family photographs.

Hook had lived like a nomad his whole life, had never owned a home, never in one place long enough to put down roots.

When his career had crashed and burned there was no thought of settling in the States. The US was a foreign country to him now, way more foreign than the lands of brown and yellow people and musical languages and fragrant food where he had fought America's wars—declared and undeclared—over the last thirty years.

Bob Carnahan called him over to the chess board. The big man lit a joint and took a hefty toke before holding it out to Hook, who, in his dry years, had still allowed himself a little weed, but he shook his head.

Carnahan was a good player and won most of their games, although Hook usually made him work hard for his victories. But today his mind wasn't on the game.

As they played, Carnahan said, "So, what about this plane crash?"

"Yeah. A mess."

"Think it has anything to do with those Israeli kids on board?"

"No."

Carnahan looked at him and his shrewd blue eyes narrowed. "You've heard something?"

"No. Why would I?"

"Aren't you a guy who keeps his ear to the ground?"

"You know what they say about people with their ears to the ground?"

"Something about not seeing the stampede coming?"

"Yeah."

They played on, but Hook was distracted, staring out the window at the cliffs, listening to the buzz of a fly.

He heard a clank as Carnahan tipped over his king, even though he was winning.

"Let's quit this, Harry."

"Sorry, Bob."

"No *problemo*, man. You okay?"

"Sure. Just the heat."

"Uh-huh, it's a bitch." Carnahan squinted at him. "Want another Coke?"

"No. I think I'll get moving."

Carnahan stood, grinning his genial stoner grin. "Go, Harry. Go get a massage. Have a swim. We'll reconvene next week, okay?"

Hook was going to walk back to the beach, but he found himself going toward the cliff and out a gate on the west side, following a footpath that wound through a souk of low-rent resorts, cramped backpackers with overburdened septic tanks, massage parlors, bars, and restaurants.

He emerged on the opposite side of the skinny peninsula from where he'd landed, in a swamp of mangrove-fringed tidal flats, and waded through black mud that sucked at his ankles like quicksand until he reached an empty long-tail that bumped in the low, brown water. He made a deal with the boatman to sail him southwest into the Andaman Sea, toward the sun that sagged like a blood orange, to where Kate Swift and her daughter were hiding.

THIRTY-FIVE

Nadja stood in the lobby of the clinic, staring out of the glass doors at the long driveway flanked by rows of snow-frosted oaks, her overnight bag on the floor beside her. She was still a little dislocated, her synapses fogged by the industrial-strength sedatives that had been pumped into her.

It was a gloomy afternoon, the tops of the trees scraping the gray sky.

At 4:00 p.m. a black Mercedes-Benz limousine from the late sixties drifted up the driveway and stopped outside the lobby, the driver invisible behind the tinted windows.

The car was her husband's conceit. Too small to drive it himself, he would sit beside her in the leather-and-walnut rear, smoking his foul cigarettes as they were chauffeured through the city, pleased with his beautiful European car and his beautiful European wife.

Nadja lifted her bag and went outside. The teeth of the wind had her hunching like a crone as she darted for the car, her feet sinking into the snow. Fighting open the rear door, she slid into an overheated interior as stifling as a drying room. There was no sign of Lucien.

The driver didn't turn and all she could see of him was a pale neck rising from his shirt collar and thin, dark hair plastered to his skull.

"Good afternoon, Mr. Morose."

Without a word Morse clicked the car into gear and the Mercedes slid off down the driveway.

"Where is my husband?" she asked, leaning forward, catching a whiff of something antiseptic beneath the cloying scent of his hair grease.

Morse's dark eyes glanced at her in the rearview mirror before sliding back to the roadway, a pair of gates opening outward like unfurling wings.

"Mr. Benway sends his regrets that he couldn't be here," he said in that parched voice.

Knowing there would be no further conversation, she sat back and watched his hands on the wheel. Broad, sallow hands, strands of dark hair lying like quills on the white skin.

When Nadja found herself conjuring up a series of brutal snapshots of those hands eviscerating Michael Emerson, she looked out the window, watching as the countryside gave way to the crumbling outskirts of the city, a blur of industrial sites that grew like a fungus from the poisoned land.

THIRTY-SIX

"Now, Lucy, it pains me that we have to meet in this clandestine-fuckin-manner. I'd like to take you for a steak the size of a Doberman over at the Capital Grille and we could chow down and catch up, but the climate, the fuckin *climate*, just will not permit that. Understand?"

"Understood, Congressman," Benway said, seated primly beside the hulking black man in the rear of the Lincoln MKZ hybrid, hidden by the tinted windows as they cruised Capitol Hill. "I'm just pleased that you can make some time for me."

"Fuck, Lucy, don't even think about it."

It was always "Lucy" with Congressman Antoine Mosley. Always had been. Benway had learned over the years not to let it grate on his nerves.

In Benway's experience, black Republican politicians either adopted a superslick persona, as smooth and purchase-free as the carapace of a stealth fighter, or they went to the other extreme, amplified their down-hominess, their street cred.

Mosley was one of the latter and his recent appointment to the House Permanent Select Committee on Intelligence had done little to mute his braggadocio or his ghetto bray—an affectation, Benway knew. The man had been reared in a middle-class Huxtable-esque household and had *graduated summa cum laude and first in his class* at Harvard Law School.

"Now, Lucy, I've always been of the opinion that you were treated like shit."

"Thank you, sir."

"I mean to say, we're talking fuckin broken eggs and omelets here, right?"

"That would be one way of looking at it, Congressman."

"And bet your ass that in Auntie Fazela's Halaal Kitchen over in What-thefuckistan, nobody's giving a good goddamn about no broken eggs."

"We do seem to be held to a higher standard, sir. One that hampers our capacity to do our jobs."

"Too fuckin true." The man shot his cuff and looked at a wristwatch the size of a fishpond.

Benway dipped his fingers into his pocket and produced a USB flash drive, which he held out to the congressman, who kept his hands in his lap and regarded it as if it were a piece of dung.

"The fuck's that?"

"It's a thumb drive, sir."

"I know *that*, Lucy. Question is, what the fuck's on it, man, that's going to get this nigger's black ass in a sling?"

Benway told him about the plane crash in Thailand and about Kate Swift's finger.

Told him about the forensic report that he'd copied to the drive.

Still not taking the flash drive, Mosley said, "This bitch, Swift, she caused you no end of grief, right?"

"She did, sir."

"So it's safe to say you got a dog in the fight?"

"I have an interest, it's true."

"Now, Lucy, you didn't shin up a palm tree with a fuckin Gadfly surface-to-air missile and shoot that motherfuckin plane down, did you?"

"No, sir, sad to say, I did not."

"Mmm, mmm. Okay, then. Who did?"

"I don't know that anybody did. The investigation is ongoing, I believe."

"No Hamas towelheads taking potshots at those Israeli kids?"

"Not that I know of, but I'm no longer inside the circle of knowledge."

"But our esteemed leader is choosing to say nothing about that traitorous bitch dyin in the crash?"

"Yes."

"Must be a reason, Lucy. Has to be a fuckin reason."

"I would agree with that, Congressman."

"Bears scrutiny, that I will allow."

"I'm pleased to hear you say that, sir."

"Leave this with me, Lucy. Leave this with me."

Mosley palmed the thumb drive and the car cruised to a halt, ejecting Benway, who stood for a few moments outside the Supreme Court Building before hailing a cab.

THIRTY-SEVEN

Morse activated the remote on the keychain and the town house's garage door rattled up like an anchor being raised. He drove into the garage, which had been extended to accommodate the limousine's length, and brought the Mercedes to a halt.

Nadja got out of the car, feeling the chill. Morse unlocked the door leading into the house and she walked through to the kitchen, setting her bag down on the counter.

Unbidden, Morse sat at the table and stared out at the gloom.

"You're going to stay here?" she said.

"Those are my orders."

"So I am your prisoner?"

"Mr. Benway has requested that you don't leave the house until he returns."

She turned away from him and went into her upstairs bedroom and stood for a few moments at the window, unsure of what to do. Desperate for some comfort she couldn't name, she searched for the secret phone Michael had bought for her.

Gone.

She opened the drawer of her vanity, lifted out an antique music box and unfastened the lid, triggering the clockwork strains of "Clair de Lune." She rifled through the jewelry inside, looking for the one gift that Michael had given her, a diamond pendant.

Gone, too.

Lucien was almost clairvoyant at times. It was what made him so good at his job.

Nadja sat and stared at her split reflection in the wing mirrors and was astonished to see tears flowing unchecked down her cheeks.

When had she last cried?

Was it when she was fourteen and her parents, prosperous bourgeoisie Muslims—a doctor and a lawyer—had been shot in front of her on a Sarajevo street? Or maybe it was after she'd fled, trying to get to relatives outside the city, and was captured and enslaved by the Serbian colonel?

In the face of the Serb's attentions her tears had dried and evaporated along with her innocence.

But here they were, flowing into her mouth. Salty.

Nadja was overcome by apathy and lost what remained of the afternoon lying on the bed in her murky room in a litter of crumpled Kleenexes, staring at the TV, uncaring if she was watching news of genocide in Africa, obscenely peppy daytime television, or jingoistic action movies. She realized how far gone she was when she spent a dazed hour in the company of Kim Kardashian and her ottoman-sized hindquarters.

Whenever Nadja felt her mind bump up against the pain of Michael's death—like a ship running aground in a deep fog—she would reach for a blister pack of tranquilizers and surrender herself to lassitude and inertia, wondering how long it would be before the pills no longer worked and she'd have to find a more permanent end to her suffering.

THIRTY-EIGHT

When a sound roused Kate from her sleep in her DC apartment, she thought at first it was Suzie, who had been restless and had needed many stories and lullabies before she'd finally closed her eyes and began snoring softly.

Kate listened but could hear nothing coming from Suzie's room. She realized that what she'd heard was an alert tone on the laptop that she'd left plugged in beside her bed.

Still bleary-eyed, she reached for the computer and ran a finger over the touch pad to wake it and saw that she had a notification: she'd been patched into a live video feed. She clicked on the link and her screen was filled with infrared images from a camera hovering above a clot of square mud houses.

It took her a second to understand that this was footage transmitted by a Predator drone and the mud houses were those of the tribes of South Waziristan.

Where Yusuf was.

She hit the speaker icon on her screen to unmute it and heard the voices of the mission controller and the pilot.

"There's a mosque. Do not engage the mosque. The rectangle is the mosque."

"Roger that."

"A group of men is oriented eastwards. You see them?"

"Affirmative."

The crosshairs found the men, maybe eight of them, walking in the narrow street between the houses, the camera zooming in tight, the image sharp and, despite the solarization of the night vision, startlingly intimate. The group broke apart and she saw Yusuf, his walk unmistakable, that loose-limbed shamble, every gesture of his imprinted on her memory.

Fighting panic, she reached for her Samsung, keying in the number of the satellite phone that he may or may not be carrying, aware that, because of image latency, what she was seeing had happened anywhere between two and five seconds ago. To overcome the great distance (and the earth's curve), the images from the drone circling over Pakistan had to travel to a satellite that bounced them to the US Air Force base in Ramstein, Germany, from where they were sent via fiber optic cable across Western Europe, the Atlantic Ocean, and the continental United States before they reached the drone's pilot and the other watchers.

And her.

She heard the satellite phone ringing, and after a few seconds she saw Yusuf reaching for his pocket.

The mission controller said, "Okay, you are clear to engage them."

The camera zoomed in even tighter and Yusuf stepped away from the men, lifting something to his face.

"Yusuf," she said. "Yusuf!"

Kate heard nothing and she knew that there was another latency, another delay, from the satellite phone.

Then she heard a crackle and Yusuf, standing still on the screen, said, "Yes?"

"Run!" she shouted, knowing that if he moved fast enough he'd keep ahead of them, that the latency could save his life, that they'd be shooting at where he had been. But he didn't hear her.

The controller was yelling now. "Engage them. Light 'em all up. Come on, fire!"

Unleashing a AGM-114 Hellfire missile with a hundred pounds of yield.

An explosion tore a white hole in the night.

Debris.

Dust.

And Yusuf, miraculously, ran from the fiery blast, stumbled, staggered, ran on.

Kate, shouting eleven thousand miles across the world, "Run! Run, Yusuf!"

The controller yelled: "We've got a squirter! Keep shootin. Keep shootin."

Another explosion and more dust and when it cleared, something that had once been her husband lay in the rubble.

Kate was sobbing, calling out Yusuf's name, when somebody touched her on the hand. She opened her eyes to pink gloom. She was lying on a cloth on the cool sand, buttery lamplight spilling from the nearby hut, and she could hear Suzie singing a song as she rocked in the hammock—something about "animals, animals, animals"—and it was JP hovering above her, concern in his eyes.

"You're okay?"

"Yes," she said, lifting herself up on an elbow, sand raining from her hair. "Just a dream. Shit. Sorry. How long have I been asleep?"

"It's okay," he said. "I hung out with Suzie. It was fun. And now she can fish like a pro."

Kate pushed the dream away and found a smile. "Are you real, JP? Huh? Seriously?"

He smiled back, but there was a hesitation. Her radar attuned.

"What's wrong?"

"Nothing." *Nussing*. "It's 'Arry."

"What about Harry?"

"He just called me. He's over there," he said, nodding toward the neighboring beach. "He wants me to go over in the Zodiac and get him."

"What's he doing here?"

JP shrugged. "He didn't say."

He headed down to the water and pushed the inflatable out. She heard the clatter of the outboard and watched him disappear.

She stood and gathered her towel and her cloth and went up onto the balcony.

Suzie, still rocking in the hammock, stopped singing and said, "Is Harry coming?"

Kate nodded and said, "Yes, Harry's coming."

As she stared out at the last bits of mauve light, fragments of the dream floated around her like bats. The calm and the peace she'd felt these last days was gone and all that remained was sadness and desolation.

And cold, corrosive rage.

THIRTY-NINE

It was dark when Nadja surfaced from slumber, woken by Morse's strangled whisper and Lucien's rumble floating up to her from downstairs.

After a minute she heard the front door of the town house closing.

Nadja wiped her face and went down to where her husband stood alone in the kitchen, dressed in one of his bespoke suits.

"Darling," he said.

She didn't reply, her nostrils flaring at a pungent fragrance.

Her imagination, surely?

But he had a paper bag with him. Takeout. Szechuan takeout.

Like a magician, he produced a series of little red cardboard tubs, each bearing the Pavilion's panda logo, releasing the perfume of the food that brought Michael back to her with breath-robbing clarity.

Lucien—the man who loathed Chinese food with a passion—licked sauce off a finger and smiled at her blandly. "Are you hungry?"

He observed her as she filled a glass of water from the faucet, her back to him, composing herself as she sipped.

Nadja turned to Lucien and smiled and said, "Of course. How thoughtful."

And as she sat and ate the food—ate it all: devouring the searing, bloodred mapo tofu; folding the salty shredded pork into the little white pancakes as delicate as hankies and tearing into them with her teeth; inhaling the squid with pepper salt. Turning the meal into a kind of a celebration of who Michael Emerson had been and how he had freed her, Nadja decided that she would not destroy herself after all.

No. She would destroy her husband.

FORTY

Kate emerged from the shower, dripping, barefoot and dressed in a loose cotton dress she'd bought in Bangkok. Harry Hook was installed at the kitchen table, drinking a glass of Coke in the draft of a fan that went *tick, tick, tick* and lifted his still-abundant and only slightly graying hair away from a forehead that shone with sweat.

He was winning hearts and minds—*love me, love me, love me* was the refrain of his breed of spook, *love me even while I betray you and torture you and kill*—and JP and Suzie were hanging on his every word as he told the story of his boat trip over, turning a two-hour hop in a long-tail into something Homeric.

He looked at Kate and smiled a smile that didn't quite take, the smile of a huckster peddling snake oil. She stood in the doorway, her eyes locked to his, and waited for him to explain why his plan hadn't worked, why her searches on JP's iPad had yielded no information about a sensational discovery at the crash site of AirStar Flight 2605.

He looked away from her and dipped a hand into the plastic bag that sat folded on the table and took out a puppet, a little female figure with a white face and a conical crown, its garments dazzlingly bejeweled.

Suzie stared at it and her mouth formed a perfect O as Hook manipulated the strings and had the little slippered feet dancing on the wooden tabletop, white hands with red painted nails waving like a twenties flapper.

Hook handed the strings to the girl. "It's for you. Go on, take it."

Suzie looked up at Kate who, in a moment of churlishness, wanted to spit out a comment about the aptness of the puppet metaphor and grab the little doll and sling it into the ocean for the tide to carry to India, but she nodded and said, "What do you say?"

"Thank you, Harry," Suzie said and planted a kiss on Hook's cheek, which caused him to flush with both embarrassment and pleasure.

Suzie took the puppet, in awe of its gaudy beauty, and went off into the bedroom to play.

Kate sat down and crossed her arms and said, "So, what brings you here?"

"Just checking in."

"Bearing gifts and bonhomie?"

"Something like that." He smiled one of his winning smiles. "How's the finger?"

"Gone, remember?"

He crinkled his eyes at her. "No pain?"

"No."

This was his time to segue into an update about his master plan, but he said nothing and sipped at his Coke, his eyes on the fan.

The silence was awkward and she felt for JP so she asked the question that she'd wanted to ask for a while, "So tell me, Harry, why did you choose Thailand?"

He looked at her and she could see him relax as he stepped off a little ledge of uncertainty onto firmer, more familiar footing.

"Let me tell you my Thailand story."

"I'll bet you've also got a Burma story and a Lebanon story and an Iran story and a Jordan story, haven't you?"

His smile soured a little. "Hey, you know what it's like. We get around."

"Oh, we do. Regular little globetrotters for Jesus."

He sighed. "Do you want to hear the story or not?"

JP topped up his Coke. "Tell us, 'Arry."

"When I first came out here, maybe fifteen years ago, I saw all these Thai guys—tough-looking little buggers with teeth like tombstones and tattoos and scars—buzzing around on scooters carrying bamboo bird-cages. Couldn't see into the cages, because they were covered with cloth, but you can guess what I thought?"

Kate said nothing, but gentlemanly JP filled in as the straight man. "Cockfighting?"

"Yeah. Cockfighting. You spend any time in Asia and you know that these guys love their blood sports. I've been to cockfights. Sickening. Never want to go near another one." He sipped his drink. "So I put those cages out of my mind, then one day I was riding a bike outside a small town when I saw maybe twenty guys in a field, standing around poles strung with wires and these cages were hanging from the wires. And this wasn't like any cockfight I'd ever seen. So I stopped the bike and went over and found a guy who could speak a little English and he told me that the birds in the cages are bulbuls. Jungle songbirds. And what these men do, once a week, is put their songbirds in competition, laying heavy beats, too. Betting on which bird can sing the sweetest and the loudest for the longest."

"So that's your Thai story?" Kate asked.

He shrugged. "No ladyboys or bar girls or ping-pong shows. Bird singing competitions. That's Thailand, for me. That's why I'm here."

She tilted her head and said, "That's a sweet story, Harry."

"I think so. And a true one, too."

"Now isn't that a rarity?"

He said nothing, looking at her, drinking his Coke.

She could no longer dam up her rage and disappointment. "What the fuck are you doing here, Harry?"

"I just told you."

"No, *here*. Here in this fucking kitchen."

JP stood and said, "Maybe I take Suzie and her puppet out onto the beach?"

They watched him walk through to the girl and lead her and the toy outside with a lantern.

"It was all fucking bullshit, wasn't it, Harry? This plan of yours? This plan to save us?"

"Now slow down."

"Why couldn't you just accept you were fucking burned out, that whatever mojo you once had was gone and let us get the hell out of your orbit? Why did you have to fuck with us?" She held up her bandaged hand. "Get me to do this?"

"Jesus, you don't flirt with bluntness, do you? You just go right in and give it the clap."

"Your little bird story was cute, Harry."

"You already said that."

"You were always one for the songbirds weren't you?" He stared at her warily. "'Find your fucking nightingale?'"

"You heard about that?"

"Oh, it was legendary. The gospel according to Harry Hook."

He sighed. "I may have expounded a little too long and a little too loud about that in times gone by."

"That was what so many of your brilliant schemes, your *coups*, turned on, right, Harry?"

"Yes."

"The poor stooge who went out there and sang what you wanted him to sing? Sang it loud and sang it clear? Loud and clear enough to change the minds of the unbelievers?"

He stared at the fan and sucked his teeth.

"But this time your plan was just a little undercooked, wasn't it? A little makeshift? A little desperate?"

He looked at her. "It had all the food groups."

"But there's nobody to sell it, is there, Harry? You cut off my finger and had it dumped at the crash site. And then you waited."

"Yes."

"In other words, you shoved a note into a fucking bottle and tossed it into the ocean?"

He closed his eyes and massaged the bridge of his nose.

"Where's your fucking nightingale, Harry? Where's your fucking songbird?"

When he didn't reply, she sighed and went out onto the balcony. She stood in the dark and watched JP and her daughter play on the sand in the light of the lantern, the puppet sending long, inky shadows out toward the water, Suzie laughing and tugging at the strings.

For the first time, Kate felt pain in her finger. Not at the joint, but up near the nail. The nail that wasn't there. Phantom pain. She'd been warned about it, in her googling, that her nervous system was still wired to believe that the digit was attached.

Just like she was wired to believe that all she had lost was still out there. Somewhere.

***

Hook hovered in the doorway, watching Kate, and said, "I never made you any promises."

"No, you didn't," she said, her eyes on her daughter on the beach.

"What I did wasn't an exact science. It was always like this, back in the day. A crapshoot. Seat-of-the-pants stuff, all guesswork and blind reckoning, like a pilot lost in a cloud."

"Sure."

"I'm sorry if I've disappointed you. Maybe you picked the wrong guy for help?"

"Yeah, maybe."

He stared at her. "Why did you come to me, anyway? Surely you've heard all the stories about how I flamed out?"

"Oh, yeah. I've heard them all."

"But you still came?"

"Yes, I still came. Because I carried my own little flame in my heart, that the magnificent Harry Hook would save my life."

"Well, as you said earlier, my powers have waned."

"I came for you because of your legendary abilities, sure, but ..." She paused.

"But what?"

She shook her head, still not looking at him. "Forget it."

Hook was withdrawing, ready to return to the kitchen, to take himself beyond the range of her anger when she spoke again, so softly that her words barely rose above the hiss of the ocean.

"I came to you because you're my father."

He produced something that resembled a laugh. "You're being metaphorical, right?"

"Nope. I really am your daughter. Your unknown and unloved spawn."

Kate turned toward him, her face catching a spill of yellow light from the doorway as she smiled sourly and said, "What, the great Harry Hook is lost for words?"

When he stayed mute, she shook her head and walked down onto the sand toward her child, leaving him standing alone in the dark.

FORTY-ONE

Dawn found Hook walking away from the bungalow, trying to reassemble himself as he followed the trail of seashells that traced the tide line on the deserted shore The rising red sun bled into the lilac wash where the flat ocean met the sky at the horizon.

Last night, when Kate had dropped her bombshell, it'd been too late to cross to the neighboring island, so he'd hidden on the beach in the dark and crept back into the bungalow when the others were asleep, crashing on the sofa.

He'd lain awake, pulling one of the all-night vigils that he'd become so good at. Listening to the soft snores of Kate and Suzie in the bedroom.

His daughter and granddaughter.

Jesus.

Exactly what he was meant to do with that information he had no idea.

Was it even true? Or was it just a fiction concocted by a woman driven mad by grief and fear and alienation?

As a retailer of untruths, Hook knew only too well that he, by authoring his narratives, had not only invented fictions, he had reinvented *himself*. Taken himself far away from what had been fragile and fearful by creating personas that were more comfortable to inhabit than the real Harry Hook.

Wasn't it possible that she had done the same? That, hunted and on the run, her life and the life of her child endangered, she had unraveled and become marooned on the far side of the fuzzy line where truth and fiction blurred?

Hook found himself standing frozen on the beach, unable to process his thoughts, feeling as if the browser window of his mind had a dozen tabs open simultaneously.

He waded into the warm ocean, letting it lap at his calves. There was enough light to see the tiny silver fish that darted around his legs in the clear water.

He sank down into the ocean, submerging his body, stilling his mind. He drifted to the surface and floated on his back, letting the gentle rocking of the water soothe him, staring at the beach and the jungle and the sky.

Bob Carnahan first brought him here three years ago. Carnahan had once owned a house on the tiny island, built on government conservation land. The 2004 tsunami had destroyed the house, along with all the other dwellings, wiping out almost the entire population of a village of sea gypsies.

The government had no wish to develop the cay after the disaster and the surviving gypsies had disappeared. The animist Thais (fearful of vengeful spirits) considered the place bad luck and the boatmen on the neighboring islands refused to venture here. Only the splintered remains of one bungalow had remained.

Over the space of a year, Hook and Carnahan had come out a few days at a time and camped on the beach while they repaired the bungalow. Carnahan was a skilled builder and what Hook lacked in expertise he'd made up for in enthusiasm. The renovation complete, they'd hauled a gasoline-powered generator over from the mainland and the place had become their refuge. Every month they spent a couple of days chilling and fishing and playing chess and smoking a little weed.

Nobody bothered them, the ghosts keeping the island safe from invasion.

The perfect hideout for Kate and Suzie Swift.

As Hook stood up out of the ocean, shaking his head like a dog and releasing silver beads of water from his hair, he remembered Kate's face as she'd turned toward him last night on the balcony when she'd said what she'd said, and goddammit if he didn't finally see—with terrifying clarity—the resemblance to the face he'd shaved thirty years ago, when he'd been young and handsome enough to get into all kinds of trouble.

And he knew in his bones that, despite all of his elaborate smoke-screens, she wasn't lying.

She was his daughter.

The acceptance of this drove him down the beach, toward the jungle beyond—not ready, yet, to go back to the bungalow and learn how and when he had unwittingly fathered that intimidating woman.

The clatter of an outboard stopped him and he turned to see the Zodiac, snout riding high in the water, take off toward the other island with JP at the tiller and Kate and Suzie in the prow.

And what did Hook feel?

A fleeting moment of regret was replaced by relief.

They were gone from his life. He was free.

Free of obligation. Free of guilt.

He shut down the traitorous thought that filled him with dread as he flashed on empty bottles and days lost to alcoholic amnesia and his life slowly sinking into the kind of drunken torpor and lassitude that had claimed so many of the foreigners he'd known in this country, and walked slowly back to bungalow.

The bedroom was empty of all female paraphernalia.

He went to the kitchen and helped himself to a bottle of water from the fridge. On the table the Burmese puppet he'd bought for the kid lay beside JP's iPad. He tossed the puppet onto the counter, and activated the iPad. Reflexively, he scanned the news sites.

What he saw caused him to cough, a spray of water dappling the screen of the tablet, and he dropped the bottle and ran out onto the balcony, searching the horizon for the Zodiac, seeing it, a tiny speck in the blue expanse of water.

Stupidly, uselessly, he waved and shouted.

Then he calmed himself and entered the front room, collected his cell phone from the floor beside the sofa, and dialed JP's number. He heard a warble from the balcony and went out to see the Frenchman's iPhone lying on the bamboo table beneath the hammock.

FORTY-TWO

Lucien Benway allowed himself a smug little smile as he sat in his office before his wall-mounted TV, channel surfing. As he flipped between the American and international news broadcasts, a delicious mosaic assembled before his eyes. Robin Roberts on *Good Morning America*: "Already dubbed Fingergate, this is set to rock the White House to its foundations"; Bret Baier on Fox: "This is an accusing finger pointing right into the face of the president"; a dour BBC anchor with marbles in his mouth: "Fingergate, a major embarrassment for an American president already battling a plummeting approval rating." Each fragment was a justification of his lobbying for Congressman Antoine Mosley.

When the White House press secretary appeared on the screen at a media briefing, looking harried and exhausted, saying, "At this moment we have no comment," and stalked away from the podium, questions hurled at his retreating back like rocks, Benway laughed out loud, feeling better than he had in the two years since his fall.

Then, as he landed on CNN's *New Day*, and saw Chris Cuomo introduce some hulking, bearded nonentity as, "David Burke, the freelance journalist who broke the Fingergate story," he sat forward in his chair, swallowing his laugh.

Cuomo said, "Okay, let's unpack this. We've got a finger—a finger that independent experts, based on fingerprint evidence, have confirmed belongs to Kate Swift—found at the crash site of AirStar Flight 2605 in southern Thailand. You contend that the administration is aware of this finger but has suppressed the information?"

"Yes."

"Where did you get the finger?"

"Chris, I can't disclose my source."

"Can't or won't?"

"All I can say is that Kate Swift's finger was given to me by a person highly placed in US intelligence."

"Why? Why would they do that?"

"In the belief that the American people deserve to know what this administration is hiding from them."

"And what is the administration hiding? Beyond the knowledge of this body part found in a crashed plane in Southeast Asia?"

"I think the White House's silence speaks of complicity."

"Let me ask you directly: Are you saying that the current American administration downed Flight 2605?"

"Let's remember what happened in 2013 when whistle-blower Edward Snowden was stuck at Moscow's Sheremetyevo airport," Burke said.

"How is that relevant?"

"A memo was leaked in which a senior intelligence official advised the president that, in the event of Snowden's escape from Moscow, he would be very confident taking down a private jet and only a little less confident taking down a commercial airliner."

"At the time that memo was rejected by the White House as being fabricated by Julian Assange and WikiLeaks."

"They would say that. What's especially relevant is that the memo was written by Lucien Benway."

"You're talking about Lucien Benway, the disgraced ex–CIA operative who was fired after Kate Swift blew the whistle on his extra-judicial activities?"

And up came a photograph of Benway leaving a Senate hearing two years ago during what he had come to call the "weeks of infamy," scowling, looking squat and toad-like, and all the fizz went out of the morning's champagne.

"Yes. Lucien Benway, one-time head of CIA Special Operations—tasked directly by the president to mount covert operations in foreign countries—until the nature of his activities were exposed by Kate Swift. I would like to hear Lucien Benway's take on this. And I'd like to hear from the White House if it's keeping silent because of its history with him."

Benway shut the TV down and sat a moment, aware that Morse had entered the room almost silently and stood near the door.

"Who is this David Burke?" Benway asked.

"Until a week ago he was a minor player at the *Washington Post*. He was fired for writing stories that were high on hysteria and low on facts."

"Well, he's had a credibility transplant now." Benway scratched his scalp, the thin hair making a whispering sound. "How did this bottom-feeder end up with Kate Swift's finger?"

"The Plumber?"

Benway shook his head. "No. He's too strategic. He'd use an intermediary."

"Who, sir?"

"I see the hand of Mrs. Danvers in this."

"What would his motive be?"

"Revenge. The old sodomite's nose is still out of joint because I unseated him. And he was always overly fond of Kate Swift."

"It's causing the administration more damage than you, sir."

"Mnnn, perhaps. But there's always blowback and I don't relish another inquisition by the press."

"Do you want me to shut Burke's mouth?"

"What is this, Morse? Open season on reporters?"

The pale man stood stolidly, staring at a spot just above Benway's head.

Benway said, "It's a tempting notion, but no, that would only enhance his credibility. Look at the Emerson thing, how quickly his brothers in the media have sanctified him. Dig around, see what you can find out about Burke. Do it as quietly as you can."

"Yes, sir."

When Morse had gone, Benway left his office, locking the door behind him, and wandered down to the kitchen to brew himself a pot of tea.

Nadja sat at the kitchen table smoking, drinking coffee, and watching the little TV set on the counter.

"So, you're back in the news," she said as she stood and clicked off the TV. "Such an unflattering photograph, dear Lucien. You look like Truman Capote after a particularly torrid night at Studio 54."

Nadja gave him a dismissive rub on the head, in the manner of a dowager patting a lap dog, and walked up the stairs, her mocking laughter reaching Benway as he throttled an oolong tea bag.

FORTY-THREE

Kate waited with Suzie in the shade of a palm tree on the beach, their bags on the white sand at their feet, while JP bought tickets for the long-tail back to the mainland. Groups of tourists lined up at the boats that rocked at anchor, a stew of accents carried on the hot, still air.

"Where are we going?" Suzie asked.

"I don't know," Kate said. "Just away from here."

"Is JP coming with us?"

"No," Kate said, "he's not."

"I like him."

"So do I."

"Then why doesn't he come with us?"

Kate could have said: because I want to get as far away from him as I can. For his own safety.

But she just shrugged. "He can't. He has to stay here."

"With Harry?"

"Yes, with Harry."

"I like Harry, too."

Kate said nothing, pretending to search for the Frenchman.

The child had tears in her eyes. "I don't want to go. As soon as I meet people I like you take me away from them."

Kate hugged her. "Hey, baby. It'll be okay. I promise."

She looked up to see JP, wearing boardshorts and a torn T-shirt, but not his usual smile, walking toward them across the sand.

He handed her the tickets. "Okay, you're good to go."

"Thanks, JP." She reached down and shouldered her backpack.

As JP helped Suzie into her pack he said to Kate, "I would be 'appy to go with you."

"No," Kate said, taking Suzie's hand.

The girl stopped and looked up at her. "Why not? Why can't he come?"

"Jesus, Suzie, stop with all the questions, okay?"

The child withdrew from her as if she'd been slapped. Kate knelt down and tried to embrace her, but the girl stepped away and walked down toward the boats.

"Shit," Kate said and felt like crying herself.

"Let me talk to her," JP said and he went after Suzie.

He put a hand on the child's shoulder and said something that had her looking up at him, squinting at the hard sunlight, and then she smiled and so did he and when the boatmen called for the passengers to board, the Frenchman lifted Suzie onto his shoulders and walked her through the shallow water to the long-tail and set her down under the canopy, giving her a kiss on the cheek.

Kate, wading toward the boat, stopped as JP turned and came abreast of her.

"Good luck, Kate," he said.

"Thanks," she said, "for everything."

But he was already walking away, back toward the beach.

Kate dumped her pack in the long-tail and climbed the little ladder, feeling the boat rock beneath her, feeling a jolt of pain in her left hand when she forgot, for a moment, to nurse it.

But the pain was good.

It cleared her mind of everything that was frivolous and stupid.

She had one job: to protect her child.

Kate settled down beside Suzie and when the boatman fired up the engine and turned the boat toward the open sea, a cockscomb fan of water spraying them, she didn't look back.

FORTY-FOUR

Hook stood on the beach, watching as a black dot detached itself from the horizon and became the Zodiac lazily bumping its way back from the neighboring island.

JP wasn't rushing, and why should he?

The situation was awkward and last night, even the Frenchman, who'd never said a bad word to Hook, had given him a certain look before he'd faded out onto the balcony to sleep in his hammock.

Maybe that debt, at least, was finally squared.

It was about time.

Years ago, when Hook had still been operational here in Thailand, he'd set up a sting to bring a Filipino scumbag with ties to Abu Sayyaf separatists into his sphere of influence, engineering a drug bust that would make the Pinoy—who'd funded his holy war by peddling cocaine and underage girls to sex tourists—his asset. But JP, just eighteen and dumb enough to supplement his scuba diving income by selling weed for the Filipino, had been a minnow caught in the net and an overzealous local cop had wanted to ride the boy hard in a country that executed drug dealers.

Hook had gained JP's release by throwing the Filipino the way of the cop at the cost of his operation. Fuck it, the kid had deserved it.

JP, although Hook had never told him the exact details, knew that Hook had saved him and had sworn eternal fealty.

Hook hadn't needed him for much more than friendship over the years. Not until this. Not until he'd known that Kate and her daughter would've been too visible on their own; but a couple and a kid, well, they would be just another trio of vacationers, making happy on the balmy shores of Thailand.

Hook, sunburned and sweating, splashed his way out to the Zodiac as it neared the shore, JP cutting the engine, letting the inflatable coast in.

"Where are they?" Hook asked.

"They've gone."

"They're on the boat?"

"Yes."

"You're sure?"

"I saw them leave."

Hook hauled himself into the Zodiac, which took water from his weight.

"Go after them."

"No."

"Why not?"

"She doesn't want to see you, 'Arry."

"Believe me, she'll want to see me now."

The Frenchman just stared at him and made no move to fire the engine.

"Come on, JP. Let's go, man."

"I don't know, 'Arry."

"Jesus, JP, have I ever fuckin lied to you?" Hook waved this away when he saw the Frenchman's face. "Okay, but I made good, didn't I? Afterwards? I saved your ass?"

"Only after you dropped me in the shit."

So he did know, after all.

No time to get into that now.

Hook mopped his sweating brow on the sleeve of his shirt. "Listen, JP, the situation has changed. Kate and Suzie need to stay under the radar. Just take me to them. Please."

The Frenchman shook his head, his sun-bronzed curls bouncing, but he yanked the outboard to life and took off, charting a course toward the open sea.

"I don't know if we will catch them, 'Arry," he said. "The long-tail left a while ago."

"Was it full?"

"Yes."

"Then it'll be slow. We'll head it off," Hook said, with a confidence he didn't feel.

FORTY-FIVE

As Kate watched the long prow of the boat ride the high waves they'd hit when they'd left the protected waters of the island, she felt her earlier certainty drain away and a sudden panic seized her.

For the first time in her life she was without options. Even after Yusuf's death, when she'd gone public with the details of Benway's actions, with the shopping list of atrocities they had all committed, she'd been fueled by disgust and by revenge, her own guilt washed away by the balm of her virtue.

And during the two years she'd spent in northern Vermont she'd been as dedicated as a method actor in assuming the role of the proprietor of a small-town gift store. She was the smiling, friendly, unthreatening single mom—the very antithesis of the spy, the bargain-basement Mata Hari and stone-cold killer she'd been for nearly a decade before.

She'd lived her life a day at a time, shutting out as best she could the terror that gnawed at the edges of her consciousness and hijacked her dreams, leaving her sweating and gasping in a roiled bed.

But there had always been a little pilot light burning in the corner of her mind, that if things went bad she would turn to the man who could make it all right.

Harry Hook.

She'd believed that Hook would save her because he was brilliant, yes, but most of all because he was her father.

Sitting in the wooden boat, beside her daughter who was asleep—or pretending to be—listening to the roar of the engine and the thump of the hull as it smacked the waves, drenched by salt water, she realized how pathetic her father fantasy had been.

Because Daddy was a delusional drunk. A lying asshole who'd collected scalps to shore up his flagging ego—who knew how many other bastards he'd spawned after his decades of one-night stands—who'd acted the savant for enthralled audiences until he'd finally overplayed his hand, costing twenty-two people their lives.

And she'd *known* all this, known he was a man of straw, and yet she'd still come to him and sat at his feet like a *giddy* acolyte and let him draw her into his lunatic plan—had sacrificed a finger to this absurdity.

And last night, even after she'd confronted him about the failure of his scheme, she'd told him she was his daughter because she'd yearned for him to clasp her to his big strong chest and make it all okay.

Instead, he'd crept off into the dark like a whipped dog.

Fucking pathetic.

Lost in this orgy of self-recrimination, Kate suddenly noticed that the boatman was waving his arms and shouting in Thai.

She turned and stared to port, and there was the Zodiac with JP at the tiller. Hook was in the prow, on his knees, red-faced, sodden, hair hanging over his eyes, beckoning and bellowing.

The boatman squawked like an enraged jungle bird, the two crafts tossed in their colliding wakes, the Thai shaking his fist and shouting for the inflatable to retreat.

But JP gunned the outboard and cut across the bow of the long-tail, and the boatman had to take evasive action, throttling back.

The passengers, soaked and angry, were in it now, yelling, and the boatman brandished a machete, as if Hook was his namesake pirate of old.

The Zodiac bumped into the side of the long-tail and Hook waved at Kate, shouting something up at her.

At first she couldn't hear him, then the long-tail's roaring engine sputtered and stalled and in the sudden quiet she heard Hook shout, "It's *sung*! The fucking nightingale has *sung*!"

FORTY-SIX

Nadja Benway sat beside her husband in the rear of his ridiculous Mercedes-Benz staring out as they cruised down Connecticut Avenue, the snow a gray blur against the night sky, tires whispering on the wet road. All the windows were closed and Lucien smoked one of his foul Turkish cigarettes that always brought back to her, no matter how hard she tried to cleanse it from her memory, the stench of the unwashed Serbian colonel who'd enslaved her; a peasant (the recipient of a battlefield commission) who'd harbored the superstitious belief that his lack of hygiene—a miasma of sweat, blood, piss, shit, plum brandy, ripe meat, and rotten teeth—would protect him from enemy bullets.

He'd left a stinking corpse lying in the black mud of rural Bosnia.

Nadja lit a Marlboro and inhaled deeply, the menthol-infused tobacco the perfect antidote to these overheated memories.

She saw the red neon of the Avalon Theater bleeding into the night and Morse slowed the car and stopped beneath the marquee advertising Michelangelo Antonioni's *L'Eclisse*. When the car halted she was still expecting a trick, expecting Lucien to laugh and order Morse to drive on.

But he waved his cigarette at the theater lobby and said, "Well, off you go. Enjoy the movie," as if he were talking to a child.

As Nadja cracked the door, the freezing wind stinging her cheeks, he grabbed her by the wrist and said, "I'm trusting you, Nadja. Morse'll be here to collect you in two-and-a-half hours."

"Of course, Lucien," she said, shivering in the cold, watching as the

Mercedes-Benz was sucked like flotsam into the wake of the nighttime traffic.

Still not quite believing that Lucien had allowed her out of the house, she dropped her cigarette in the gutter, crossed the sidewalk to the box office, and bought a ticket, expecting at any moment to feel Mr. Morose's hand on her arm.

But, unmolested, she took her ticket and walked into the overheated lobby, mingling with the mainly older, moneyed art-house crowd. She bought a cup of coffee but ignored the snacks on offer—Godiva chocolates waited in her purse.

She'd removed them from the refrigerator and stashed them in her Chanel bag as Lucien had stared at the kitchen TV as it burbled on about the Fingergate scandal—her husband cropping up in almost every news report as "the disgraced ex–CIA operative Lucien Benway."

His eyes had been on the screen but she knew he was observing her reflection, illuminated by the interior light of the Viking refrigerator, as she removed the Belgian chocolates and placed them in her purse.

She was proud of this little piece of tradecraft. It was vital that Lucien believe she was intending nothing but an evening watching a film that he found pretentious and boring.

After she'd stowed the chocolates, he'd muted the TV and turned to her saying, "This campaign against me is in danger of metastasizing and I can't afford to show any vulnerability. I'm counting on your support, Nadja. The sharks are circling and there can't be any blood in the water."

"Dear god, Lucien, what a mélange of metaphors. You *must* be upset."

"I'd caution you to remember that you are dependent on my goodwill and kindness."

She'd bitten back a sarcastic retort and shut her purse, the little click of its clasp like a gunshot echoing through the kitchen, and manufactured a smile that was all innocence.

"Naturally, Lucien," she'd said, as obedient as a chattel slave.

Nadja took her coffee and made her way into the cinema, enchanted as always by its huge screen and rows of padded seats.

She seated herself on the aisle and drank her coffee and ate a chocolate she had no appetite for, watching the giant images of Monica Vitti and Alain Delon on the screen, still expecting her husband or his creature to materialize in the doorway, observing her.

But neither of them appeared and, even though she'd seen the film too many times to count, Nadja was drawn into the tale of the beautiful woman who leaves an older lover and has an affair with a young stockbroker.

The last time she'd seen the film had been on Netflix with Michael Emerson, lying naked on his bed after hours of lovemaking, drinking wine, and smoking. Now, watching Vitti and Delon embrace, she felt a sudden lurch, as if something deep inside her had broken free and was falling into endless space.

She closed her eyes and she was back in that bed with Michael, smelling his scent, feeling his semen still warm and tacky between her thighs.

Michael had reached for the remote and paused the film and turned to her.

"Why do you stay with him, Nadja?"

"Michael, please, not now."

"Answer me."

"He saved me."

"Is that enough?"

She'd laughed. "He quite literally saved my life. Yes, I'd say that's *enough*."

"So you're content now to live half a life?"

"Is that what I'm doing?"

"Aren't you?"

She'd touched the hair on his chest. "I feel completely alive now."

"And why is that?"

She'd lit a cigarette to cover her discomfort. "Come on, Michael, let's watch the film."

Nadja had reached for the remote but his hand covered hers and he turned her face to his.

"He doesn't make love to you, does he?"

"Michael …"

"Does he?"

"No."

"Has he ever?"

"No."

"Has he ever even kissed you?"

She'd sighed smoke. "No."

"But he condones your promiscuity?"

"Yes."

"Welcomes it, even?"

She'd said nothing. Smoked. Drank. Stared at the frozen image of the lovers on the screen.

He'd moved so that she was forced to look at him.

"He's trapped you, Nadja. And you've enabled him to. Why?"

She'd felt a rush of anger. "What do you fucking know, Michael, with your bloody American certainties? What were you doing when you were fourteen? Playing Little League?"

"Actually, I was playing Junior League by then."

"Well, I was lying on my back being raped by a Serbian colonel who passed me around his troops for sloppy seconds when he was done. This went on for a year until Lucien saved me and brought me here."

"I get it, Nadja. I do. But you can move on now."

"What are you saying, Michael?"

He'd taken her fingers and kissed them and said, "I know that I'm risking losing you by saying this, but I love you, Nadja. I fucking love you."

She hadn't replied, not ready.

Not yet.

She hadn't replied with words, but the sex that had followed immediately after this declaration had been transcendent.

And now he was gone.

On the big screen, the Roman cityscape was blurred by her tears. She delved into her purse for a Kleenex and dabbed her eyes and then washed her dry, heaving throat with coffee.

She tossed the empty Styrofoam cup under the seat in front of her, stood, and made her way out of the theater to the street, where she flagged down a cab and ordered the driver to take her to the bar where Michael Emerson's wake was being held.

FORTY-SEVEN

Philip Danvers sat by the fireside in his living room listening to Erik Satie's "Gymnopédies," sipping a glass of Cutty Sark and smoking the single cigarette he permitted himself each night. The melancholy beauty of the music—in combination with the scotch, the mildly narcotic tobacco, and the industrial-strength painkillers he swallowed by the fistful—infused the room with a dreamlike quality, and Danvers, in the way of very old men, found himself dozing.

The Satie ended and, with a series of delicate clucks, the turntable arm lifted and settled itself back in its cradle.

Danvers roused himself, set down his glass, stood, and, willing away the spike of agony that defied the analgesics in his bloodstream, crossed to the stereo perched beneath shelves of long-playing records. He lifted the plastic lid of the turntable and sheathed the disc in its sleeve, which he returned to the shelf.

He spent a moment pondering his vast collection before he withdrew another LP—the Fischer-Dieskau and Weissenborn rendition of Schubert's lieder—and settled it on the turntable. When he lifted the curved tone arm from its little cradle the record started to rotate slowly and he gently lowered the stylus onto the grooved vinyl.

There was a sucking hiss, like distant surf breaking, before the trill of Weissenborn's piano and Fischer-Dieskau's honeyed voice rose through the static.

Had Danvers allowed himself to be seduced by the digital era, each note and phrase would have been rendered with sterile clarity, but the vinyl, despite the surface noise and ticking scratches, had a warmth, a humanity, that made the record uniquely his, the way the dog-eared pages and broken spines branded his books forever his and his alone.

He returned to his chair, closed his eyes, and lost himself in the music until he heard the sound of a car in the driveway and the crunch of tires on the gravel.

Danvers recognized the low rumble of the powerful engine, and wondered for a moment whether he should trek upstairs to where he kept a handgun.

He dismissed the thought and sipped his drink, waiting for the knock on the front door.

When it came, Danvers walked to the door and opened it, seeing the pale bulk of Dudley Morse standing behind Lucien Benway, who looked small enough to be the big man's hand puppet.

The noxious Lilliputian winked and said, "Hello, Philip. I hope you don't mind me dropping in?"

By way of an answer, Danvers stepped back and gestured for the men to enter.

Benway, who'd been to the house on several occasions years before, walked into the living room and made a show of warming himself at the fire, rubbing his palms together and smiling a counterfeit smile.

Morse stood beneath the archway to the hall, his hands behind his back.

"Sit, Lucien," Danvers said, and the little man lowered himself to the couch, the toes of his boots just brushing the floor.

Danvers crossed to the sideboard and lifted the bottle of Cutty Sark. "Drink?"

"Why not?" Benway said. "For old times."

Danvers poured an inch of scotch into a cut glass tumbler, used tongs to add two cubes of ice from a bucket, and took the drink across to Benway who raised it and said, "Here's mud in your eye."

A salutation stolen from Danvers. Along with his accent and locutions.

No matter, there had been more egregious thefts.

Danvers seated himself, hands on his knees, and stared at Benway. "So?"

Benway took a sip, pursed his lips in a moue of distaste and set the glass down on the side table. "I needn't ask if you've been following this Kate Swift debacle?"

"Fingergate? Quite the story. And there you'd had me believing that Kate was hiding out in Moscow having bikini waxes with Anna Chapman."

Benway smirked. "I only reported what I heard."

"So you say." The old man coughed a phlegmy laugh.

"I'm here to tell you that I'll play, Philip."

Danvers raised his eyebrows, a pair of caterpillars crawling up the corrugations of his brow. "Play?"

"Yes. We both know that you saw Kate Swift in Berlin and directed her toward Harry Hook in balmy Thailand. We both know that he authored this finger business. A classic piece of Hookian opportunism. And we both know that Kate, and her child, are alive and well and slurping Tom Yum soup and getting suntans."

"We do?"

"Yes, we do."

"Well."

"Who gave you the finger? The Plumber?"

"Hardly. He's always been very polite."

Benway allowed a small smile. "That's very funny, Philip."

"Thank you."

"Surely you understand, Philip, that the Plumber is using you? He surrendered the finger so you could do what you did: stir up the media and embarrass the administration. The Plumber hasn't survived all these years by being shortsighted, he's looking ahead to his next master. Preparing the ground, if you like."

"Fascinating."

"Now, I'm happy to see this administration embarrassed."

"I'm sure you are."

"And, despite my history with Kate Swift, I'm prepared to go along with all of this. To swallow the fiction that she died in an Asian rice paddy. Bygones, I say. Bygones."

"That's big of you, Lucien."

The little man blinked this away. "What becomes tough to swallow however is when I get dragged into this mess, when I'm associated with the downing of that plane. I smell a scapegoat turning slowly on a spit: me."

"Colorfully put."

"If you're the person who tied me to this story, untie me. If not, use your influence to direct the media hounds in another direction."

"You're overestimating me, Lucien. I'm just an old man watching the world from his fireside."

"Bullshit." For just a moment the careful diction slipped, but Benway composed himself. "David Burke is your useful idiot, mouthing lines scripted by you. Take his focus away from me."

"I'm tired, Lucien. And old. Too old to play these games."

"Fix this, Philip."

"Or?"

"Or I'll send Morse to Thailand to track down Kate Swift and her spawn and prove they're still alive." Benway stood. "And then he'll kill them both."

FORTY-EIGHT

Kate sat at the kitchen table of the bungalow, sweating in the yellow light of a paraffin lamp, waving away mosquitoes and sipping a tepid Chang beer. What with the chaos of the day, nobody had thought to stock up on gasoline and the generator had spluttered and died just after dark, stilling the fans and dousing the lights.

Harry Hook had fished four paraffin lamps out of a kitchen closet and lit them. He'd taken one into the living room and delighted Suzie with—Kate had to grudgingly admit—a surprisingly skillful display of hand-shadow puppetry, casting birds and hares and wolves and galloping horses on the walls of the room.

Then—there was no end to his showmanship—he'd asked Kate if he could take Suzie down to the beach and show her the marine phosphorescence the waters were famous for.

She'd nodded and said, "Not for too long. And stay where I can see you, Suze, okay?"

Kate stood on the balcony watching as Hook walked the girl down to the water, Suzie yelping as giant fruit bats wheeled overhead. He took her into the shallows, stirring the water and igniting the phosphorescence that surrounded them like glimmers of fairy dust. The girl's laughter and delighted squeals carried up to Kate.

By the time Kate had gotten Suzie washed and into bed, there was no sign of Hook and JP, and Kate wondered if they were out on the beach smoking weed.

So she sat and drank beer and sweated and, despite herself, felt curiously happy that the day was ending very differently from the way it had begun.

Once they'd returned to the island on the Zodiac—mother and daughter abandoning the long-tail amidst polylingual protests from the boatmen and the tourists—Kate and Hook had grabbed a moment in the bedroom of the bungalow to talk about what was happening in Washington. Hook fired up JP's iPad and showed her the bearded David Burke raining down righteous indignation and hinting at dark conspiracies.

"Who is that guy?" Kate asked.

"I have no idea," Hook said, "but since Benway is getting drawn into this, I'm prepared to wager that Mrs. Danvers does."

"So Philip found you your songbird?"

"Yes, I believe he did."

From then on the day had belonged to Suzie, and Kate had watched as all of her daughter's unhappiness was washed away by Harry Hook at his most seductive.

Hook, alone, appeared in the doorway to the kitchen.

"Can we talk?"

"Sure." She pointed at a chair.

He sat and looked everywhere but at Kate before he finally stared into her eyes. "I had no idea that you were my daughter. That I *had* a daughter."

"I know that."

"How long have you known about me?"

"A long time."

"Does Philip know?"

"Yes. My mother died when I was fourteen and she left me a letter telling me you were my father. When I was eighteen I started digging into your background and it led to the Agency. They thought it was a security breach, but then Philip saw I was just a kid."

"A formidable and resourceful kid."

She shrugged. "He must have thought so. He recruited me."

"Smart guy. He always had an eye for talent. We never overlapped?"

"No, while I was in training you were busy melting down and by the time I graduated you were gone. Philip explained your fragile condition and asked that I leave you be. I agreed."

Hook cracked open a can of Coke and took a sip. "Tell me about your mother."

"She was in publishing. Worked for a small outfit that didn't make much money. We lived in Manhattan. She never married, always told me that my father was dead. She was a good mother. I loved her."

"What was her name?"

"Sarah Swift."

Hook toyed with the Coke can. "I don't remember her."

"I know."

"We're talking the mideighties. When I was stateside, which wasn't often, I partied hard. Booze and chemicals. I remember sticking a straw in a big Bufferin bottle of killer coke before I hit the New York clubs. I guess that's when I met her?"

"I guess."

"I'm not sure why I'm apologizing, but …"

"Don't apologize. It was her decision to have me. And to not tell you."

"Yeah, okay." He fiddled with the tab of the can, then he looked up at her. "What happened to her?"

"She died on 9/11."

He stared at her. "The Towers?"

"No. In a car wreck in New Jersey. She'd been at a bookstore in Hackensack when the planes hit and she was trying to get back to Manhattan, to me, and collided with a bus and that was that."

"I'm sorry."

"Yeah."

There was a silence, and they listened to the wash of the ocean and the drone of mosquitoes and then, to fill the void, Kate reached for the iPad and searched the news sites. She found a White House press briefing, the press secretary at the podium saying that it had taken time to verify, the administration didn't want to misinform, but yes, they could now confirm that Kate Swift, and presumably her daughter, Susan, had perished on AirStar Flight 2605.

The press secretary paused meaningfully. "Kate Swift betrayed her country, but the loss of the lives of her and her daughter is no less tragic for that."

"So it worked?" Kate said, looking up at Hook who loomed over her shoulder. "Your crazy fucking plan? It seems that I'm dead."

"Yes." Hook smiled and ran a hand through his hair and said, "Which, if you know your New Testament, is the necessary precursor to being resurrected."

FORTY-NINE

Even though she was thirty-two, child-sized Janey Burke still got carded going into bars. Every fucking time. Now, she wasn't the world's most ardent barfly, but she and David hit DC cocktail lounges a couple of times a month. They got pleasantly loaded then headed back home to make the bedsprings wail, and it'd become a habit to enter a drinkery with her driver's license in her hand, ready to have it scrutinized.

Bearded, bearlike David, who, ironically, was a year younger than his tiny wife, never got asked for ID. While Janey went through the formalities, he just stood with his hands big as catcher's mitts bulging out of his pockets and a stupid grin on his face, whistling "Young Girl." Which had been funny maybe the first half-dozen or so times but now was just a pain in the ass.

But he persisted, like the big fucking overgrown boy that he was.

So, when they walked into the Point of View bar on the eleventh floor of DC's W Hotel and a young guy bore down on them, Janey was already flashing plastic.

But the guy ignored her and smacked David on the shoulder, saying, "Bro, you are getting some *heat*."

David all but shuffled his size thirteens, squeezed into the pair of leather dress shoes he'd last worn on the day they were wed six years ago at the Brooklyn Marriage Bureau, and said, "I got lucky."

"A lot luckier than Mike, man."

"Hell, yeah."

"Bummer."

"Major bummer."

The guy was moving off and they got drawn into the crowd in the bar, all media types, all there to raise a glass to their departed comrade, Michael Emerson.

It wasn't a formal memorial, just a gathering to drink and share war stories. Emerson had been buried the day before in his native Pennsylvania with much hoopla, a phalanx of lenses trained on his family—steelworkers who were numbed and shell-shocked at having to grieve on the world stage. This, by contrast, was all hip and mellow—high on irony and low on sentiment.

Janey hadn't wanted David to come, even though a bunch of people—people who, a week ago, would have walked past him on the street—had called and asked him to be there.

Because he was hot.

Because he'd scooped all the heavy hitters.

Because, in the unspoken superstition of these Fourth Estate vampires, just by being in his orbit might result in some magic rubbing off on them.

"It's hypocritical," she'd said, pacing their cramped living room that afternoon, dressed in sweats and a baggy hoodie, her red hair uncombed and her pixie face wearing a scowl and a blush of annoyance that made her freckles pop.

"Jesus, Janey," David had said, "stop being so Emily Post."

"Emily Post?"

"Yeah, you know, so old school. So all the about the etiquette."

"Have you even fucking read Emily Post?"

David had sighed and raised a hand in surrender. "Okay, let's drop the Emily Post metaphor—"

"Analogy."

"Whatever." He shook his head. "I've always been outside staring through the fucking window, Janey. Now I've been invited to the buffet I've been trying to get at for years."

"Michael Emerson's *wake*?"

"Hell, you know it's just an excuse for networking. Nobody even fucking liked the guy."

She'd dragged one side of her mouth down and crossed her arms across her boyish chest. "Why did I expect more of you?"

"Jesus, this is my chance, Janey. You know how narrow these windows are. Next week it'll be something else and I'll just be that guy again. I want to go to this Emerson thing. I want to hustle. I want to land a job, for Chrissakes. We need it."

What he'd left unspoken was that a year ago she'd walked out on a gig contributing political pieces to the *Huffington Post* to write a novel, a roman à clef set inside the Beltway, seen through the eyes of a jaundiced journalist not unlike herself.

The novel, though, had been becalmed for months, and David—a good man and true—had never once called her on this, had just brought home the paychecks and let her sit at her desk and write.

Or pretend to.

So they'd gone to the W Hotel. She'd insisted on being there, in the misguided belief that she could protect him.

She huddled against a wall, drinking a dirty martini, standing on tiptoe to watch him, hulking and awkward and sweating, as he was danced through the room of poised and charming and voracious sharks.

Janey caught up with him near a window framing the Lincoln Memorial, which seemed to float above a ghostly bed of snow.

"You okay?" she asked.

"Yeah. People are making me crazy offers."

"I'll bet."

"But I'm staying cool and aloof, biding my time."

"You? Cool and aloof?"

"Hey, I'm trying."

Her eyes were drawn across the room to a tall, dark-haired woman in jeans and a sweater under a black cashmere coat. She moved through the crowd effortlessly, people parting before her, until she was at the bar and getting the attention of the bartender ahead of a crush of other drinkers without seeming to do anything more than raise an eyebrow.

"Who's that?" Janey asked

"Who?"

She nodded toward the brunette who rested an elbow on the bar, surveying the room with an air of infinite boredom; a woman who'd perfected the art of making ennui look sexy.

"That's Lucien Benway's wife," David said.

"As in 'the disgraced ex–CIA operative Lucien Benway'?"

"Yep. Nadine or Nadia. Something foreign. She's Croatian. Or maybe Bosnian."

"Bos*niak*."

"Really?"

"Yeah." Janey stared at the woman. "She's gorgeous."

"If you like the just-slightly-dissipated ex-supermodel type."

"Which you obviously do."

"Not me," he said. "Why eat goulash when I can eat carrot cake?"

Janey punched him on the upper arm hard enough to make him wince.

"What's she doing here, do you think?" she asked.

"Rumor has it that she was banging Mike Emerson."

"For real?"

"Uh-huh."

"Emerson was screwing Lucien Benway's wife? Are you sure it was the jihadists who got him?"

"Oh, yeah. Jesus, if you had to behead all the guys who've boned the lovely Mrs. B, the road to Damascus would be lined with skulls."

"She's easy?"

"As a sleeper sofa, baby. You can be sure she won't leave here alone tonight."

A correspondent for *Newsweek*, a toothsome man with a hair weave who was a frequent pundit on political chat shows—reliably glib and simplistic as he gnawed on the week's news—barged up and started talking to David as if he'd known him forever, and Janey turned and downed her martini as she watched planes take off from Reagan National Airport, trying to let the booze wash away the nameless terror that lurked in her gut.

FIFTY

Nadja Benway *did* leave the W Hotel with a man: a New Zealander named Eddie Jones, a photographer specializing in images of conflict and suffering. One of his pictures—a carrion bird eating the eyes of a skeletal Somali toddler—had been a contender for a Pulitzer in the nineties.

It was a widely held belief that the child had still been alive when the vulture had started its snacking and Jones had been criticized for not scaring the bird away, to which he'd replied, "I document the fucking news; I don't make it."

An unsightly man, shading fifty with a sagging gut and skin as pock-marked as one of the bullet-scarred ruins in his photographs, he'd stood alone at the bar, drinking a steady succession of vodkas as Nadja had observed him from her vantage point farther along the counter.

He was one of those drunks who seem to become more grounded and steady the more they consume. When the stool beside his was vacated and she slid onto it, he took an age to look up from his drink and into her face.

"My, my," Jones said in his strangled Kiwi accent, "a beauty."

"Thank you."

"Don't thank me, darling, thank whatever gene pool you doggy-paddled out of."

His eyes were back on his drink.

Michael Emerson had worked with him frequently, out of necessity rather than choice. Jones was one of the few photographers who'd been prepared to accompany Emerson on his increasingly kamikaze quests.

"He's brave," Michael had once said of Jones.

"Or sociopathic," she'd said.

"The distinction," he'd said as he shoveled moo shu pork into his mouth, "is a fine one."

When Nadja placed her hand on Jones', feeling the scrofulous texture of his skin, he sighed and stared at her in the mirror behind the bar, raising his eyebrows.

"Would you like to fuck me?" she asked.

"What's the price of admission?"

"Why should there be a price?"

"When I look like me and you look like you there's always a bloody price."

She nodded. "Okay. I understand you were in Jordan with Michael?"

His eyes narrowed. "So?"

"Tell me about his last days and I'll let you do whatever you want to me."

"What's your interest? Professional?"

"No."

Jones pointed a nicotine-stained finger at her and wagged it slowly. "Ah."

"*Ah* what?"

"You're *her*."

"Who?"

"The love of his fucking life."

Despite herself she felt a quickening of her heart. "He called me that?"

"No, darling, he didn't say one bloody word about you. But I knew. You always know."

"How?"

"All of a sudden he was being careful. Like he had something to lose. In my experience there's only one thing that does that to a man."

"What?"

"The big-fucking-*L*." He smiled at her, revealing long yellow teeth.

"So if he was being careful, why did he leave Amman for Syria?"

"That, my beauty, is the fucking twenty-million-dinar question. Well, one of them."

"What's the other?"

"Why didn't he take me with him?"

She stood. "Can we go somewhere?"

He shrugged. "Sure." He threw back his drink and sighed. "I'll tell you what little I know. And you don't even have to fuck me."

"No," she said. "I want to."

"You do?"

"Yes."

"Why?"

"Because every man I fuck helps me remember Michael. Does that make any sense?"

"You know, it does. It does."

Jones stood, keeping a hand on the counter for a moment, steadying himself, then he walked slowly and with great purpose from the bar, not once looking back to see if she was following.

FIFTY-ONE

Harry Hook emerged from the ocean just after dawn wearing the ratty pair of black swimming shorts he hadn't removed since his impulsive decision to come to the island two days before. He had no fresh clothes in the bungalow, so when he'd risen an hour ago he'd washed his T-shirt (rank with sweat) at the kitchen sink and hung it from the branch of a tree to dry.

While searching the kitchen closet for detergent he'd stumbled upon a plastic Tesco bag containing a Grumbacher tin with a tray of twelve virgin watercolor cakes, a clutch of new sable-haired brushes of various sizes, a couple of 2b pencils, and a spiral-bound book of white cotton paper. He'd brought the painting supplies on a long-ago trip with Bob Carnahan and forgotten about them.

Hook filled a plastic tumbler with water and walked down the beach until he had a view of the ocean in the foreground, the bungalow behind framed by the jungle and the cliff. A notion had taken him to paint the scene and give it to the child.

To his granddaughter.

He sat on the sand, dripping, and watched the sun rise until there was enough light to open the watercolor book on his knees and sketch the scene in pencil.

Satisfied, he started to paint a wash of azure and pink that captured the flat mirror of the ocean. The jungle, verdant green and dense, he rendered in quick strokes, as he did the sky that changed before his eyes from rose to lemon yellow to the flat blue of the tropics.

He was busy contemplating the bungalow, trying to formulate a strategy that would allow him to portray it realistically without getting fussy and overdetailed—a failing of his—when a small figure came out on the balcony and waved.

Hook waved back and the girl skipped down onto the beach. As she approached, he laid the watercolor book face up on the sand, unable to close it, even though he wanted to, for fear of smudging the paint.

The child stood and squinted down at his handiwork.

"That's pretty."

"It's not done yet."

"I know. But it's still pretty."

"Well, I'm nothing more than a Sunday painter."

"But today's Thursday."

Hook laughed. "Yes, it is." He saw her bemused expression. "A Sunday painter is someone who dabbles, does it as a hobby. Someone who isn't very good."

"Well, I like it."

"Thank you."

"Can I have it, when it's done?"

"Yes. I was painting it for you, actually."

She blinked and looked at him for a long time. "You were?"

"Yes."

"Why?"

"I thought it might be a little souvenir. A memento, for when you go." Hook saw her face and regretted his words. Unused to the exacting business of talking to a child.

"I don't want to go," she said and looked close to tears.

"Oh, you'll still be here for a while."

"And you?"

"Yes, me too," he said, knowing he was lying to the girl.

For the truth was that he had no plan, and it shamed him to admit that beyond the wild melodrama of the finger in the plane wreck (a by-product of terrible coincidence and his toxic postbinge imagination) he'd had no strategy. The coming days were a blank canvas.

"Suzie!"

They both turned and saw Kate in the doorway of the hut, beckoning.

"You go on," Hook said. "I'll catch up with you later."

The girl ran back toward the bungalow and stood on the balcony with her mother and JP, who had risen from his hammock, and then the three of them went inside.

Hook selected a medium-sized brush—a corrective to his tendency toward fussiness—and wet the bristles in the water container. He applied the brush to the umber watercolor pan, dabbed it in the mixing tray, then rinsed the brush in the glass and lifted some yellow ochre to mix with the umber.

The resulting hue was close enough to the bamboo of the bungalow. He kept his wrist loose, allowing himself to paint in easy strokes. So absorbed was he in capturing the essence of the hut without losing himself in detail that it was only when her shadow fell across the page that he realized that Kate was standing over him.

Hook felt embarrassed, as if he'd been caught at something trivial and somehow humiliating.

He put the watercolor book down on the sand.

"A man of many talents," Kate said.

The roar of the Zodiac's outboard rescued Hook from having to reply and they watched JP and Suzie bump away toward the neighboring island.

"Are they going for provisions?"

"Yes," she said.

Neither spoke again until the inflatable disappeared.

"Look," he said, unable to bear the silence, "I think what we're busy with here is kind of an improvisation."

"You're not talking about the painting, are you?"

"No, I'm not."

"You mean you don't have this thing all figured out and tightly plotted?"

"No, I don't. I'm sorry."

She looked at him and he saw something in the line of her jaw and the squint of her eye that was uncomfortably familiar.

"Did you ever?"

"Well, I saw that plane crash on TV and—"

"No, I mean years ago."

"Back in my heyday?"

"Yes."

"No. No, I didn't. I always liked to leave room for happenstance. I believed that you could sketch out a scenario and then you had to step back just a little and let life fill in the blanks."

"Very Zen."

"Or something."

Kate sat on the sand, wrapping her arms around her knees and looking out over the water.

"It's okay," she said .

"What's okay?"

"That you don't have it all mapped out."

"That's not what you said the other night."

"I was pissed off the other night. Mostly about a lot of stuff that had nothing to do with you."

"Well, I was a participant."

"Only tangentially."

"Now that's a nice five-dollar word."

She smiled. "And look what happened. That Burke guy showed up and moved it all along."

"He's just a puppet. Mrs. Danvers has an arm up his ass."

"That's an unfortunate image."

They both laughed.

"What's Philip doing, do you think?" she said.

"I think he's doing what he does best. Bending circumstances to his whim."

"Meaning?"

"Look, he has it in for Lucien. What Lucien did was a form of patricide, or at least Philip would see it that way, shafting him and taking control of what he had spent years creating. Mrs. Danvers is lighting a fire under Benway's feet, and he'll sit back and watch him dance."

"A dangerous sport."

"Very."

"And there I was thinking he was doing it all for me."

"Oh, Philip has his sentimental side, of course. And you better believe he's convinced himself that he's doing something noble, doing this to help you and maybe even me. But he's a master at biding his time. And here's his opportunity."

Kate lifted a handful of sand and let it seep through her fingers.

"How did you get involved with him?"

"With Philip?"

"Yes."

He shrugged. "That's long ago and far away."

"Tell me."

Hook shook his head. "The past is just another fucking lie." He stared out over the ocean. "Let's stick with the present."

She stared at him. "We're going to have to deal with Lucien, aren't we?"

"Yes, we are."

"So," she said, "what would you do if you were me?"

"Well, I wouldn't buy any green bananas."

Laughing, she stood and set off down the beach, back toward the bungalow. Hook sat a moment, listening to the small waves kissing the sand, then he started to paint again. Before he was even conscious of what he was doing, he had, with a few dabs of the brush, captured his daughter walking away from him, the wind teasing at her hair which, by the day, was returning to the same shade of brown as his own.

FIFTY-TWO

Waking in the morning, Nadja felt like a seabird washed up on some befouled and blackened beach, plumage matted and viscous with crude oil.

Gray light dribbled through a gap in the curtains of Eddie Jones' hotel room and found her still lying in bed beside the photographer, who gargled and grunted in his sleep.

The empty bottle of Stolichnaya on the bedside table explained why she had slept until nearly 8:00 a.m.

Nadja eased her throbbing body—the cameraman had been relentless in collecting his reward—from beneath the covers and dressed. She recovered her purse from under the bed and as she lifted it, her phone fell out, the message light blinking in admonishment.

Making her way out of the room to the bank of elevators, she rode down alone, avoiding her reflection in the mirror.

She walked through the lobby into the cauterizing cold, a fresh fall of snow icing the low-rise cake that was DC, and stood huddled in the entrance while the doorman flagged a cab for her.

On the drive home, she assembled what she could of the photographer's testimony.

It had been brief.

Michael Emerson had gone to Jordan to do a piece on the kingdom's role in the war against Islamic State. He'd had no intention of crossing into Syria. The night he arrived, he'd met up with Eddie Jones for a few drinks and then left the photographer in the bar saying he'd see him in the morning when they were to travel together to the Muwaffaq Salti Air Base.

When Michael hadn't shown, Jones had spoken to the hotel desk clerk who told him the reporter had checked out sometime during the night. Jones could get no other details.

Jones had stared at Nadja over his vodka glass as he'd lounged on the bed, shirtless, his hairy white gut swimming over his belt. "I had a feeling, though, that palms had been greased. There's the story I was told and then there's the truth, and there's a fucking desert between the two. Those towelheads are born liars, darling."

Yes, she'd wanted to say, we are.

But she'd merely spread herself across his bed and let him drip his flab and his sweat onto her, and she'd shut down and thought of Michael.

The taxi dropped her outside the town house, and she walked up the steps and opened the door.

The TV was gabbling in the kitchen and she saw Lucien sitting in his shirtsleeves, smoking a cigarette.

"Good morning," he said.

"Good morning." She didn't look his way as she headed in the direction of the stairs.

"Not so fast, my dear," he said, lifting a Boone & Sons Jewelers gift bag from the table and holding it out toward her. "I have something for you."

"What is it, Lucien?"

"Oh, you'll love it," he said, flashing one of his most lethal smiles. "It's a bracelet."

Nadja opened the bag and saw a matte black box the size of a pack of cigarettes with a black rubber belt looping from it.

It took her a moment to understand what she was looking at.

"Fuck you," she said, "I'm not wearing that."

"Oh, yes, you are," he said, "unless you want to return to the detox facility on a, shall we say, permanent basis."

She heard a scuff and Mr. Morose stood in the kitchen doorway, his hands behind his back, his face impassive.

"Put it on," Lucien said.

Nadja sat at the table and removed the penny loafer from her right foot, lifted her jeans to her calf and slid on the ankle monitor. She battled to attach the device and Morse, as unctuous as a sales assistant in a shoe store, kneeled before her, pulled the strap tight enough to bite into her flesh, and clicked the connector closed.

FIFTY-THREE

Hook, sluggish after the late lunch of freshly caught kingfish that JP had grilled on an open fire, was dozing on the balcony of the bungalow when the warble of his cell phone roused him from a dream that dispersed like smoke the moment he opened his eyes.

Disoriented, he thought for a moment that he was back in his house in the jungle. But then Kate, wearing a brightly patterned cloth over her bikini, stepped out of the bungalow and handed him his cell, and he remembered where he was. The phone fell silent as he took it from her.

He saw Bob Carnahan's name on the caller ID and dumped the phone on the wooden floor beside his chair.

"Nothing urgent?" Kate asked.

"No, just a guy I play chess with."

"You play chess?"

"The way I paint. Poorly."

"Don't be coy. You know that painting was a big hit."

"I'm just pleased she liked it."

"She loved it. Thank you."

After lunch he'd presented the watercolor to Suzie who'd gushed and kissed him, which had made him feel happy and melancholy all at once.

"Are you going to tell her?" he asked. "About me?"

Kate found a few grains of beach sand trapped in the crease of her elbow and dusted them off with her index finger while staring at him.

"I haven't decided yet. She's lost so much in the last few years, I need to be careful."

Hook nodded and looked away from her gaze.

JP appeared from the jungle carrying the spade he used to bury their garbage. He dropped the spade near the steps and came up off the beach smelling of wood smoke. As he passed Kate in the doorway, she touched him on the hand and smiled up at him and Hook knew they were sleeping together. They were being discreet, but the signs were unmistakable.

The man in him was pleased for her. The ex-spy wasn't. Distractions were dangerous. As a creature prone to distractions, he'd learned that the hard way.

Kate followed JP into the bungalow as the Frenchman whispered something, and she laughed softly.

Hook sat and watched the lazy swell of the ocean, the small waves nibbling silently at the shore. His cell rang again.

Carnahan.

Hook grabbed the phone and walked down the three steps onto the beach, scuttling like a crab for the shade of a tree, the molten sand torching his bare soles.

"Bob?"

"Permission to come aboard, Skipper," Carnahan said.

"Where are you?"

"Across the way from you, Harry. When I got here the Zodiac wasn't moored on the beach so I figured you were over there."

"You're alone?" Hook asked.

"Hell, yes," Bob said. "Just me and a little baggie of primo weed."

Hook hesitated. "Okay, Bob, I'll come and get you. Give me a couple of minutes, okay?"

"Sure."

Hook ended the call and loped across the sand like a firewalker, and went into the house to where Kate sat reading the dog-eared paperback of *The Quiet American* that he'd left there months ago. JP was in the kitchen washing dishes. Suzie helped him and they chatted about fishing and the ocean.

Hook beckoned Kate out onto the balcony and told her about Carnahan. Told her that she should pack up all of her and Suzie's things and get JP to pack his, too.

"You believe this joker's here on a whim?" Kate said, her hands on her hips, leaning in toward Hook, her face gaunt and serious in the slant of hard yellow sun.

"Yes," Hook said, "I think so."

"*Think*? There's no fucking room for 'think.'"

He held up a placating hand. "I'll get you and Suzie and JP across to a resort on the south beach on the big island."

"There's another beach?"

"Yeah, it's a little more remote."

"And?"

"Then I'll collect Bob and bring him here. If he's set on staying a couple of days, I'll tell him I've got to get back to the mainland and he can take me across in the morning. We'll connect and figure out what to do next."

She shook her head. "I don't like it."

"Relax. He's just an old geezer escaping his wife."

"What if he's not?" Hook just stared at her. "Do you have a gun?"

"No."

"Jesus."

"I was never much good with them, anyway."

"Why don't you stay over on the big island?"

"And what do I tell Bob?"

"That you're leaving early in the morning."

"He won't buy it. He'll be suspicious." Hook was about to put a hand on her arm, but he let it drop. "Okay, get moving. He's waiting for me."

Hook stepped into his flip-flops, rescued his T-shirt from the tree, and dragged the Zodiac from the beach to the ocean. The tide was low and he was sweating freely by the time he got the craft into water deep enough to float it. He clambered inside and lowered the outboard into the water, checking that the propeller had clearance.

Kate, Suzie, and JP hurried across the sand and splashed through the low water to the inflatable, throwing their packs onto the PVC floor and climbing aboard.

"You didn't leave anything?" Hook said.

"I've done this before, Harry," Kate said. "Too many times."

He nodded and yanked at the pull cord twice before it caught. Taking hold of the tiller he set course for the trio of limestone cliffs that rose like sentinels from the ocean. Once the Zodiac was behind them, they were shielded from view from the neighboring beach.

Hook approached the big island from its south side. This beach was smaller and rockier. No long-tails plied their trade here, the stretch of coastline accessible only by road. Or by a shallow draft vessel like the inflatable.

Hook got the Zodiac as close to the shore as he could and his three passengers clambered out, JP taking Suzie on his shoulders. Hook watched them wading in toward land and then he gunned the outboard and went back around the cliffs, the restaurants, bars, and wooden boats growing larger as he neared them, the low thump of a reggae backbeat reaching him as he cut the engine and elevated it, allowing the inflatable to beach itself beside a row of long-tails.

Carnahan was sitting in the shade of a palm, away from the tourists, and raised a hand in salute. He stood, slung a small pack from his shoulder, and walked over to the Zodiac.

"Hey, Harry."

"This is a surprise."

"Yeah. My fuckin beach is overrun with *farang*, man—it's like Rockaway on the Fourth of July. I need some air. Some space. You down with that?"

"Sure."

Carnahan dumped his pack and clambered into the inflatable. Hook gunned the outboard and pointed the nose toward the bungalow.

Wiping his forehead on his arm Carnahan said, "Jesus, it's wicked hot."

He dug into his pocket and emerged with a spliff. Sitting with his back to the breeze he set it alight, took a mighty hit, and offered it to Hook, who shook his head.

Carnahan shrugged and sat smoking and staring out at the ocean, the bandanna around his head, the droopy mustache and stubble bringing to mind Dennis Hopper in *Apocalypse Now*.

A cell phone rang. An old Credence number that Hook couldn't quite name.

Carnahan fished the phone from his shorts and jabbed at it with a thick finger.

"Hey, baby," he said as he sucked on the joint. "Yeah, I'm on a boat. Uh-huh. Well, you know, Phuket is fuckin Phuket." He winked at Hook. "Okay, miss you too, sugar." He sheathed the phone.

"You told Betty you're going to Phuket?" Hook asked.

"Yeah. Truth is, I've had a few hassles with the old ticker," he tapped a finger against his chest. "Nothing serious, but Betty doesn't like me being alone out here."

"But you're not alone."

"Sure, but I didn't know that when I left home, now did I?" He took a hefty toke on the blunt. "Women just don't fuckin get it about us, do they, Harry?"

"Get what?"

"That we have to kid ourselves that, like gods and despots, we're beyond the reach of custom, obligation, and law."

"And cell phones."

"Amen to that, brother. Amen to that." Carnahan sucked the last life out of the joint and flicked the end into the ocean, exhaling a plume of fragrant smoke at the sky.

FIFTY-FOUR

Kate went out onto the tiny balcony of the beach hut that stood in the sand on rickety wooden legs, watching Suzie play at the water's edge. JP emerged from the one room that was almost filled by a double bed and stood beside her.

"I have asked you no questions," he said.

"I'm grateful for that."

"But I know who you are."

"Okay," she looked at him.

"Don't worry. I will say nothing." *Nussing.*

"Thanks, JP."

"I also know you are 'Arry's daughter." When she stared at him he shrugged. "I have ears. And eyes."

"Yeah, well, daughter in name only."

"You trust him?"

"Don't you?"

He held up a hand. "Maybe that is the wrong word. Trust. I mean, you're sure he can get you through this?"

"Yes, I'm sure." Even though she wasn't.

"His heart is good, I think."

"Yes, it is."

"And long ago he was sharp up here." He tapped his temple. "But now, maybe, not so much."

"What are you saying, JP?"

"I know some people. On the mainland. Who can help."

"This isn't your fight."

"Now, maybe, it is."

Kate touched his face and felt a flare of desire. "No, it's not. It's mine. And Harry's."

She left him and walked down onto the beach where her child was playing against a sky wild with the colors of sunset.

FIFTY-FIVE

Hook cut the outboard, and he and Carnahan dragged the Zodiac up onto the beach near the bungalow as the red sun drowned itself in the ocean and a sudden mauve dusk fell.

Carnahan turned to admire the view. "Fuckin paradise, Harry. Right?"

"Yeah, it's paradise, okay."

Hook turned and walked across to the bungalow, hearing the low chug of the generator, fruit bats bursting from the trees like shrapnel and buzzing around the balcony. He entered the house before Carnahan and saw no sign that anybody but him had been here.

Carnahan came in and gave the place a once-over, then headed for the kitchen and opened the fridge. He held up a sweating bottle of Heineken, JP's brew of choice, overlooked in the hasty clean up.

"Fallen off the old wagon, Harry?"

Hook shrugged. "You've got me cold, man."

"Good for you. What did Bogart say? 'Never trust a bastard who doesn't drink'?"

"I thought he said that the whole world was three drinks behind."

Carnahan laughed. "Here, catch up."

He slung the bottle at Hook, who caught it and popped the cap. He didn't want the beer but he couldn't refuse it now, so he took a slug.

"Your health, sport," Hook said.

"Uh-huh." Carnahan stood with his back to the kitchen sink. "So you just decided to head on down here?"

"Yeah, when I left your house the other day. On a whim. I brought nothing, only what I'm wearing."

Hook set the beer down on the table and wandered across to the window and looked out at the jungle. The cicadas had kicked in, a high-pitched whine.

By the time Hook heard Carnahan behind him it was too late. Carnahan hit him with his full weight, grabbed him by the hair, and smashed his face against the wooden window frame, stunning him.

Carnahan kneed him in the liver, and Hook whinnied and folded. The big man kicked him in the gut, and Hook sank to the floor.

Carnahan flipped him onto his back and straddled him. Hook could smell his sour sweat, the recently smoked weed, and some kind of lemony hair product.

When Hook tried to speak, Carnahan punched him in the mouth and he felt the salty heat of blood on his lip.

Carnahan had a filleting knife in his hand, the one JP had used on the kingfish a few hours before, and he prodded the tip into the flesh between Hook's eyelid and eyebrow.

"Where are they?" he said.

"Who?"

"Harry, don't fuck with me. Tell me where they are or I'll take your eye, man. I'm goddamn serious."

"Jesus, Bob, who the hell are you?" Hook said.

"Who I've always been."

"You're working for Lucien Benway, aren't you?" Hook took the man's blink as an affirmative. "When you were building those dams in third-world shitholes you were a fucking *asset*?"

Carnahan shrugged one shoulder. "Strictly small time, Harry. After I retired and moved here I put all that behind me—until you washed up on my beach."

"And, what, Benway got you to keep tabs on me?"

"In a low-key way. He just wanted to know your movements."

"Why didn't you tell me, Bob? Why'd you pretend to be my fucking friend?"

"That wasn't a pretense. But Benway has threatened me, Harry. Threatened Betty."

"Jesus."

"Now, I'm sorry as all hell about this, but I fuckin mean it, Harry. You tell me where Kate Swift and her kid are or I'll take this eye. And then the other."

Carnahan jabbed the knife tip into his skin again and Hook closed his eyes and said, "Okay, Bob. Okay, man. They're on the big island."

"You came over alone."

"They're on the south beach. I went behind the cliffs for cover and then doubled back to get you."

Carnahan relaxed slightly and the knife moved from Hook's eye.

"You're not shittin me?"

"I am not shitting you."

Carnahan reached up and wiped sweat from his walrus mustache. This displaced his weight a little and Hook wrenched a fist free and punched up into his trachea. The big man gagged and tried to bring the knife into play, but Hook drove the heel of his hand into Carnahan's nose and felt the bone break.

Blood dripped from Carnahan's nostrils as Hook bucked, unseating the bigger man. Hook stood and kicked Carnahan in the ribs. He went down, gasping and spewing and bleeding.

Hook was catching his breath when Carnahan gripped him around the legs and toppled him, his forehead striking the edge of the table as he fell.

Carnahan reached for the knife that had spun under the table.

The beer bottle had shattered on the floor when Hook dropped it, and he seized a blade-sized shard of glass—immune to the pain when it cut his own hand—and threw himself at the big man's back. He grasped Carnahan by the hair, lifting his head, exposing his thick neck, as furrowed as a bull seal's. He cut Carnahan's throat and blood geysered, spraying hot across Hook's hands and flinging wet red gouts onto the wall.

Impossibly, Carnahan, a hand gripping his torn gullet, regained his feet and blundered toward the door, gasping and sobbing, toppling the kitchen table and chairs.

Hook tried to get up but slipped in the blood and fell to the floor. As he clutched onto the counter and hauled himself upright, Carnahan exited the kitchen and staggered toward the balcony, leaving a swathe of blood in his wake.

Hook, puke dribbling down his jaw, followed and saw the man plunge from the balcony to the beach, where he lay face down.

Surely to God this had to be the end of him …

But by the time Hook jumped down onto the sand that was still warm beneath his feet, Carnahan was lurching toward the Zodiac.

Hook's foot caught the spade that JP had abandoned earlier, and he lifted it and ran at Carnahan, swinging the blade.

Carnahan fell to his knees, crawling on all fours despite the blows that rained down on him and, blinded by blood, floundered into the water.

Hook, gasping, exhausted, took the spade back as if he were wielding a Louisville Slugger and swung it with everything he had left, the steel chiming like a dinner gong against the white-haired man's skull.

Carnahan collapsed into the water and lay still, the surf fizzing around his prone form.

Hook stood leaning on the shovel, sucking air, waiting for a sign of life from his erstwhile friend.

Nothing.

Under the baleful yellow eye of the fat moon that rose from behind the palms, Hook folded to his knees in the tepid water, the hiss of the surf and the drill-bit whine of the cicadas drowned out by his ragged, sawing breath.

FIFTY-SIX

Philip Danvers sat on the bench in Battery Lane Park, waiting for the journalist who was fifteen minutes late. Danvers knew he was too conspicuous, bathed in the cold glare of a streetlight, but standing in the shadows near the restrooms, he'd found his knees trembling from more than the cold and had he not sat he'd have collapsed in the snow.

So he waited, bundled in his Burberry, his head warmed by his Tyrolean hat, holding a brown envelope in his gloved hands, his breath ghostly in the lamplight, each exhalation bringing him closer to his inevitable end.

He forced away the images of blood spattering the porcelain of his toilet bowl earlier as he'd sweated and shaken as he'd tried to piss. The liver-spotted hands clutching the cistern were those of an ancient stranger.

Since Benway and Morse had left him the night before, Danvers had not slept. He'd driven to a 7-Eleven, purchased a disposable cell phone, and sat in front of his fire making calls to a list of numbers he kept in a small notebook.

Many of the numbers were no longer in service, and it had saddened but not surprised him that most of the people who did answer had hung up when they heard his voice.

He was reaching out to the men and women who had once belonged to his shadowy unit. Who had once been *his* people, operatives he'd groomed and nurtured and guided through marital strife and addiction and sexual confusion and paralyzing fear until they'd realized their true potential.

Only to be taken from him when Lucien Benway had staged his

little *putsch* and Danvers had been pushed out into the cold, scorned and useless, like an unwanted codger.

When Kate Swift had done what she'd done and ripped the unit apart, leaving Lucien the exiled pariah—ah, how the mad world spins—there had been both a purge and a diaspora. Those most loyal to Lucien Benway had been pruned away like diseased elm branches, their silence bought with golden handshakes and threats.

The rest of the personnel had been absorbed into the greater corpus of the intelligence apparatus, demoted and sent to hardship posts in grim third-world countries, posts that were dangerous—or worse, cripplingly humdrum.

Of the handful of people who *had* spoken to him, only two had mustered sufficient loyalty—Danvers coaxing and cajoling like a painted old roué—to do his bidding.

He'd gathered their offerings via email (sent to a desolate internet café in a strip mall) and he'd driven home and downloaded the intelligence from a thumb drive onto his computer. There, he constructed a collage of lies and half-truths in the manner of Harry Hook, his inkjet printer clattering and spitting photographs, flight manifests, and what would pass for classified CIA communiqués.

His work had none of Hook's sparkle and genius—a little like the inferior efforts of an Old Master's apprentice—but he felt it would suffice.

He heard the growl of an engine, and a car bumped to a halt at the entrance to the park. A door closed and he waited, the footsteps of whoever was approaching muffled by the recent fall of snow. Then the burly reporter hove into view, wearing a knit cap and a scarf.

David Burke waved his gloved hands and said, "I'm sorry. My wife had the car. Her yoga class ran late."

Danvers almost laughed at this glimpse into Burke's prosaic little world.

"No matter," he said as the hefty man flopped down beside him, his breath coming in the great, steamy snorts of a plow horse. "I need you to listen very carefully."

"I'm listening."

"I don't know if you are aware of the war being waged on Thailand's border with Malaysia?"

"Vaguely. Some provinces wanting to secede from Thailand?"

"Yes. Provinces that are overwhelmingly Muslim in a predominantly Buddhist country."

"Yeah, rings a bell."

"There are a number of insurgent groups at work. The usual alphabet soup of acronyms. One of them, the GMIP, is rumored to have al-Qaeda connections. More significantly, for the purposes of our conversation, they receive support, both financial and in terms of manpower, from the sultan who rules over the sovereign state of Palang, a fly speck in the Indonesia archipelago. A place where the clock is turning back, where shari'a law prevails, where adulterers are stoned and homosexuals are lynched in public. Three men from the sultan's bodyguard have been on the CIA's radar for years. One of them was killed by the Thai army in their southernmost province last month. The other two were seen at a Thai airport five days ago. The airport from which AirStar Flight 2605 departed."

Burke looked at him. "What are you saying?"

Danvers flapped the envelope. "It's all in here. But, in brief, a little less than a decade ago, Lucien Benway was instrumental in helping the sultan wrest power from a secular government and has continued to provide his services. Two of the passengers on that aircraft were traveling on stolen passports: one belonging to a Greek, the other to a Spaniard. I believe that Benway put those men on that aircraft along with Kate Swift and her child."

"And they what? Blew up the plane?"

"I don't know. Perhaps."

"Just to kill Kate Swift? What was in it for them?"

"Well, the eighteen Israelis on board would have sweetened the deal."

"Fuck."

"Yes."

"But nobody has claimed responsibility."

"Not yet, no."

The big man scratched at his beard and stared at the snow.

Danvers stood and held out the envelope. "Keep fighting the good fight."

Burke took the envelope, looked down at it, and then up at Danvers. "I don't know."

"You don't know what?"

"This is heavy shit, man."

"It is."

"Dangerous shit."

"It's a story that deserves to be told."

"Sure, but maybe not by me."

"You're the man of integrity, Mr. Burke. It's your story to tell."

"Integrity?" The big man laughed. "Is *integrity* going to console my wife when I'm lying on a slab wearing a nifty little toe tag?"

"Oh, come, don't be melodramatic. You're a public figure now. With all the protection that affords you."

Danvers walked away, feeling feverish and faint, desperate not to crumple to the snow under the eyes of his songbird.

FIFTY-SEVEN

Nadja Benway woke before dawn, sprawled facedown on her bed, still dressed in the soiled clothes she'd worn to Michael's wake, her mouth dry and bitter from the handful of pills she had swallowed upon returning home to hurl herself into oblivion.

She sat up and clicked on the bedside lamp, wincing at the light, her thoughts moving as slow as mud. Her alarm clock told her it was 6:00 a.m. She had been asleep—or unconscious, rather—for close to eighteen hours.

A memory had her gazing down at her right ankle, just to make sure that the faceless black thing secured to her lower leg was real, and not a figment of her imagination.

It was real.

Yesterday morning, in the kitchen, when the ankle monitor had locked onto her leg with that smug little click, she'd known that a circle had closed. She was trapped again. Just as she had been trapped more than twenty years ago.

Once again, with some terrible symmetry, a man was holding her captive.

She'd looked up into Lucien's face and seen his smile of satisfaction and known that this was what he'd always wanted from her. Complete subjugation.

She'd gone up to her room and popped five pills out of the blister pack, swallowed them, and passed out.

A terrible desperation suddenly had her gagging, and she ran to the bathroom and vomited into the sink. Then she pulled off her underwear and sank down on the toilet, sitting with her eyes closed, listening to the dribble of her urine. Afterward, she stood and looked at her reflection in the mirror and the understanding of the terrible loop that she seemed doomed to repeat left her breathless. She stripped off the rest of her clothes, drew a steamy bath, and used a carbolic soap to scrub herself clean, the astringent, tarry smell an antidote to the musky residue of sweat and sex that clung to her body, which was still sticky with the photographer's fluids.

She dried herself with such vigor that it was almost an act of self-mortification, her skin red and stinging as she went through to her bedroom closet and stepped into cotton panties fragrant with lavender detergent. She found a very plain white bra and a white silk blouse that she slipped on over a dark skirt that ended at her knees.

Her legs were bare and the ankle monitor was hard and black.

She gathered all the pills in her bedroom and took them to the bathroom and popped them out of their blister packs and flushed them.

Barefoot, she went down to the kitchen and removed the bottle of vodka from the refrigerator. She opened it, caught the strong whiff of the liquor, and almost weakened, but she shook her head and poured it down the sink. She uncapped a bottle of spring water and drank a long swallow from it.

If she was going to take on her husband she would have to recalibrate her mind and achieve some balance and stability.

Nadja sat down at the kitchen table, the blue of dawn leaking in through the windows, and clicked on the TV and waited for the world to speak to her.

FIFTY-EIGHT

First light woke Hook and he lay a moment in the hammock on the balcony of the bungalow, perfectly calm in the lilac dawn, listening to the mutter of the ocean and the mournful wails of the gibbon monkeys.

Then recall of the previous evening's bloodshed had him sitting up, rocking the hammock, staring out across the beach to where a dark form lay in the mud; the tide, under the spell of the moon, had retreated far back during the night.

He put a finger to his lip. It was swollen and throbbed and one of his teeth felt as loose as a toggle switch.

Hook, naked, climbed out of the hammock and stood holding onto the bamboo railing, quelling a sudden dizziness.

His shorts and T-shirt, heavy with gore, lay on the beach by the stairs where he'd discarded them last night, unable to bear the sticky chafe of Carnahan's blood on his flesh and its old iron smell in his nostrils.

He stepped down onto the sand, soft and cool to his bare feet, and lifted the clothes. The pale cotton T-shirt was rigid with dried blood and would never be worn again, but the black shorts were made of a non-porous fabric and could be salvaged.

He walked down to the ocean—avoiding the corpse—the mud sucking at his feet until he reached the water's edge. He knelt down, his sad balls scraping the cold ooze, and washed his shorts in the sea, a smear of red drawn away on the receding surf.

Hook stood and pulled on the dripping pants, tying the cord under his burgeoning paunch. He steeled himself and crossed to where Carnahan lay with one cheek flat to the mud, his visible eye open and milky, staring out to sea.

A small white hermit crab scuttled out of the tear in Carnahan's throat and Hook gagged. He stood with his hands on his knees, retching, but there was nothing left in his gut to vomit. Using the back of his hand, Hook wiped slime from his mouth, then he took a deep breath, reached down, and grabbed Carnahan by his hairy ankles and pulled.

With a suck the mud released the dead man, and Hook dragged him onto the beach.

The sun was up now, the heat already oppressive, and Hook was sweating from the exertion. He sat down beside the body and thought of Carnahan placing his hand on Betty's, his roguish blue eyes disappearing into a maze of wrinkles as he'd smiled at her.

Pushing this from his mind, Hook frisked the corpse. He found Carnahan's cell phone, waterlogged, its gray face blank, as well as a wallet that held a couple of thousand baht in cash, Carnahan's passport and Thai driver's license, and a photograph of a young Bob and Betty standing in the garden of a tract house.

Hook put the money in his pocket and carried the phone and the wallet over to the balcony and dumped them by the hammock. He went inside and found Carnahan's pack on the couch in the front room beside his Ray-Ban aviators. Hook unzipped the pack. Two T-shirts. Two pairs of shorts. A couple of pairs of skivvies.

And an automatic pistol.

Hook was no gunman but he knew enough about weapons to see that the automatic was well maintained and that there was a round in the chamber.

He left the pistol on the couch and put the sunglasses in the pack and zipped it up, slinging it over his shoulder. On his way down to the beach, he stepped into his flip-flops, scooped up the phone, wallet, and his soiled T-shirt and carried them over to the circle of blackened stones and charred wood where JP had grilled his fish. A book of matches lay beside the stones.

Hook dumped the bag, the wallet, and the T-shirt on the ashes, then opened the cell phone and removed the SIM card, dropping it on the pile. He detached the battery from the phone and flung it into the jungle, pocketing the cell. Then he went to the rear of the hut, where the generator still chugged. He killed the motor and dug out the jerry can of fuel that stood beside the generator.

Hook carried the can out to the beach and poured gasoline over the fire pit. He struck two matches and dropped them onto the pile. The gasoline flared with a soft whump and the flames started eating away at the canvas of the pack.

Hook went back to Carnahan and grabbed his ankles again and dragged him into the jungle, waving away mosquitoes. He went deep enough to lose the beach from sight and left the corpse in a dense thicket. He tossed the cell phone into the undergrowth and went back for the spade that still lay in the mud.

After returning to the jungle, he dug a hole, sweating, plagued by flies, mosquitoes, and gnats. When the hole was deep enough, he rolled Carnahan inside and shoveled sand over him, packing it tight. He found a few stones, a thick branch, and a few dried palm fronds and covered the grave.

Returning to the beach he checked on the fire. The flames were dead and the pack and most of its contents, the wallet, and his T-shirt were ash. The Ray-Bans were the only thing still intact, the glass shattered and the frame buckled and blackened. Hook hurled them into the jungle. He stirred at the remnants with a stick and took the jerry can back to its home near the generator.

Hook kicked off his flops and went back into the bungalow and surveyed the carnage.

Resisting the temptation to torch the place—the blaze and the smoke would be visible from the neighboring island—he plundered the kitchen for cleaning solvents and rags and set about the long and messy task of cleansing the bungalow of Bob Carnahan's blood.

FIFTY-NINE

Lucien Benway had not slept. He'd spent the night sitting behind his desk in his ergonomic chair dressed in yesterday's clothes, still reeking of Turkish tobacco and his unwashed body, stocking feet resting on a carpeted ottoman, drinking more than he should have from a bottle of Cutty Sark as he'd stared into space.

His glass, made of the fine lead crystal he favored, was smudged and still held a finger of scotch the color of urine. The elephant's foot ashtray stationed beside his chair was filled with white cigarette butts, an overflow of them lying on the polished wooden floor.

The heavy curtains were drawn, but gray early morning light bled in around the edges. Benway sighed and ran a hand over the pale stubble that grew like weeds in irregular clumps on his creased face. He stared at the smeared glass then lifted it and swallowed the liquor that burned down to his empty, dyspeptic gut.

Where had the hours gone since Morse had left the previous night?

Benway couldn't account for them—they'd slipped away from him like untethered skiffs floating away on the black river of his musings.

Benway had been an atheist since the age of twelve, when he'd killed the drunken preacher who'd attempted to sodomize him in a double-wide in Beaumont, Texas—he'd bludgeoned the pedophile to death with a heavy skillet and walked away without a backward glance, the authorities never thinking to question the stunted boy. However, that night had found him caught up in a stream of mumbled incantations that were too darkly primitive to be any of the long-forgotten prayers of his childhood, taking the form of a bargain but with what or whom he couldn't say.

A bargain in which he offered his eternal fealty in exchange for the subjugation of the enemies that circled him like wolves.

Benway smacked the glass down onto the desktop and laughed away this barbaric impulse, something inhuman and low, that had squeezed itself through his consciousness like curd cheese through muslin.

He stood, the shrapnel from his old injury knifing into a nerve in his spine, and let the pain clear his head. Crossing to the window, he opened the drapes and stared out at a day as gloomy and monochromatic as a scene from the Ingmar Bergman movies his wife liked to watch on the TV in the living room, curled up with her legs tucked beneath her, eating chocolates and drinking vodka.

The thought of Nadja had him wincing at more than the pain in his back and he marveled at how oftentimes love and hate couldn't be separated by a cigarette paper.

A familiar sharp knock had him turning from the window.

"Yes?" he said, and Morse entered, bringing with him a faint whiff of disinfectant.

Did he bathe in Lysol?

Morse closed the door and stood with his back to it, at parade rest. He said nothing as he stared at a spot above Benway's head. An irritating habit.

"Okay, spit it out. Did you hear from our man in Thailand?"

Morse shook his head. "He's gone dark, sir."

"I'm hoping that's a reference to his tan?"

Morse, a humorless creature, merely shook his head again.

"What were your instructions?" asked Benway. "Just to keep tabs on Hook?"

"I may have incentivized him a little, sir."

"How?"

"I may have mentioned that if he didn't find proof positive that Kate Swift is alive Burmese pirates would take his wife."

Benway stared at Morse. "Jesus Christ, Morse, this is farcical."

"He's a stoner, sir. A slacker. A lazy man given to evasions and eliding."

There was another knock at the door, this time the light drumming of fingertips on the wood.

Benway waved Morse from his path as he crossed to the door and opened it.

Nadja stood outside. She wore a very plain black dress and black pumps. Her legs were bare of nylons, the ankle monitor an obscene limpet clinging to her right talus.

"Lucien, darling, I think you should turn on your TV." She smiled poisonously and walked away.

Benway closed the door and located the remote on his desk, activating the TV set, *Good Morning America* fading up. He heard his own name spoken by David Burke, the bearded hack, who was in conversation with George Stephanopoulos, spewing a confection of fiction and falsehood that could only be the work of Philip Danvers.

SIXTY

When Janey Burke was nervous, she ate. No, she fucking *gorged* herself, stuffing everything from ice cream to candy bars to leftover mac and cheese down her throat. Not that it ever showed on her skinny frame.

Her yoga teacher had once told her that her Ayurvedic constitution was vata. She'd googled it and found that vata women were tiny and flat-chested with turned-up noses; were highly imaginative, spendthrift, anxious, easily sexually aroused but quickly satiated, produced little urine and their shit was dry, hard, and small. Like a hamster's.

All true, but still—*eew.*

Waiting for David to return to the apartment after his morning as a media man-whore (she'd killed the TV and powered down her laptop and iPad, so intense was her consternation at what she'd seen and read), she'd raided the fridge and stuffed herself.

When she heard the scrape of his key in the lock she capped the Ben and Jerry's Boom Chocolatta and shoved it back into the freezer, wiped her mouth and stood with her flat ass to the counter wearing, she hoped, a neutral expression.

"Hey, babe," he said, shedding his jacket and scarf and flinging them onto the couch as he crossed to the coffee maker.

"Dave, what are you doing?"

"I'm getting some coffee."

"No, what are you doing to yourself? To *us*?"

He blinked at her as he pushed down on the plunger. "You're talking about the Fingergate thing?"

"Don't."

"Don't what?"

"Do *not* reduce it to a buzzword."

"Hey, it's more than a *buzzword*, baby. It's a hashtag. It's a goddamn *meme*."

"Fuck off, Dave. A woman is dead. A child, too. Not to mention all the other people on that plane. And you're soundbiting it like some Fox hack?"

"Christ, Janey, I'm the one who's out there shouting about this."

"Slow the fuck down, Mr. Sockpuppet." She saw she had stung him and lifted her hand. "Dave, I'm sorry. You've been brave and you've done good, but I'm scared for you, don't you get it?"

"What? So I should just shut up?"

"No. But realize how vulnerable you are. You're the mouthpiece of Philip Danvers and how sure can you be of his agenda?"

"Jesus, I resent that, Janey. I'm not just a mouthpiece. I've researched this. I've dug deep into this fucking cesspit."

"And now you're as good as accusing Lucien Benway of downing that plane?"

"With good reason. Look at the evidence."

"Evidence? Where did you get this evidence, Dave?" He stared at her without replying. "It was handed to you by Danvers, wasn't it?"

"It checks out."

"You think you're Woodward and Bernstein all rolled into one, don't you? You want to be forever legendary as the guy who brought down an administration?"

"Only if that administration deserves to be brought down."

"You're winging it, Dave. Flying solo. You don't have the *Post* or the *Times* or some monster network with their lawyers and their ombudsmen and their fucking muscle behind you."

Glugging coffee from the mug he burned his tongue and cursed.

"Let's go away, Dave."

He furrowed his brow. "Go away where?"

"Anywhere. Let's just get out of DC. Away from all this craziness."

"Janey, Jesus, this is a career-defining moment for me. This is where it all comes together."

"I'm scared, Dave." She sat down at the table and felt tears on her face.

He crossed to her and touched her with one of his big, warm, clumsy hands. "Hey, baby."

She shrugged him off. "Do you believe Benway did it?"

"Took down that plane?"

"Yes."

He scratched his beard. "Yeah. I believe it."

"So, if he did that half a world a way, just think what he'll do to you, right here in his own fucking backyard."

David shook his stupid head. "I'm visible, now, Janey. I'm known."

"You can't see past your megaego, can you?"

"I'm not being egocentric, I'm being practical. The more visible you are, the safer you are. Fame is like a fucking superpower, baby. It keeps you safe."

Janey stood and walked back to the refrigerator. She removed the Ben and Jerry's from the freezer while her husband carried on talking, filling the apartment with his addle-headed rationales, but she didn't listen to him, just dug deep into the tub and ate ice cream until she was ready to puke.

SIXTY-ONE

When Harry Hook emerged from the pathway through the jungle, Kate, prowling the beach, saw that something was different. It wasn't only the new outfit he sported (red and blue check shorts made from a nasty synthetic fabric, a canary-yellow T-shirt, and a Nike cap pulled low over his face—the cheap clothes typical of the tourist stalls on the main beach), but there was a change in his walk; the determined jauntiness that had made him, at a distance, appear almost youthful was gone, replaced by a tread both slower and heavier.

Kate crossed the sand, meeting him near the hut. Suzie and JP were far down the beach, foraging for shells, and hadn't seen him arriving.

"What happened?" Kate asked.

He sat down in the shade of a palm and told her everything in the kind of forensic detail that only a man with his training could have mustered. But it was more than a hyperdetailed debriefing, it brought with it shadows of the confessional, and she had to remind herself how different he was from her.

When he was done she asked, "Are you okay?"

"Yes."

"You're sure?"

He shrugged one shoulder. "I've never killed anyone before." He smiled sourly. "Back in the day there were always others to do the dirty work."

"I'm sorry," she said. "He was your friend."

Hook shook his head. "He was Lucien's lackey."

"You never suspected?"

He rubbed his swollen lip. "Nope. Naive of me, I suppose, to think Lucien would let me drop off the grid."

"Yes." She looked at him, and saw her twin self reflected in his sunglasses. "There are going to be repercussions, Harry. You said this Bob guy had a wife."

"Yeah, but he told her he was in Phuket."

"He called you from the beach and he spoke to his wife from the Zodiac. The cell phone tower on this island will tell the real story."

"Any kind of investigation is days away. We have time."

She looked down the beach at Suzie and JP. The girl waved and as Kate waved back she came to a decision. "I'm taking Suzie and going, Harry."

"Going where?"

Kate shook her head. "Anywhere. Just far away from Thailand. I feel like we're fish in a barrel."

He stood and moved close to her. She could smell soap on his skin. "What about you wanting to go back to America?" he asked.

"I think it's time to retire that pipe dream."

"So you're going to raise Suzie on the run? Always looking over your shoulder?"

"Your plan worked, Harry. Well, the first part, anyway. As far as the administration is concerned, we're dead."

"For now."

She stared at him, moving a tendril of hair from her face.

"Lucien isn't going to give up," Hook said.

"Lucien's resources are limited. I'll outrun him."

"That may be true today, but there'll be a new administration in office next year. And Lucien could well be back in favor. And the new guys will be keen to discredit their predecessors."

"You think they'll question our deaths?"

"Yes, I do. There's more than enough doubt for that." He glanced across to Suzie and JP who were walking their way. "We need to finish this now."

"How?"

"By finishing Lucien."

"He'll never come here. He'll send Morse."

"Yes. But if we capture Morse we can finish Benway."

Hook watched the approaching man and child. Suzie called his name and started to run toward him.

"So let's return to the mainland and bait the hook," he said.

"And I'm the bait?"

"Yes," Hook said as he waved to the little girl, "you're the bait."

SIXTY-TWO

Nadja sat on the edge of her bed, her knees together, her spine as straight as if she were in deportment class, listening for something.

Quite what she didn't yet know.

It wasn't the avid growl of the media who were camped out on their sidewalk, growing in number throughout the day as Lucien's supposed role in taking down that plane in Thailand had gone viral. Reporters had pounded on the front door like debt collectors, demanding a statement from Lucien—who'd stayed barricaded in his office—until a patrol car arrived and a couple of cops shoved the mob back onto the sidewalk and threatened them with arrest if they approached the door again. So Lucien, even in his reduced state, still had a little clout with the police.

Nadja heard Mr. Morose leave Lucien's office, closing the door behind him. For a big man, his movements were ominously soundless and the only clue that he was on his way down to the hallway was the creaking of the stairs. When the gabble of the news hacks rose in volume she knew that he had exited the house.

A few minutes later she heard the distinctive whisper of Lucien's office door opening, the fit so secure it was almost like an airlock. She waited for the soft click as it closed and the deadbolt engaged, but it never came and instead she heard the scuff of Lucien's shoes on the carpet as he walked from his office to his bedroom and closed the door. A minute later she caught the soft hiss of the shower in his en suite bathroom.

And then it struck her: what she had been listening for had not been a sound, but rather the absence of one.

Nadja, barefoot, crossed her bedroom and peered out into the corridor. Astonishingly, the door to Lucien's office stood slightly ajar, which spoke volumes about his alcohol consumption and state of mind.

She quelled a sudden, paralyzing jolt of fear and walked silently toward the room that she was forbidden to enter.

Lucien had said that to her in as many words two years ago when he'd had to move his operation here, into what had been a never-used guest room.

Once the bedroom furniture had been replaced with a desk, a file cabinet, and a wall-mounted TV he'd stood in the doorway one evening, waiting for her as she was on her way to bed and said, "Nadja?"

"Yes?" she'd said, her fingers on the antique brass handle of her bedroom door.

"Think of this room as my lair."

"How very *feral*, Lucien. What do you do in there? Strip naked and bay at the moon?"

He'd smiled one of his smiles that never touched his cold little eyes and said, "I'd appreciate you never coming in here."

"Oh, I wouldn't dream of it, Lucien," she'd said and disappeared into her bedroom.

And she never had. The closest she'd come had been that morning, when she'd tapped on the door.

Fear consumed her as she approached the office. Fear that very nearly had her turning on her heels and fleeing back to the sanctuary of her bedroom.

But she breathed through the terror and pushed open the door. The heavy curtains were drawn against the media horde and the only light came from the Anglepoise on the desktop.

The air was heavy with the stink of Lucien's cigarettes. She saw the overflowing ashtray, the empty bottle of Cutty Sark on the desk and the dirty glass.

These very visible signs of Lucien's unraveling cheered her.

She went behind the desk and looked at his computer. It was off and she knew that he would have it password protected.

The drawers of the desk were locked.

There was nothing for her to find, nothing that would bolster her intuition about what had really happened in the Levant.

Disappointed, she was about to leave the room when her eyes were drawn to the wire wastebasket that stood beneath the desk, almost invisible behind the black leather chair.

She shifted the chair, its casters making a little ticking sound, and kneeled down by the wastebasket.

It held a few empty Samsun packs and today's *Washington Post*, the headline yelling about Lucien and the Fingergate business. But there was something under the newspaper, something crumpled. Moving the *Post* aside she saw it was an airplane boarding pass stub.

The light was too poor to read it, so she lifted the stub and palmed it, ready to rise from beneath the desk.

Nadja froze when she heard the click of Lucien's bedroom door opening. He'd been uncharacteristically rapid in his shower.

She listened to the whisper of his shoes on the carpeted corridor and then the drumming as he stepped into the office and walked across the wooden floor, the sickly sweet smell of his aftershave setting her nostrils twitching.

Feeling at once terrified and absurd, she shrank beneath the desk.

In the gap between the desk and the floor she could see Lucien's tiny chukka boots. A succession of clicks and a fume of tobacco reached her as he lit a cigarette. He coughed and she saw his feet moving her way.

A glass chimed and she knew he had lifted the empty scotch bottle and the tumbler. His footsteps receded and the light was extinguished. The door closed and the lock caught.

She waited a few moments and hurried to the door, a new terror tightening her chest.

What if she couldn't open the door from the interior?

Fumbling in the dark, she found the cool plastic of a recessed button on the wall. She pressed it and with a little cluck, like a tongue against a palate, the lock released and she opened the door and stepped into the corridor, shutting it behind her.

Heart pounding she flew into her bedroom and locked herself inside. She sat on the bed and unfolded the boarding pass stub.

And there it was.

Below the red Emirates logo was proof that Lucien had flown from Amman to Dubai on the day Michael was killed.

She opened her desk drawer, removed a copy of Kundera's *Life Is Elsewhere* and slipped the stub inside. She walked to the window, staring out blindly at the vultures below. They spotted her and pointed cameras and microphones and yelled questions, calling her "Nadja" in their overfamiliar manner.

She pulled the drapes closed and stood a moment with her forehead against the cool plaster of the wall, hugging herself, wild thoughts of revenge setting her pulse racing.

SIXTY-THREE

As the long-tail skirted the last of the limestone cliffs and hit open water, Hook was thrust against the side of the boat, and Bob Carnahan's pistol, which was shoved into the waistband of his shorts, jammed into his ribs. He'd offered the weapon to Kate but she'd refused, insisting that he keep it.

Keep it to protect her daughter.

Waves buffeted the boat, drenching the passengers, and Hook put an arm around Suzie, the girl made bulky by the orange life jacket he'd insisted she wear. The jackets, shoved under the seats of the boat, were soiled and poorly maintained, and the other passengers (five Korean tourists) had ignored them. But Hook had searched for the smallest and cleanest and tied her into it, shaking his head at her protests.

She'd moaned and tugged at the belts, but once the boat was underway, she'd been distracted by the noise and the spray, the life jacket forgotten.

It had been Hook's idea, back on the island, that they split up on the trip to the mainland. That Kate and JP take a boat together and once they'd gone, he and Suzie would follow. It would make them less conspicuous. Kate and JP would be just another couple of suntanned lovers and Hook and Suzie a grandfather and granddaughter off on a jaunt.

Kate hadn't liked the idea, but she'd finally agreed.

She'd walked Suzie down the beach and spoken to her for a while. The girl had looked back at Hook and then said something to her mother, nodded, and smiled, and why this should have filled him with some sort of pride he couldn't fathom. But it had.

The ocean flattened out and Hook removed his arm from around Suzie's shoulders, but the child stayed close to him.

"Can I tell you something?" she said.

"Sure."

"I have a grandmother and a grandfather back in America. My daddy's mommy and daddy."

"Okay."

"I called her Grammy and I called him Papa."

"That's nice," he said.

"I haven't seen them for a long time."

"I'm sorry."

"I miss them."

"You would."

"Do you think they miss me?"

"I know they do."

"I don't think I'll ever see them again."

He put a hand on her knee. "What your mom did was a very brave thing. Do you know that?"

She stared up at him. "When she fought the people who killed my daddy?"

"Yes. It wasn't easy. And it has made your life tough, I know. But she did it because she had to do it. Because it was the right thing to do. Do you understand?"

"Yes, I understand."

"Okay then."

They sailed a while in silence, the rocking of the boat, the endless flat ocean and the treacly sunshine lulling Hook into a kind of stupor. He thought the kid had fallen asleep when she said, "Harry?"

"Yes?"

"My mommy told me."

"Told you what?"

"Told me who you are."

He couldn't think of what to say, so he said nothing.

"So, can I call you Grandpa?" she asked.

Hook, overcome by some emotion he battled to name, couldn't find his voice, the roar of the long-tail's engine filling the yawning silence.

Then he cleared the block in his throat and said, "Yes. I'd like that."

Suzie wrapped her little pipe-cleaner arm around him, laid her head on his chest, and fell asleep, and for a moment he forgot about the dead man's gun in his waistband, forgot about what he'd done the night before, even forgot about what awaited them on the shore and allowed himself to be happy.

SIXTY-FOUR

For the first time in over forty years Philip Danvers was actually spying, was out there in the field, covertly tailing a man.

He'd spent so long behind a desk—the last decades of his career feverishly devoted to politicking, to keeping afloat the great lie that he and he alone, given endless resources and almost limitless power, could set the skewed world back on its axis—that he'd forgotten the primal charge that came with stalking another human being.

Of course following David Burke was a cakewalk, even for a septuagenarian who was busy dying of prostate cancer that was metastasizing at the speed of a bullet train. Very different than Danvers' last operation in the field, in still-bisected Berlin. There he'd tailed a KGB agent codenamed Nijinsky because he'd been so light on his feet, a man so skittish that he'd jumped at shadows and fled at the whiff of a tail, disappearing into a warren of alleys in Kreuzberg or evaporating into Kaiser's supermarket on Ku'damm, even the most expert of followers left looking silly.

At last it had fallen to him to do the legwork. Danvers, the case officer, the desk man, the urbane figure propping up the bar at the Hotel Zoo with the Brits, matching them pink gin for pink gin and bettering them, frequently, in banter and sarcasm, winning their admiration if not their trust; or wallowing in smoky *bierstube* with Bundesnachrichtendienst agents, conversing with them in Berlinisch German with such easy fluency that many refused to believe he wasn't a son of the soil.

He'd shadowed Nijinsky unseen and had finally captured him on film meeting with the senior British diplomat who (so it emerged) he had turned years before.

Ah, how the pink gins had flowed at the Zoo's cocktail bar …

But that, as they say, was then and this was now.

Now being Nineteenth Street Northwest, Washington, DC. Danvers sat in his parked Volvo and watched as David Burke, sumo-sized in his bulky jacket, left a taxi, sidestepped a brace of bicycles chained to low poles and found a path between the snow-filled flowerbeds that lined the sidewalk outside the Palm restaurant.

The man moved with a new sense of purpose and confidence. He was riding high on the latest Fingergate revelations: it was now taken as gospel that Lucien Benway had swatted that plane from the Asian sky on the orders of the POTUS himself.

Danvers' little homage to Harry Hook had been more successful than he had dared hope or imagine, and the outsized man disappearing into the eatery had sung the libretto to perfection.

Knowing Burke's whereabouts was not an act of clairvoyance— Danvers had called him an hour ago, from his burner phone.

"What are your movements today?" he'd asked.

"The editor of the *Post* is taking me to lunch at the Palm," Burke had said, unable to hide his smugness. "Why do you ask?"

"I may have something more for you."

"What?"

"Just keep your phone on and we'll talk."

Danvers had killed the call, stood up from behind his desk, gripping the wooden top so hard his knuckles had turned white as he'd waited for the pain in his nether regions to pass. He'd wiped his brow with a handkerchief, gathered his old leather satchel from the sofa, and made his way down to his Volvo, driving slowly into the city.

As he'd driven, his mind had traveled back two decades, to that restaurant in Beirut when Harry Hook had regaled the young acolytes with tales of deception and birdsong.

The Bryn Mawr blond, the one Hook had ignored so studiously that he could not have made his attraction plainer to Danvers, had won her place in his bed by leaning forward, her pert young breasts (fetchingly displayed in a tight knit top) brushing the white linen tablecloth, and saying, "Harry?" in a Marilynesque whisper.

None of the other neophytes had dared address Hook—least of all by his given name—but here she was, leaning in and smiling and saying, again, "Harry?"

Hook had paused his monologue, blinked, moved a stray lock of dark hair that dangled over his left eye, sipped at his arrak, and said, "Yes?"

"Surely the time must come when the little dickey bird," the pink tip of her tongue had peeped through her lips as she'd said this, and Danvers could almost feel the sexual smolder rising from Hook like heat from blacktop, "has sung all he needs to sing? When, if he sang any more, he may, well, *ruin* things?"

Hook, his slightly bloodshot eyes for her and her alone, had smiled and said, "Oh, you're a clever little thing, aren't you?" He'd waited until two colored spots the size of poker chips had appeared on the coquette's cheekbones before he'd continued. "Yes. Just as important as finding the nightingale and letting it sing is choosing the moment when it must come down from the rooftop and be still."

"But, Harry," she'd said, "what if it has fallen in love with the sound of its own voice? What then?"

Hook, smiling so broadly his eyes were almost lost in the laugh lines that radiated out from their corners (lines that women had found so irresistible) had shaken his head and said, "Now, now, that's more than enough shoptalk."

And he'd stood and taken the blond's hand and led her out into the hot Beirut night, leaving behind him a vacuum that even Danvers, no slouch as an orator, had struggled to fill.

The aged Danvers sat outside the DC restaurant and listened to the radio, hearing report after report that damned Lucien Benway as the tool of a murderous administration.

He was so lost in this drama of his creation that he almost missed Burke, who shook the hand of a sleek, gray-haired man—a frequent, somewhat self-satisfied media presence—who stepped into a waiting taxi. Burke was about to hail his own cab when Danvers hit speed dial on his disposable phone and stopped the bearded man's arm as he raised it and caused his hand to dip into the folds of his fleecy jacket.

He watched Burke lift out his phone. "Yes?"

"Turn up Jefferson Place."

"Why?"

"Just do as I say."

Obedient as a St. Bernard, the big man turned left and strolled past a brutalist office building that loomed over a series of row houses. Danvers, wearing his coat and hat, was behind him and hit redial again. The reporter lifted his phone to his ear.

"Go into the alleyway," Danvers said.

Danvers rang off and the big man stopped, looked around, then walked down the alley that opened up after the houses, deserted but for a box truck that blocked it midway: a Sysco vehicle making a delivery to the service entrance of one of the many restaurants. The cab of the truck was empty.

When Burke reached the truck, he turned and saw Danvers advancing toward him. "Hey, why're we rendezvousing here?"

By way of reply, Danvers produced a .38 pistol with a silencer from the folds of his Burberry and fired twice into Burke's chest. Burke folded to his knees as if to pray and Danvers placed the silencer against the big man's skull and finished him off.

He stepped over the corpse, squeezed past the truck, and continued along the alleyway to N Street, turned left, and walked slowly back toward his car.

He was invisible. Nobody saw an old man.

SIXTY-FIVE

Janey Burke had never been in a peep-show booth, but she felt a powerfully voyeuristic sensation as she stood at the glass window and watched the morgue attendant hover over the sheet-covered corpse on the gurney.

The uniformed woman at her side asked her if she was ready and when Janey said she was—in a voice that was admirably level—the cop nodded and the attendant lifted the sheet with a flourish worthy of a magician's assistant.

Seeing her husband's dead face—even though she'd been preparing herself for this since the woman cop and her male partner had appeared at her door a half hour before and told her that David had been shot dead in a Northwest alleyway—prompted a rush of emotion so intense that her knees buckled and she had to send out a hand to the wall to steady herself.

The cop took her arm. "Are you okay, Mrs. Burke?"

"Yes," Janey said, filling her lungs with air thick with formalin and something more sinister that she didn't care to name.

But she wasn't *okay*.

Never, ever again would she be fucking *okay*.

When the cops had broken the news to her in her hallway Janey had wanted to swing around and shout at David (the David, who in her imagination was in the kitchen making coffee and eating leftovers straight out of the fridge in the way that made her crazy) and say, "You see, asshole? I fucking *told* you so!"

But she'd just nodded and said, "Where is he?"

"At the morgue. We need you to identify him. If you want to call somebody to be with you?"

She'd shaken her head. "Take me to him."

Janey had pulled on a coat and a hat and when the cops led her down to the patrol car, apologizing that she had to sit in the back, she must have looked like some juvenile offender to the couple of rubberneckers who stood watching.

On the drive over, talking to the police officers through the dividing mesh, the male cop, who had atypically (at least to Janey's mind) surrendered the wheel to his colleague, told her that a truck driver had found David's body. Nobody had seen who had shot him, although the cop assured her that because David had been such a well-known media figure—his words—he was certain that more information would surface.

The woman cop, looking at Janey in the rearview, had said, "We have to ask you this, Mrs. Burke, but do you know who might have done this? Did your husband have any enemies?"

When Janey had replied, "Why don't you knock on the door of 1600 Pennsylvania Avenue and ask them?" the cops had exchanged a look and then shut up for the rest of the ride to the morgue.

Janey turned away from the viewing window and walked down the corridor, the cop in her chunky uniform, all aclatter with walkie-talkie, handcuffs, nightstick, gun, and a can of mace, dogging her heels.

At a desk near the door of the morgue, Janey was asked to sign for a plastic bag containing David's personal effects. The bag was discreetly opaque and she had no impulse to peer inside. Just as she'd had no desire to see the rest of David's body beneath the sheet.

She would remember him as big and furry and warm and horny. There was no room in her consciousness for the cold husk back in the freezer room.

She signed for her dead husband's things and left the morgue, the police-woman taking her arm when a bank of flashbulbs detonated in her face, the other cop clearing a path through the media who shouted questions at her.

Janey was shamed by the memory of, back when she was still a reporter, doorstopping the family of a just-dead ten-year-old boy (the victim of gang violence in Washington Highlands) and lobbing questions at them, not even noticing their stunned, folded-in faces, so convinced was she of the importance of her journalistic calling.

The cops got her in the back of the car and the woman whooped the siren to clear the media vultures, and as the car nosed out into the street, Janey listened to the light tap of rain on the roof, drops like tears trickling down the windshield, mocking her dry ducts.

There would be no tears for David.

Not until Lucien Benway had paid for this.

SIXTY-SIX

"Is this your handiwork?" Benway asked, standing by his desk with his arms folded, the lamplight glancing off his silk shirt as he stared up at Morse.

"No, sir, it is not."

"You did not follow David Burke down that alleyway and put a bullet in his skull?"

"No, sir."

Benway swung away from Morse, grabbing for the TV remote to silence the whorish CNN anchorette with the Tartar cheekbones who insisted on pronouncing his name "Lootcheen Banway" while she as good as tried and convicted him of the "assassination" of David Burke.

In the act of twisting, a searing white-hot pain shot up Benway's back and neck and into his right temple, where it seemed to explode. For a few seconds, he saw flashes of light and bile rose in his throat.

Gasping, feeling cold sweat on his grooved forehead, he sank into his chair and waited for the agony to pass.

Morse said nothing, staring down at him as if he were a lab rat.

When he could speak again, Benway, through clenched teeth, said, "Then the question is, who did?"

"I can't offer an opinion, sir."

"Because all they've done is martyr that addled-headed hack and left me directly in the line of fire."

"We need to prove that Kate Swift is alive," Morse said.

"Yes, we do. By Jesus, we do. Any ideas?"

"Yes, sir."

"Yes?"

"I reached out to a Mossad connection in Jerusalem and he shared with me something that I feel is significant, sir. A member of the Israeli disaster team recovering bodies from the wreckage of AirStar Flight 2605 was also in Thailand during the 2004 tsunami." Morse paused. "Harry Hook was still operational at that time. They were both on the island of Phuket." Pronouncing it *Foo*-ket.

"That's *Poo*-ket, Morse. Like doggy doo-doo."

"Noted, sir."

The pain in Benway's back was momentarily forgotten as he stared up at Morse. "That *is* significant."

"I'm pleased you share my excitement, sir," the tall man said, deadpan.

"Where is this Israeli now?"

"Still in Thailand. The recovery of the remains of the gymnasts is expected to take a few more days."

"You enjoyed your visits to Thailand, Morse?"

"Yes, sir. Except for the climate, the people, and the food."

Despite himself, Benway laughed and immediately regretted it when a spur of bone plucked at his thoracic nerve like a lute and the pain flared.

"Well, pack your Speedo and some weapons-grade sunblock and hop on over to the Land of Smiles and have a word with this Haredi."

Benway closed his eyes and waved a tiny hand at the pallid man who evaporated like a twist of smoke.

SIXTY-SEVEN

Kate licked a smear of massaman green curry off her finger as she plated the cornucopia of street food that Hook had brought with him when he'd delivered Suzie to JP's house. She realized that she was presiding over a bizarre family dinner: grandfather, daughter, granddaughter, and the daughter's love interest, all seated at the kitchen table of the Frenchman's charmingly scruffy bungalow.

This was the closest she'd come to a family gathering since Yusuf had died, and a sudden sadness washed away the lingering balm of sun and sea and sex that had allowed her to consciously forget what was still coming her way.

JP, as if reading her mind, touched her hand and said, "You're okay?"

"Yes," she said, but she ate in silence.

The others made up for her lack of conversation. Hook told wild stories about Thailand—cannily tailored to a six-year-old audience of one—and JP played along, feeding him lines and allowing himself to be the butt of jokes.

Kate tuned out the conversation, feeling the way she used to before a mission. Focusing her thoughts, toughening herself.

Suzie giggled at some jest of Hook's and said, "That is so lame, Grandpa."

Kate saw the look of delight on her daughter's face and her heart broke a little more. This won't last, she told herself. It never does.

When the food was done, JP asked Suzie if she wanted to watch a cartoon DVD. She nodded and he took her through to the cramped living room where a sofa, a cane chair, and a TV stood among a mess of diving gear.

The soundtrack of the movie was loud enough to drown out conversation in the kitchen. Kate leaned closer to Hook and said, "How do you think it's going to go?"

"You heard about that reporter getting hit?"

"Yes. Benway?"

Hook shook his head. "I can't see it. It's too obvious."

"Who then?"

"I don't know. But it's upped the heat on Lucien and his only way out is to prove you didn't die on that plane."

"Enter Dudley Morse?"

"Yes."

"And you reckon we can take him?"

"I can create the scenario. You can take him." He looked at her. "That's what you do, isn't it?"

"Did."

"Okay, did."

"Yeah, there were none of the Cold War niceties that you cut your teeth on."

"I know that. I was there, remember, after 9/11?"

"Yes, but you faded from the picture when things got really interesting. These days it's all about either getting the bad guys positioned for interrogation or taking them down."

"It never bothered you?"

"The killing?"

"Yes."

"No."

"Some Manhattan kid just woke up one day and found out she could do that?"

"Not quite. You're to blame."

"Me?"

"Yes. I was fourteen when the Towers fell and my mother died. A friend of hers took me in and I spent the next few years in a sort of daze. I was okay at school but not brilliant. I was pretty but not beautiful. I had no idea what to do with my life and I started making the wrong choices that kids make. Got into some trouble. Then I decided to look for you."

"Why?"

"Some romantic daddy thing. That I'd find you and you'd change my life."

"Sorry."

"Don't be." She drank beer from the bottle. "You weren't easy to find."

"No."

"Google didn't hack it."

"I'll bet not. What did you do?"

"I was a teenager. Every teenager knows a kid who knows computer shit. Mine knew how to penetrate firewalls and bypass security systems. He found you. It cost me a six pack of beer and a blow job."

"Cheap at the price."

"I thought so. When he saw who you were, who you worked for, he backed off, but he'd gotten me far enough in to let me fumble on. Of course I was detected and Philip sent some people. Anyway, as I told you before, he decided to take me under his wing and suddenly my life had a purpose. I started out looking for a father and I found a calling. I found out what I was good at." She laughed. "Imagine my surprise."

"Be all you can be."

"Hell, yes."

"You're not angry with him?"

"Philip?"

"Yes."

"Why would I be?"

"You were just a kid. He bloody indoctrinated you."

"Oh, he did, as only that fucking old Svengali could." She shrugged.

"But I would've used that skill set in another way. Probably would've ended up in prison by the time I was twenty. Or worse."

"You never questioned what you had to do?"

"No. I loved the certainty of it all. The us and them thing. We were right. We were good. They were wrong and they were bad. Simple. No ambiguities."

"I was all about the ambiguities. That's where I thrived, out in the place where certainties crumbled, where people could be turned and bought and corrupted."

"We were different weapons, you and me. With different purposes."

"Yes, we were."

"Why did *you* do it Harry?"

"Same as you: because I was good at it."

"But you were never a believer?"

"In flag and country?"

"Yes."

"No. Not like you were."

"Yes, I drank that fucking Kool-Aid. If, a decade ago, you'd asked me what I loved the most in the world I would've said, without hesitation and not a whiff of irony, 'I love my country. I love the United States of America.' So if I had to use my body, I used it. If I had to kill, I killed."

"And now?"

"What do I love now?"

"Yes."

"My daughter."

"That's it?"

"Yeah, that's it." She smudged a finger in a puddle of beer. "I've been through too much. I still want to live in America and I still want my kid to grow up there, but I see it for what it is. And I'll make sure Suzie sees that, too, when she's old enough."

"Do you have any regrets?"

"Well, Jesus, my husband's dead."

"I'm not talking about what was done to you, as grievous as it was." He looked at her. "I'm talking about what you did."

"You really want to open that door?"

He shrugged. "I'm thinking you haven't had a chance to talk about this stuff."

"No. For the last two years all I've spoken about is kids and the PTA and double glazing and television. And you know what?"

"What?"

"It was okay. It was numbing. But I had the dreams."

"Yes. That happens. The septic tank has to be emptied."

"Nicely put."

"Thank you."

"And you? You had the booze?"

"Yes. And the sex."

"Okay."

"I'm done with that."

"Hell, I'm not judging."

"I didn't think you were. I live quietly. I try to stay sober. I try to still my mind. I reread books I've already read and I paint badly."

"And then we came along."

"Yes, and then you came along."

She drank and looked at him. "So, lay it on me."

"What?"

"Your master plan."

"It's a work in progress."

"Don't try and snow me with that Zen shit, Harry."

"I'm not. It's organic. That's how I work. Which, for you, must be a nightmare."

"Yeah. You don't take a haiku to a gunfight."

"I think you mean a koan."

He laughed and for a moment she saw how devastatingly charming he must've been, back when that had been his thing. Then he was serious again.

"I want you to hide in plain sight."

"Jesus, now here he comes with the aphorisms."

"I want it to *appear* that you're in hiding, but you'll be visible enough for Morse to find you."

"And then I take him down?"

"No. The other option."

"Get him positioned for interrogation?"

"Yes. Can you do that?" He stared at her over his Coke can.

"Relax. I'm not squeamish."

"Good, because Morse isn't going to be easy to crack."

"What do we want from him?"

"To know what he knows."

"About Lucien?"

"Yes, about what Lucien has on the great and the good. That's the path to you being resurrected and invited back to the table."

They sat without speaking for a minute, listening to the cartoon babble from the other room, then Hook stood. "You okay with me taking the kid to town for ice cream?"

"You sure you want to do that?"

"Yes. And maybe you need to start saying au revoir to JP?"

"Yeah, maybe."

Hook disappeared into the living room and got Suzie. Kate heard the clatter of the dirt bike and she went through to where the Frenchman sat on the couch drinking beer, staring at her.

"Everything's fine?" he asked.

"Yes," she said.

"If you want my help, I am here."

She hesitated before she spoke. "You said you have connections?"

"Yeah."

"Can you get weapons?"

"Guns?"

"Yes."

"What do you need?"

"Do you know guns?"

"A little."

"I need a Glock 19 and something smaller. Like a .32 snub-nose."

"Anything else?"

"A sawed-off shotgun."

"Double or single barrel?"

"Double."

"Are you starting a war?"

She said nothing and stared at the static on the TV screen.

JP set down his beer, took his cell phone and went into the kitchen and she heard him speaking in makeshift Thai.

He came back into the room. "I will hear in the morning." He sat beside her. "What is going to 'appen, Kate?"

"Let's not talk, okay?" she said and straddled him, kissing him.

He kissed her back and then he lifted her and carried her into his bedroom.

SIXTY-EIGHT

"Motherfuckin groundhog day," Congressman Antoine Mosley said to himself as his MKZ hybrid came to a halt on Capitol Hill and yet another white man with an agenda lowered himself into the seat beside him.

As the driver accelerated, the Plumber said, "Thanks for meeting with me, Congressman."

"Let's make this speedy, okay? I got me a lunch engagement."

"Then I'll get straight to it: How would you like to be appointed chairman of the House Permanent Select Committee on Intelligence?"

Mosley stared at the Plumber. "You fuckin with me?"

"I am not. We can make it happen."

"Yeah?"

"Yes."

"And how much of his soul does this nigger have to sell?"

"All we need is for you to spearhead an investigation into Lucien Benway."

Mosley sucked his teeth. "Last time I heard Benway was an independent contractor with no ties to the intelligence community. Therefore he does not fall within our remit."

"Come on, Congressman, surely there's enough motivation now with all these allegations around AirStar Flight 2605? With the assassination of David Burke?"

"Assassination?"

"What would you call it?"

Mosley shrugged.

"The administration has to act," the Plumber said. "The Thais are furious and the Israelis are threatening to recall their ambassador."

"Understandably."

"And the governments of Australia, Great Britain, and China are righteously aggrieved that all signs point to their nationals having been murdered by a senior intelligence officer who was until recently in the employ of this country."

"Do you believe that Kate Swift died on that plane?"

"I believe that if it quacks it's a duck."

"It was expedient, wasn't it, for the White House to say that she did?"

"It brought some closure, yes."

"So you want me to steer an investigation into Benway? You want me to find that he has no connection to this administration and that his actions regarding AirStar Flight 2605—if any—were his and his alone?"

"That would be the ideal outcome."

"Are you sayin he took that plane down?"

"For the purposes of this conversation, yes."

"Do *you* believe he did?"

"That's not germane," the Plumber said.

"Germane? *Germane?*"

"It means not relevant to this conversation."

"I know what the fuck it *means*. I need to know what you *believe*. You and your handlers, before I agree to participate in some bright and shiny motherfuckin lie."

The Plumber shrugged again. "I don't know, Congressman. Nobody does. What we do know is that Lucien Benway needs to be stopped."

"Then why don't you stop him?"

"The way he stopped that journalist yesterday?"

"Is it *germane* to ask if you believe he killed that poor fool?"

"I think he did, yes. But proving it is another matter."

"My question stands. Why don't you stop him?"

"We have to be seen to be going after Benway legitimately."

"Even though the outcome is predetermined?"

The Plumber shrugged. "Let's call it house advantage."

"Hmmm, mnnn. I dunno. There's a shitload of heat here."

"Standing up to Benway will bring you a lot of visibility."

"I'm already visible."

"In the Thirteenth Congressional District, maybe. What I'm offering you is the national stage."

"And what makes you so goddamn sure this nigger is just going to leap up onto that stage and dance like Bojangles? Tippy-tappin his feet and smilin his watermelon smile?"

"I know you're ambitious."

Mosley stayed uncharacteristically silent.

"I need an answer, Congressman."

"What if the propeller heads investigating that plane crash come back with pilot error, or turbulence or metal fatigue?"

"That's not going to happen."

"No?"

"No."

"You guys got your thumb on the scale?"

"It's what we do."

"Yeah, that's why there's an oversight committee."

"Exactly. So?"

"I'll admit your offer is appealin."

"I'm pleased."

"Chairman? For real you'll make that happen, if I do this?"

"Yes, we will."

"Damn," Mosley said with a sigh, "then I guess old Bojangles is lacin up his tap shoes."

SIXTY-NINE

It took Janey Burke just two phone calls to track down Lucien Benway's Q Street address.

When the first person she'd spoken to, her once-upon-a-time journalistic mentor (a hard-bitten second-wave feminist who'd been in the trenches with Steinem) had tried to interview her about David's murder—*cunt!*—she'd hung up and called her most recent editor, a Waspy ex-jock with a crush on her, who'd made awkward attempts at sympathy before giving her the address and a warning: "Now, don't you go and do anything impetuous, Janey."

She'd thanked him, wrapped herself up against the cold, and caught a taxi over to Georgetown, not trusting herself to drive their rusted old Toyota since she was lately given to sudden, violent fits of shaking.

Still no tears, just these savage expressions of convulsive grief that shook her tiny frame, causing her to flail her skinny limbs and shake her head, making her look as if she were in the mosh pit of her very own death metal club.

The first such attack had hit her after she'd drifted out of an Ambien-assisted slumber around dawn and, still more asleep than awake, had reached for David's big, warm, furry body and had found only pillows and the rumpled comforter.

When her fogged memory had, at last, reminded her that David was gone, gone, *gone* forever—no warm and fuzzy notions of the afterlife for godless Janey—her body had started flinging itself around the bed like she was auditioning for a part in the latest installment of the *Exorcist* franchise, the first of which—her wildly raging mind had spewed up at her—had been set (but of course) in Georgetown.

When she'd finally quietened her body, she'd padded across to the window, cracked the curtains and peered down, relieved to see that none of her erstwhile colleagues were lurking outside. There'd been a contingent when she'd returned from the morgue the night before, some familiar voices trying to lure her to them by sprinkling their barked questions with nuggets of griefspeak, but she'd dashed inside, locked her door, and ripped the battery from the buzzer before unplugging the landline, muting her cell, and shutting herself down with a trio of oblong white pills.

She was sitting in the cab as it passed Georgetown University, watching with blank eyes as the snow fluttered around the Neo-Medieval spires of Healy Hall, when David spoke to her: "Who the fuck do you think you are, Janey? Nancy Drew?"

She answered out loud, "No, Veronica Mars, fuckhead. And I'm only doing this because you Woodward-Bernsteined your lard ass onto a morgue slab, buster."

When the driver, an Arab by his looks, regarded her suspiciously in the rearview, she bit on her woolen glove to shut herself up for the rest of the ride.

Any questions Janey might have had about where the media contingent had gone were answered when she arrived at Lucien Benway's house: a swarm of journalists, cameramen, and primping news reporters doing stand-ups occupied the sidewalk and spilled over into the street, to the ire of the genteel locals returning home from Union Market with their organic provisions or Banana Republic with tasteful tropical wear for their snowbird jaunts to St. Kitts.

She paid the taxi driver and, as she stepped out into the chill, said out loud, "So what the fuck are you doing here, Janey?"

Which in the way of many good questions had no easy answer.

For a mad moment, she considered shoving her way through the throng, tripping up the eight steps to Lucien Benway's ivy-fringed door, and addressing the media in some sweeping Evita-like tirade in which she demanded justice and swore vengeance.

But she didn't; she just walked away (unrecognizable in her coat and her ski hat) and circumnavigated the block. When she arrived back ten minutes later, nothing had changed.

So she walked again, a little farther this time.

And she kept on doing this until she knew this part of Georgetown better than Google Earth did. And as she walked, her eidetic memory channeled the campy voice of a long-ago college professor waxing lyrical about the row houses' architectural styles (Federal town houses, ornate Italianate bracketed houses, late-nineteenth-century press brick houses) until she felt sick and totally unhinged.

It was getting dark when she returned after her umpteenth circuit, and the lights were on in Benway's house. It was snowing and it was cold and she hadn't eaten the whole day. Or peed since she'd left home. And she suddenly desperately needed to do both.

Then she saw a cab ease up to the house adjacent to Benway's, and when she heard a rattling sound she watched as the green door of a garage rolled up and a man scuttled out. A very small man with a very big head.

Janey, standing not ten feet away from him, wished that somehow a gun could manifest in her gloved hand, that she may smite him like he had smote her David.

These atypically biblical fantasies were brought to an end when the press squad spotted Benway and converged, yelling and jostling and flashing and whirring and clicking. Benway ducked into the taxi and the car blared its horn and shook off the media like a dog shaking off fleas.

They were left muttering and stamping their feet, and then the cold and the advancing dark worked their magic and they started to leak away. Within a half hour there were only two paparazzi left—bouncer-sized men who were famously locked in some grim blood feud—until they both, without looking at one another, folded away their massive lenses, straddled matching Japanese superbikes, and roared off in opposite directions.

Janey waited a moment before she crossed the road and climbed the steps and rang the bell. No reply. She knocked. And knocked again.

With a squeal and a clatter, a sash window was raised and she saw a shadowy figure looming over her.

"If you don't go away, I'll have you arrested for criminal trespass," Nadja Benway said in that cultivated accent of hers, part Brit, part something Balkan.

"I'm not a reporter, Mrs. Benway," Janey said, resisting the old hack impulse to get all chummy and call the woman by her first name.

"Who are you then?"

"My name's Janey Burke and I believe your husband killed my husband."

***

When Nadja opened the front door and the light spilled out and caught the elfin face of the small figure standing on her top step she thought she had been duped.

This was a child, surely?

But as Mrs. Burke stepped closer, Nadja realized she was at least thirty.

"Please, come through to the kitchen," Nadja said, taking the woman's coat.

Janey Burke followed her and said, "I'm sorry, but I'm really desperate to pee."

Nadja pointed to the bathroom and went on through to the kitchen and fidgeted, wanting to drink and smoke. But she did neither.

The day had been arduous. She'd been kept prisoner in a house that was under siege. Lucien had stayed holed up in his office, emerging only a few minutes ago, leaving without telling her where he was going.

The only relief had been the absence of Mr. Morose.

The toilet flushed and the Burke woman appeared in the doorway.

"Please," Nadja said, pointing at the chair opposite her. "Sit."

Janey Burke sat.

"So, why have you come here, Mrs. Burke?"

"Janey, please."

"Janey."

"As I said, I believe that your husband killed my husband."

Nadja kept her gaze level. She almost, out of some misguided sense of sisterhood, voiced her true feelings, that whatever Lucien may be he was not a fool. It was one thing to kill her lover in some desert wasteland, quite another to eliminate the man who had been pointing a very big finger at him in his own backyard.

But, instead, she said, "But why have you come to *me?*"

"Because I think he also killed somebody you loved."

This rocked Nadja and she felt the blood drain from her face. She reached across and grabbed the small woman by the arm hard enough to bruise her.

"What do you know? Tell me!"

Janey shook her head. "I'm sorry, I don't know much, honestly. But I've heard rumors that you and Mike Emerson were lovers."

"It's true. We were. I was going to leave my husband to be with Michael."

"Would your husband have allowed that?"

"Apparently not."

"So you do believe he killed Mike Emerson?"

Nadja looked at the portrait of the peasant girl hanging on the wall, remembered all she had sacrificed in her life to be here, and then she looked at this small carrot-haired woman—who might just be her savior—and said, "Yes. Yes, I do."

"Then you'll help me?"

"Help you how?"

"To make him pay for the death of David."

"What I can tell you, Janey, is that Lucien hasn't survived all these years in his toxic profession without being cunning. He will have covered his tracks very carefully. Despite all the hullabaloo, has anyone come forward with any tangible evidence linking him to the death of your husband?"

"Not yet."

"Exactly. Just as there are all these wild, unsubstantiated rumors about his involvement in that plane crash in Asia." She shook her head. "Lucien will weather this storm."

"I can't let that happen." Nadja shrugged. "So you won't help me?"

"I can't help you."

The small woman flushed and shot to her feet, knocking her chair over. "You're trying to protect him!"

Then she started to shake and flail and Nadja was certain she was experiencing some kind of grand mal epileptic seizure.

Janey grabbed hold of the table and with sheer force of her will she stilled the shaking.

"I'm sorry," she said. "It's the shock, I think."

"Of course. I'm afraid I can't offer you a drink." The only alcohol left in the house was locked in Lucien's office.

Janey shook her head. "No, I think it's better if I don't drink."

"Probably wise."

Nadja extended one of her long legs and raised the hem of her jeans, exposing the ankle monitor. "Do you know what this is?"

"Yes," Janey said.

"My husband fitted it. I can't leave the house."

"Jesus. And you let him do that to you?"

"It was either that or be committed to a psychiatric hospital. Indefinitely."

"The fucking bastard."

"I'm showing you this to impress upon you that I hate my husband with a singular passion. The last thing I would want to do is protect him."

"So?"

"I want as badly as you do to see him destroyed. But we have to be strategic. I understand you feel that you have a crusade. That you want to expose to the world that Lucien killed your husband. But you may have to accept that that will never happen."

"I can't accept that."

"Ask yourself a question, Janey. Do you want Lucien brought down, by any means possible?"

"Yes. Yes I do."

"Then kindly sit and listen to me. I have a plan."

SEVENTY

When Benyamin Klein, sitting slumped on his bed beneath the lethargic ceiling fan, heard a soft knock at the door, he assumed that his evening meal—donated by a kosher restaurant in Bangkok and shipped each day to the hotel where he and his Haredi colleagues were billeted—was being delivered by one of the silent Thai men who staffed the establishment.

Klein had requested that only men serve him and clean his room. He did not trust himself after what had happened over a decade ago, and the photographs taken by the American still dangled over his neck like a sword.

When the knock came again, a little louder, Klein rose, grunting as the mechanism of his bad knee grated and stuttered, steadying himself on the scuffed green wall before he limped to the door.

This would be his last meal here. His job was done, the gobbets of charred flesh and spikes of bone, all that remained of the young gymnasts and their coaches, had been scraped from the blackened earth and plucked from the branches of trees, identified and laid in coffins that had been flown to Bangkok for transfer to Jerusalem.

And tomorrow, Klein, too, would fly home, back to his wife and the certainties of the old stone buildings of the Mea She'arim, where he would, once again, spend his days at the yeshiva, fervently rocking backward and forward as he studied the Torah, *shockelling* as the years blew away like dust and his blood thinned and cooled, and all these sinful thoughts became as nothing.

But when Klein opened the door, the man standing in the corridor was not small and brown and dressed in a tunic. Instead he was very tall and cadaverously pale, wearing an ugly floral shirt—so new it was still stiff and bore a checkerboard of creases from where it had lain folded in a store—and a pair of khaki trousers over running shoes.

The big goy reached out and placed the flat of his hand on Klein's sweaty chest and shoved, sending the Haredi sprawling onto his back on the wooden floor.

The man stepped into the room, closed the door, and crouched beside Klein, putting a long white finger to his bloodless lips.

When Klein, panting, tried to rise, the goy pushed him back down with no effort at all.

He dipped a hand into the pocket of his khaki pants and withdrew a large cell phone. He squinted at the face for a second, swiped at it a couple of times, and then turned the display toward Klein, who, blinking through sweat, thought he was suffering some heat-induced hallucination. For on the screen of the phone was his beloved wife, Batsheva, seen from behind, her bewigged head covered by a scarf, a cloth bag hanging from the shoulder of her dark dress as she walked through the narrow streets of the Mea She'arim, passing a trio of bearded men in black hats and long coats.

It was late afternoon and she was on her daily shopping trip to the fruit and vegetable market, the butcher, and the bakery.

As Klein wondered when this had been shot, the pale man said in an American accent, "This is live. This is right now."

A hand appeared on the screen and waved, and then was removed from the frame, the cell phone camera jiggling and bumping as it followed close behind Batsheva.

"Show me what you have under your coat," the tall man said into the phone.

The camera panned down over the familiar black garb of a Haredi and then the coat gaped and Klein saw a suicide bomber's belt: cylinders of high explosive strapped to the man's body. The coat was closed and the camera swung back to Batsheva who had stopped at a fruit stall where she lifted a Jaffa orange and inspected it.

The pale man stared down at Klein. "If you answer my questions honestly your wife will be spared. If you don't …" He shrugged.

"What do you want?" Klein said in a thick whisper.

"A finger was given to you, was it not? To plant at the crash site?"

Klein couldn't find his voice.

The man raised the cell phone toward his mouth.

"Wait," Klein said. "Yes. Yes. Please, don't hurt her."

"Was it given to you by this man?"

The goy swiped again at the phone and when he turned it back toward Klein, it showed the face of the American who was blackmailing him. The picture had been taken maybe ten years ago, but it was unmistakably him.

Klein nodded, his sidecurls dancing. "Yes. He gave it to me."

"Do you know his name?"

"No."

"Do you know where he is now?"

"No."

The pale man brought back the view of Batsheva shopping and spoke into the phone, "Okay, stand down."

The camera swung away from his wife and bumped and shook as it moved down the sidewalk and turned a corner and then the face of the phone went dark.

"You did good," the man said, looking into Klein's eyes.

He had a hypodermic in his hand, and as he shoved aside the Haredi's thick beard and plunged the needle into his carotid, Klein just had time to say "*Oy, gottenyu*," as he saw his whole life rushing toward him.

Then he saw nothing.

SEVENTY-ONE

Harry Hook, seated beneath a light at the table in his little wooden house in the jungle, sharpened an HB pencil to a lethal point with an X-Acto knife while he squinted through cigarette smoke and his smudged reading glasses at his drawing.

He was breaking from his formula of land and seascapes that were remarkable only by their lack of human presence, which, he supposed, said a lot about him. This was a portrait. Drawn from memory. A portrait of Suzie. His granddaughter. And, surprisingly, it wasn't half bad. The likeness pleased him and he'd captured something of her essence, an intriguing mixture of playfulness and a kind of melancholy that was way too old for her years.

On impulse Hook had opened the sketchpad when he'd found himself lusting after the bottle of Cutty Sark that he'd stashed in the kitchen closet. He'd somehow convinced himself that pouring the liquor down the sink was as much an act of weakness as drinking it.

When he'd returned from prowling the small tourist strip of bars, restaurants, and stalls down on the beachfront—the night air thick with spices, fried foods, gasoline, laughter, and snatches of music—he'd been sped up by adrenaline, and knew he wouldn't sleep.

It was either boozing or sketching.

So he sketched.

He'd been in town as a lure, making himself visible in the belief that Morse was watching, Hook using all his tradecraft to try and draw the man out.

But he hadn't caught a glimpse of the walking cadaver. Which meant that he was betting on something that might never happen. What if Morse was a no-show?

What if he were back in DC chewing on glass or lying on a bed of nails or whatever a Liddyesque freak like him did in his downtime?

Hook, his attention drifting, applied the blade of the knife too zealously and broke the tip of the pencil, a little rain of lead joining the whorls of shavings that lay on floor at his feet.

Hook dropped the pencil onto the table and removed his glasses. As he massaged his sinuses, he felt the sudden dragging weight of impending loss and almost gave himself up to a sadness so deep that if he let it take him, he'd have no way of getting free.

He stood, frisking himself for his cigarettes, and brought a pack of Camels to his mouth, extracting one with his lips as he wandered across to the window. Hook lit the cigarette, staring out at the night through the mesh of mosquito net, wiping sweat from his forehead with the back of his hand. The jungle was dense and dark, but the stars were as bright as pinholes in black paper, a silvery rash that rose from behind the trees and the luminous limestone cliffs.

The cigarette tasted bitter. He ground it dead in an ashtray then found himself at his laptop, nudging the mouse, hearing the hard drive grind and moan. He opened the *Bangkok Post* online and scrolled past the international news until a link caught his eye: ISRAELI DISASTER VOLUNTEER FOUND DEAD.

He clicked on the link and scanned the article. The body of Benyamin Klein had been found in his hotel room earlier that evening. He'd apparently been the victim of a heart attack.

Hook closed his eyes and felt the old familiar cocktail of elation and terror.

It was on.

SEVENTY-TWO

Kate field-stripped the weapons on the bed in the cramped resort bungalow, fingers practiced and assured as she spread out the working parts and wiped them with a cloth. The guns were clean and well maintained, but the labor kept her calm and focused. Like a meditation, almost.

That morning, when she'd woken next to Suzie in JP's bed (the Frenchman had gallantly taken the couch when Hook and the girl had returned from their ice cream mission) Kate had lain staring at the stained ceiling, listening to the calls of the gibbon monkeys and, later, the distant whine of scooter traffic, feeling more relaxed than she had in a long while. Last night's sex had something to do with it, but the knowledge that she was about to go into battle had always calmed her. Stilled her mind.

She remembered one of her instructors from years ago, a tough old combat veteran, telling her that she was a natural, one of the rare breed who grew more chilled in the face of danger.

"You're like a fuckin athlete, girl, an elite performer. Time slows down for you when things get critical and that lets you do shit that nobody else can. I'd go to war with you in a fuckin heartbeat."

She left the bed and went through to where JP was making coffee in the kitchen. He put his arms around her and tried to kiss her, but she withdrew and hurt bloomed in his eyes for a second before he turned away and stirred his coffee.

"I'm sorry," she said. "Things are about to happen."

"What things?"

"I can't tell you."

He swung on her, angry. "You don't trust me?"

"Of course I trust you. This is for your own good."

He laughed a very cynical, very French laugh. "That's a bit like when you break up and say, 'It's not *you* it's *me*.'"

"Hey, let's not do this," she said, walking away.

She only realized he was gone when she heard the squeak of his scooter's kickstand and the scratch of the electric starter followed by the sewing machine whine of the small engine.

She went into the bedroom and woke Suzie and the two of them showered together, washing their hair and laughing, but Kate was vigilant the whole time, listening for anyone approaching the house, waiting for that indefinable sensation, like a change in barometric pressure, that for her had always signaled the coming of danger.

They were dressed by the time JP returned with a backpack slung over his shoulder. Kate got Suzie watching cartoons on JP's iPad in the bedroom and went into the kitchen with him where he removed a few objects wrapped in old T-shirts from the pack.

He opened them to reveal the Glock, a .32 Smith & Wesson, and a Remington sawed-off.

"Are they okay?" he asked.

Kate inspected the weapons and could find no fault. "What about money?"

"It's taken care of."

"No, JP."

He shrugged. "Somebody owed me a favor."

He set about making breakfast and she went and packed up their belongings.

JP appeared in the doorway, watching. "Where are you going?"

"To a hotel."

"Why?"

She jerked her head toward the kitchen and he followed her.

"I told you before, JP, this isn't your fight."

"So you just go?"

"For now."

"Okay," he said, and he walked back to the bedroom, She heard him speaking to Suzie and she had to dam up an emotion that threatened to soften her.

He didn't return to the kitchen and she heard his scooter clatter away.

She'd called Hook who'd come in his friend's *tuk-tuk* and brought them to this rundown resort far from the beach and the tourist spots. It was built on the slope of a hill, with good sight lines.

Hook had hovered a while before leaving to go and dangle his lure. Or throw shark bait in the waters.

Kate rose from the bed and rotated her shoulder blades, loosening little pockets of tension. The TV flickered silently: a seventies action movie with Thai subtitles, Charles Bronson as a vigilante, wasting the trash who'd killed his wife and raped his daughter. Kate remembered watching it years ago with Yusuf, the two of them busting a gut at the flared jeans and bandito mustaches.

She felt a pang of loss that was counterproductive and clicked off the TV.

Kate walked over to where Suzie slept on a sofa by the window and touched her hair, listening to her breathe.

The burner phone Hook had given her earlier rang, and she walked into the bathroom to answer it.

"Yes?"

"He's here," Hook said and told her about the dead Israeli. "Do you want me to come over there?"

"No," she said and ended the call before he could argue.

Kate returned to the bed, reassembling the weapons, feeling serene now that things were underway. Back on familiar ground.

Locked and loaded and ready to kill.

SEVENTY-THREE

Rising with the sun, Hook took a tepid shower, his entry into the bathroom sending a flock of small khaki geckos scuttling for the safety of the roof where they would bask in the heat all day, their tails dangling like commas through cracks in the ceiling board.

Hook patted his body dry with a mildewed towel and, running his hands over a scrape of graying beard, decided he needed a shave.

He lathered up and snapped a disposable Bic razor from a pack of three. Confronting the stained bathroom mirror, he swore to himself that he would make this about hygiene, not self-flagellation. After a promising start, watching the double blades of the Bic scraping a path through the white foam and revealing his wrinkled, sun-browned skin, Hook's gaze was drawn to his eyes and he was done for.

He couldn't look into his eyes without taking his own measure, without seeing a lifetime of deception (of others, sure, but mostly of himself) and self-obsession. Without seeing a man who had worn a threadbare cloak of patriotism to excuse and enable his essential narcissism, to feed his ego and his intemperate urges. A man who'd been nothing but a cheap huckster, seducing the gullible with his oratory and his showmanship, while others—more stolid, more adult, braver—had done the hard yards, and when his time had come, when there had been no grown-ups to turn to, when it had been left to him to make the call, he'd cost twenty-two people their lives.

And now he was gambling with the lives of his daughter and his grandchild.

Hook dropped the razor in the sink and shut his eyes, gripping the porcelain, riding the sudden rush of panic that threatened to unman him.

His cell phone warbled in the bedroom and he hurried through to where it lay on the rumpled sheet. When he lifted it he saw it wasn't Kate—it was Betty Carnahan.

Feeling sick he set the phone down and waited until it stopped ringing, still staring at the device as it vibrated. Then he lifted it and played the message.

"Harry, this is Betty. I was wondering if you'd seen Bob? He's gone off the reservation. Maybe you could call me when you get this?" She was trying for levity, but Hook could hear the anxiety in her voice.

He set the phone down, wiping a dollop of foam from its face, and returned to the bathroom.

Hook finished shaving briskly. Too briskly, and he had to stick a square of toilet paper onto his upper lip where he had nicked himself.

He dressed in a knock-off Lacoste golf shirt and a pair of blue shorts. When he opened the drawer beside his bed to retrieve his wristwatch, he saw the grip of Bob Carnahan's pistol protruding from beneath the tattered paperback of *Henderson the Rain King*.

Hook pondered whether to take the weapon or not. In the end he grabbed it, checked the safety was on, and shoved it in the waistband of his shorts, covering it with his shirt.

He went out the door to the house, slamming it behind him, and thundered down the stairs, the wooden structure shaking under his weight.

He kicked his Yamaha to life, bumped his way down to the main road, and, watching his mirrors, rode slowly through the light morning scooter traffic—a few uniformed hotel workers on their way to the early shift and a mosquito swarm of miniskirted bar girls, smeared and tousled and still drunk or drugged as they made their unsteady way home, as afraid as vampires of the pulverizing sun that winched its way up over the cliffs.

Hook stopped at a bakery and bought a half-dozen croissants, a container of chocolate brownies, and two coffees to go. Back on the bike, he took a few turns, doubling back on himself (typical idle *farang* behavior), but seeing nobody in pursuit, he headed for the resort, riding up a track carved through the thick green foliage, past a toppled wooden fence, and over the grass to Kate's bungalow, sounding the horn of the Yamaha.

The door opened and Kate emerged, Suzie in the doorway behind her.

"Everything okay?" he asked.

"Sure."

As he walked inside carrying the bag from the bakery, Hook ruffled Suzie's hair and she hugged his waist.

He set the food and drinks down beside the TV. Kate tore off a strand of croissant and ate it slowly, washing it down with coffee. Suzie went straight into the chocolate brownies.

Hook couldn't stomach food and just sipped at his espresso.

His phone rang. Betty Carnahan again. He almost sent the call to voice mail but an impulse had him standing and hitting the green button.

"Hey, Betty," he said as he wandered out onto the porch, staring out over the trees at the amber cliffs.

"Hi, Harry."

"I just got your message, I was about to get back to you."

"I'm sorry to call so early."

"That's okay."

"You haven't seen Bob have you?"

"No, not since I was at your house."

"He took himself off to Phuket a few days ago. I spoke to him when he got there but now his phone goes straight to voice mail. I'm starting to get worried."

"Why is he in Phuket?"

"Oh, some boat show. You know Bob, always talking about buying a boat." She paused. "Look, Bob's done this before. Disappeared. Tomcatting, you know?" She laughed but he heard the pain of old betrayals. "But three days? I don't know whether to call the police or ..."

Hook looked back into the room and saw that Kate was watching him.

"Harry, you couldn't come across and see me could you? I'm a little stressed?"

Hook said, "Betty, a guy is here delivering water and I have to pay him. I'll call you back in a minute, okay?"

He ended the call and Kate came out onto the balcony.

"Is that Bob's wife?"

"Yes."

"Wanting to know if you've seen him?"

"Yeah. She's debating whether to involve the cops. Wants me to get a boat across and talk to her."

"Go," Kate said.

"What about you and Suzie?"

"Take Suzie with you." She leaned in closer. "Go there and try to persuade this woman to keep away from the cops for a day or two, Harry. The last thing we need right now is the Thai police coming to question you."

"And Morse?"

"I can handle Morse."

He shook his head. "I don't know."

"Harry, it's better this way. You take Suzie away from here and I'll go into town and make myself visible and draw him in. It'll be easier for me if I know she's safe."

"You can't handle Morse alone."

"I'm not some damsel in distress. It's what I do."

"You haven't done it in a while."

"It's like riding a bike."

"Yeah?"

"Yeah." Kate sighed and moved a strand of hair away from her face. "Harry, to be blunt, you'd just get in the way." She saw his face. "Sorry."

"No, you're right."

"I'll be fine."

He nodded. "You'll call me?"

"I'll call you."

"Okay."

Kate turned and went into the room and said, "Come on, Suze, you're going on a boat ride with Harry."

"Where are you taking me, Grandpa?" the kid asked, walking out onto the porch.

"To visit a nice lady."

"Is she your girlfriend?"

"No, she's married."

"Does that even matter?"

Hook laughed. "You watch too much TV."

She took his hand and they crossed to the bike, Hook lifting her up onto the saddle. As he straddled the Yamaha, he looked back at the bungalow and saw Kate standing in the doorway. She waved and closed the door and he started the bike, taking off toward the road, the child wrapping her arms around him, hugging him tightly.

SEVENTY-FOUR

Holding Suzie's hand, Hook walked along the pathway to the Carnahan's house, leading the girl past a koi pond strewn with purple water lilies and around the hibiscus shrub that hid the doorway from view. Hearing the soft jangle of wind chimes as a hot breeze ruffled his hair, Hook was able, for a moment, to imagine that this was his house and that the beautiful, gracious Betty was his wife, and that he was bringing his granddaughter home.

The fantasy stalled when Betty appeared in the doorway, moving aside a diaphanous silk curtain. She had aged ten years since he last saw her, her face hollow and drawn, her eyes dark holes in her skull. "Harry," she said and stopped when she saw the child. "Who is this?"

"This is Suzie. Suzie, say hi to Mrs. Carnahan."

Betty, rather than step backward to invite them into the house, seemed deliberately to block the doorway, her eyes on the child, her suddenly elderly mouth moving soundlessly, like one of the fish in the pond. Then she looked up at Harry, her eyes widening in terror and she started to shake her head.

Suddenly she flew backward from the doorway and landed in a heap on the wooden floor with a sick thud. Hook gaped and it took him far too long to fumble for the pistol in his belt.

By then Dudley Morse had appeared from behind the curtain and seized Hook's throat and flung him into the room, landing a kick to his solar plexus that had him curling like an inchworm, the pistol spinning across the polished floor.

Suzie screamed and tried to run, but Morse pivoted and reached out one of his impossibly long arms and grabbed the child by the hair, dragging her into the room and smothering her to him, her legs pedaling and arms flailing as she fought him.

He shut down her scream by gripping her throat, throttling her.

Hook, gasping and retching, tried to get himself to his knees, flailing at the pale man. Morse kicked him in the face and Hook felt teeth break and hot blood flow from his nose and mouth and he went down again, viewing the world through a distorted lens that was irising slowly closed as he saw Morse remove a small bottle from his pocket and pour the contents onto a cloth that he pressed to the child's face.

Then Hook fell back, unconscious before his head hit the floor like a mallet striking a xylophone.

SEVENTY-FIVE

Lucien Benway was drunk. Not shit-faced, the term his father used to use to describe his own frequent condition. When the elder Benway—like his son, short in stature but as wide as a brick outhouse—would often stagger around their trailer, weeping into the silk nightgown Lucien's mother had left behind in her haste to flee to Biloxi with a Collier's Encyclopedia salesman.

No, Benway was in what he'd call a state of controlled inebriation, akin to the controlled burn that culled undesirable forest vegetation. It was his contention that alcohol, imbibed with scientific care, cauterized the fear, anger, and resentment he carried like a poisoned well deep in his gut, leaving him primed for action.

Sitting behind his desk, dressed in a winter weight Herringbone tweed suit, white shirt, port-wine colored tie (the full Windsor knotted to perfection), and a pair of oxblood brogues buffed to such a high sheen that the face of Congressman Antoine Mosley appeared in each stippled toecap.

Mosley was everywhere. As Benway surfed from channel to channel he was confronted with the Congressman's dark scowl and ghetto locutions. Benway landed on Fox News where Mosley, pointing a finger as beringed as a rapper's, said, "This time Lucien Benway, and this administration, *will* be held accountable. Benway's chances of dodging prison are slim to none and slim just up and left town."

Benway clicked off the TV and sat staring at its mute gray screen, listening to the low, insectile murmur of the hacks camped out on his doorstep, increasing in number as Mosley's witch hunt increased in venom.

Benway's cell phone (a new number, his last was clogged with the hectoring demands of the media) burped once and he clicked open the text message. His cab awaited him downstairs, which meant running the gauntlet.

He emptied the last finger of Cutty Sark from his glass, brushed nonexistent lint from his jacket, and walked to the door. Locking his office behind him, Benway made his way down the stairs. Nadja sat at the kitchen table watching Mosley on the small TV, her beautiful legs crossed at the knee, the ankle monitor gleaming darkly in the fluorescent light.

"Darling," she said, in the sitcomy delivery she'd adopted these last few days, "do you have a dinner engagement? Perhaps you can bring me a doggy bag?"

All that was missing was the canned laughter.

He ignored her and walked to the front door, determined not to do what he had done yesterday evening and try to sneak out through his garage like a furtive adulterer.

Benway took a deep breath and opened the door onto a constellation of flashbulbs, the voices of his interrogators like the baying of rabid dogs.

SEVENTY-SIX

The flies woke Harry Hook. Their mad buzzing and their legs tickling his eyelids and lips. He blinked and looked into the dead face of Betty Carnahan, her eyes, nostrils, and mouth thick with a seething black mass of meat flies. The wooden handle of a carving knife protruded from her chest, and the floor was tacky with her blood and voided waste.

Hook sat up, his head spinning, the taste of vomit in his mouth. Vomit and something chemical, like ammonia. He remembered Morse smothering Suzie with a cloth soaked in some anesthetic and understood that Morse had used it on him, too.

Suzie.

Hook scanned the room and saw the curtain billowing in the open doorway, the wind chimes jangling atonally.

He looked at his watch, battling to focus on the dial. He had lost nearly five hours.

Jesus.

He stood and was suddenly aboard a Tilt-A-Whirl. He reached out a hand to the wall to steady himself, dislodging a framed photograph of Bob and Betty taken in happier days.

Rushing toward the door, Hook fumbled for his cell phone, speed-dialing as he emerged into the burst-fruit glare of late sunset.

***

Kate, in her shorts and T-shirt, sat on the beach near the boats as the last of the light faded from the sky, a pack slung from her shoulder.

The pack held the sawed-off Remington—old school, but still the most effective and destructive close-quarters weapon she'd ever used. The Glock was under her T-shirt and the snub-nose was tucked into the fanny pack that she had clipped around her waist.

The serenity she'd felt when Hook and Suzie had left her that morning had slowly ebbed, replaced by a nagging sense of foreboding, and she'd become increasingly edgy as she'd wandered the tourist town, sweating in the molten heat, the colors of the ocean, the sky, the foliage, the kitsch-laden stalls, and profusion of sidewalk food suddenly too intense, too visceral for her northern palate, and she'd longed for the monochrome calm of a snowscape.

Of Morse there had been no sign.

When Hook hadn't answered her calls, her agitation had edged toward alarm, despite Kate telling herself that he was doing the smart thing, lying low, keeping Suzie safe. And with the cliffs and atmospheric conditions, who knew how reliable cell phone signals even were?

And then her phone had rung, and Hook, his voice thick with panic, had told her that Morse had taken Suzie.

Rather than causing her to mirror his panic, Hook's call had calmed Kate.

Now that her greatest fear had been made manifest, she felt a sense of predestination, as if her whole life had been lived in preparation for this moment, that each day, each minute, each second had ticked by in order for her to be here, facing this.

She knew it was essential that she forget the times she had put others into this very position and what the outcomes had been, and manage her imagination.

So, anchored in the moment, Kate sat on the beach, the sand beneath her slowly cooling, listening to the shouts of the boatmen, the roars of their engines, and the fizz of the ocean and emptied her mind of all thoughts.

Just waiting.

She heard a boat blast in, the tillerman cutting the engine, letting the prow find the sand with a wet scrape. Before the long-tail had fully beached, Hook plunged from the boat, splashing through the low water.

She stood and walked toward him and when he saw her he grabbed her hand and said, "Kate, I'm sorry. Jesus, I'm sorry," his breath coming in shallow gusts, the stink of vomit, blood, and terror cloaking him.

"Calm down, Harry."

"He set an ambush for me with Betty as the bait and I fucking walked right into it. And now he's got Suzie."

Kate put an arm around his shoulders and, as if he were elderly and infirm, led him away from the boats and the tourists, to a quieter part of the beach, where they were hidden in the dark, whispering palms.

Seating him on the sand, crouching before him, her face close to his, she said, "Talk to me, Harry. Tell me everything."

Hook nodded and, fighting to control his sawing breath, he told her what had happened in the Carnahan's house and how, when he'd gained consciousness and run to the beach, he'd tracked down a boatman who'd remembered a tall *farung* carrying a sleeping girl onto a long-tail.

Told her that Morse and Suzie could be anywhere by now, traveling into the night on the mainland or hidden on one the countless small islands that spread like buckshot across the Andaman Sea.

SEVENTY-SEVEN

Philip Danvers sat at his fireside, his legs covered by a quilt—despite all his efforts he could not get warm—and sipped from a glass of Cutty Sark.

Tonight he didn't listen to music. He'd tried, but even the gentlest sonata hurt his ears, the strings too strident, the horns too harsh. It was one of the mysteries of his failing body that even as his eyesight dimmed, his hearing seemed to have become more acute.

Earlier, he'd had to get very close to his television set to catch the latest on Fingergate, to see the smug face of Congressman Antoine Mosley who had appeared from stage left and anointed himself Lucien Benway's dark inquisitor.

Did it please Danvers, what he had wrought?

Less than he would have imagined.

Vengeance, he supposed, always left a bitter taste in the mouth.

And what he had spent his dwindling days doing had been out of anger. A very particular old man's anger that had come not from the heart or the belly, but from the liver and the low, muddy entrails, a by-product of disillusionment, disappointment, and spite.

Well, that anger was spent.

And now that it had lifted from him like a broken fever, he supposed he should contemplate nobler feelings. Like love.

Given his sexual proclivities, he'd never allowed himself the indulgence of romantic love. He'd had to make do with lust. Lust that had demanded of him clandestine gropings and couplings that, after a brief frisson of excitement, had left him hollow and ashamed.

Was it a coincidence, he'd often pondered, that so many spies of his generation and the one that preceded it—Guy Burgess, Anthony Blunt, et al.—were homosexuals?

Didn't hiding a man's true nature perfectly equip him for a life of espionage?

So, he wondered, watching the flames and hearing the wood spit and spark, what was it he loved now?

Not his surrogate family.

Not anymore.

Lucien Benway was a sociopath, Harry Hook a burned-out wreck, and Kate Swift— no matter how he parsed it—a traitor.

He felt for them what he imagined most elderly parents felt for their adult issue: disappointment, guilt, sadness, recrimination, and (when it came to Harry and Kate) the melancholy that is left when love has cooled.

So what was it that he loved?

Nothing.

There it was. He loved nothing.

He sighed and finished his drink and was trying to summon the energy to stand and cross to the sideboard and pour another when he heard the crunch of footsteps on the gravel of his driveway.

The steps grew louder as the visitor crossed the paving stones and approached the door.

He heard a rusty squeal as the ring of the brass knocker—bolted to the mandible of the Pharaoh Ramses—was lifted, followed by a sharp smack as it connected with the striking plate. Just one knock, as if whoever was out there was certain he would hear it.

Danvers levered himself from his chair and walked slowly toward the door.

When he opened it he was unsurprised to see Lucien Benway standing on his doorstep, a coil of frigid breath escaping his lips.

"Lucien."

"Philip."

"You're alone?"

"Yes."

Danvers stepped back and gestured toward the fireside. "Then come on in."

Benway shook his head. "No, thank you."

"What? Are we going to stand out here and natter?"

"No, we're going for a walk."

"Are we now?"

"Yes."

"And what if I'm not in the mood for a walk?'

"I have to insist."

"Well, then. Let me get my coat."

Danvers lifted the Burberry that hung from the coat rack, grunting as he battled to get his arms into it. He buttoned the coat and joined Benway on the porch.

"Where's your car, Lucien?"

"I took a cab to that god-awful strip mall and then walked here."

"I see. A night for walking, is it?"

"Yes, it is."

With that, Benway set off across the flagstones toward the trees. He paused and looked back, waiting for Danvers, who employed a geezer's shuffle to catch up with him.

Together they walked slowly through the snow into the trees, the bare branches of the silver birches ghostly in the dim moonlight.

When the lights of the house had been lost to sight, Benway said, "I think this is far enough, Philip."

"Far enough for what?"

Benway seized Danvers by the shoulders and flung him to the ground. His hip struck a snow-covered rock and he heard it shatter like a piece of Meissen china.

Pain had been Danvers' constant companion these last days, a dull, throbbing pain that seemed to radiate from somewhere low outward into the rest of his body. But this pain was loud and sharp and intense and he felt tears in his eyes.

Tears that would freeze all too soon.

Lucien had a sturdy branch in his hand and he swung it and broke Danvers' left knee. More pain.

Benway crouched and frisked him.

"My telephone is in the house, Lucien."

"You'll forgive me if I don't believe a fucking word that comes from your mouth, won't you, Philip?"

Benway finished patting him down and stood, breathing heavily.

"Goodbye, Philip."

"*Auf Wiedersehen*, Lucien."

The little man spat a laugh before he turned and trudged away like a malevolent goblin from a children's fable, his footsteps filling with snow and disappearing within seconds.

Philip Danvers lay and looked up at the snow falling like blown cotton from the dark heavens.

So, he thought, this is how it ends.

SEVENTY-EIGHT

Hook and Kate were in the house up in the jungle. Hook paced, his heavy tread causing the house to creak and sway. Kate sat in the cane chair, looking composed and almost tranquil, only the occasional swiping away of a tendril of hair from her face a tell that she was anxious.

Hook's cell phone lay on the table and he stared at it as he paced, willing it to ring.

"Relax, Harry, he'll call," Kate said.

"Why is he taking so long?"

"Now you're talking like a grandfather, which is kind of endearing, but not exactly reassuring, if you get me."

"I do," he said. He stopped by the window and looked out into the night. "He's softening us up."

"Exactly. And he knows he can do it, because this isn't just some operation. This is personal."

"Yes."

Hook had to push away an image of the child lying dead.

As if reading his mind, Kate said, "He can't kill Suzie, Harry. Not yet. We may be personally invested but we're still pros, and if he wants something from us, he's going to have to give us proof of life."

She spoke calmly, dispassionately, and he knew it was her way of tamping down her apprehension, of keeping alive the belief that she would see her daughter again.

Kate had managed the situation—and him—since meeting Hook at the beach. He'd wanted to question more boatmen, question taxi drivers and touts, question anybody who may have seen anything, even though he knew that it was just a form of busy work, a way of keeping himself distracted, but Kate had insisted that they return to his house and wait.

And stay focused.

When they'd arrived, she asked for his phone and sat down with it at the table, her fingers a blur on its face.

"What are you doing?" he'd asked.

"Downloading an app that'll allow us to record incoming calls."

"Can't the phone do that?"

"No cell phone can. Privacy laws have the manufacturers running scared. But some tech head, who's probably a twelve-year-old kid in Seoul or Minsk, has that one licked."

She finished her task and placed the phone on the table, where it still lay. Silent.

Kate looked at him as he paced and asked, "Would a scotch help, Harry?"

He swung on her. "Jesus, are you crazy? What good would I be drunk?"

"I'm not talking drunk, Harry, I'm talking maintaining. Having you jonesing for a drink is about as bad as having you drunk."

Hook didn't reply and she stood and went into the kitchen. He could see her through the doorway as she opened the closet above the sink and removed the bottle of Cutty Sark. When she broke the seal he may not have heard the "Hallelujah Chorus," but it was close. She poured two fingers into a shot glass, added an ice cube and brought the drink through to him.

"Just this one," she said. "And take it slow, okay?"

He nodded, too desperate to feel affronted by her mothering, and raised the glass to his lips, catching the peaty vapor of the booze before he felt its bitterness on his tongue. He took a sip and let the alcohol warm his belly and almost immediately felt an easing of his tension as the liquor worked its dark magic.

The alchemical moment was enhanced when he heard the chirp of his cell phone.

He set the drink down and approached the phone, seeing UNKNOWN CALLER on its face.

Kate hit the green button and speakerphone, then activated the app and nodded at Hook.

"Yes?" he said.

"Hook, you know who this is?" Morse said.

"Yes."

"Is Kate Swift with you?"

"First I need to know the girl is alive," Hook said, his eyes fixed on Kate's.

There was a bump and a scrape then Suzie said, "Grandpa?"

"Yes. Are you okay?"

"I'm scared, Grandpa."

More bumps and scuffs and then Morse was back. "Let me talk to Swift."

"I'm here," Kate said.

"Well, well," Morse said, "in the pink."

"What do you want?"

"You're going to go public that you're alive and well, that you faked your death in that plane crash. You'll call the *New York Times*, the *Washington Post*, CNN, Al-fucking-Jazeera. You'll video call to show that you're you. You'll send them fuckin stool samples if they want, are you getting me?"

"Yes, I hear you."

"Once the news of your miraculous return from the dead hits the mass media, I'll release your brat. Okay?"

"I'll do it. But I need to see her."

Silence, then a video image appeared on the screen: Suzie, bound and gagged, tied to a chair.

The image disintegrated and Morse said, "Okay, you do what you need to do."

He was gone.

When Kate tried to speak, Hook shut her up and grabbed her arm and walked her to the window.

"Listen."

"To what?"

"Hear that amplified voice?"

"What is it?"

"A truck that drives around town with a message on a loop advertising a titty bar."

When she nodded, he said, "Play back the last moments of the call."

She worked the phone, turned up the volume and played back Morse telling her to do what she needed to do.

"Hear what I hear, in the background?" Hook asked.

"That message. Jesus. They're here. They're in town."

"Let's go," Hook said, running for the door.

Kate grabbed her arsenal and followed. Hook already had his bike started by the time she reached the bottom of the stairs and they flew down the rutted trail, hit blacktop, and then they were on the main road.

Hook turned a corner and there was the truck, heading their way, with its speakers and girlie banners and blaring looped message in Thai-accented English: "Lucky Bar. Open now. Beautiful girl. Beautiful supermodel from Bangkok."

He sped along the road in the direction from which the Toyota had come. This was Thai Town, away from the tourist center. Small sidewalk restaurants, a 7-Eleven, cell phone suppliers, the post office, a computer shop, a florist, a hair stylist, most of the buildings shuttered and closed.

No hotels. Not even a backpacker hostel. The buildings dwindled into the jungle and Hook began to lose hope, when he spotted a couple of lights through the bush.

A small dirt road led off the main drag to three rundown resorts lost in the tangled vegetation.

Hook turned onto the track, killed the engine, and they freewheeled until they reached a fork and saw two sets of bungalows in the jungle to their left, and one to their right.

He stopped the Yamaha and they sat in silence for few moments, listening to the sounds of insects and cicadas and night birds. The air was hot and thick and the smell of cooking drifted in.

Kate was off the bike, the Remington already free of the backpack, its amputated barrels gleaming in the light of the fat yellow moon that floated above the cliffs.

Hook put a hand on her arm.

"Wait," he said.

SEVENTY-NINE

When she heard the scratch of Lucien's key in the lock of the front door, Nadja opened the refrigerator and took out the ice tray, twisting it like she was breaking a chicken's neck, and freed two cubes. She dropped the cubes into Lucien's favorite glass and poured a stiff jolt from the bottle of Cutty Sark.

That he persisted with this inferior whiskey irritated her, particularly since his relationship with his erstwhile mentor had soured.

But persist he did.

Like he persisted with those disgusting Turkish cigarettes that were imported for him, at great cost, by a downtown tobacconist. Perhaps, because so much of Lucien's life was manufactured (his name, his almost neutral accent, his veneer of sophistication, his absurdly conservative wardrobe) these little habits were the bolts that held the whole rickety construction in place.

Why she was thinking these things she didn't know.

Or, rather, she *did* know. Only too well.

She was thinking them so as not to think about the other thing.

The thing she was about to do.

Lucien ditched his jacket in the hallway and walked along the corridor in his shirtsleeves, looking distracted and preoccupied. No doubt because of his brush with the media outside, though with the weather and the hour only a few lowly diehards remained.

He made for the stairs, ignoring her.

"Lucien?" she said.

He stopped with one foot on the bottom step and a hand on the banister. "Yes?"

"Have a drink with me." She held out the glass.

"Where did you get that?" he asked, his eyes narrowing suspiciously.

"I had it delivered."

"What's the catch?"

"There is no catch."

"No?"

"No." She shrugged. "I spent my day cooped up in this house all alone."

"So even my company is better than none at all?"

She produced a reasonably convincing laugh. "I suppose so."

"You could talk to the rabble outside."

"And what would I say to them?"

"You've led a colorful life. You'd fascinate them with your tales of soft beds and hard battles."

She shook her head at him in mock admonishment. "Lucien, really." Then she smiled. "See. This is fun. Just like the good old days."

"There were no good old days."

She lifted the glass again. "Oh, come on."

He shrugged and walked into the kitchen toward where she stood positioned so that he had his back to the pantry as he approached her, just as she and Janey Burke had planned.

The sliding door to the pantry rolled open silently and Janey stood frozen for a moment in the glare of the strip lights.

Nadja met her eyes, silently willing her into motion, all the while posing with a smile fixed to her face and the scotch in her hand like a greeter at a convention.

Lucien took the glass from her and lifted it to his lips. "Cheers."

Finally Janey moved, bursting from the pantry, holding a plastic laundry bag in her gloved hands, raising it like a parachute and dropping it over Lucien's head in one rapid movement.

Shocked, Lucien spilled whiskey onto his shirt and the glass fell from his hand and shattered on the tiled floor.

Just as they had rehearsed earlier—using a large cushion from the couch in the living room as a stand-in for Lucien—Janey pressed the bag to his face while Nadja kneeled and took him by the knees. Lifting his flailing feet from the ground (and catching a child-sized brogue in the mouth that she hoped would not result in a swollen lip) she toppled him to the floor, Janey sliding a cushion under his head to prevent visible injuries. Lucien fought them with manic strength, bucking and twisting, nearly unseating the two women piled atop him, pressing him down with their bodies, both of them using their hands to mash the bag to his face, his features visible through the transparent plastic, his eyes bulging and his mouth sucking at air that wasn't there.

After what seemed like an eternity, his struggles stopped and he lay still.

Gasping and sweating, Nadja and Janey stood up from Lucien, their hair and clothes awry, Janey's cheeks a violent crimson.

Nadja whipped the bag from his head. "Oh, god," she said.

"He's not? Fuck. Is he?" Janey said.

Nadja put her fingers to his neck. Nothing.

"There's no pulse," she said, panicking.

"Oh, shit. Oh, shit." Janey said. "We kept the bag on too long."

"Pump his chest," Nadja said. Janey just stared at her. "Pump his fucking chest!"

The tiny woman fell to her knees and started compressing Lucien's chest with her gloved hands.

Nadja knelt beside him and opened his mouth, saying, "Don't you fucking die on me, you miserable little shit. Not yet."

She dipped down and for the first time in all the years she'd known him she put her mouth to his. She breathed into him, feeling his lungs expand and carried on until she was exhausted. Janey, tireless, machinelike, pumped away.

And then Nadja felt something, a twitch, a flicker, and she put her fingers to the carotid and a faint pulse throbbed against her fingertips.

She sat back, sweating and panting, and when Janey removed her hands, they watched his narrow chest rise and fall.

Nadja stood and said, "Okay, now let's kill the little ogre for real."

EIGHTY

Kate stared up at the endless sweep of stars and felt a sudden loss of equilibrium. Closing her eyes, she slowed her breath and heard the clatter of the *tuk-tuk* and smelled the warm, dry dust that it threw up as it neared them.

The little green taxi rattled up the road from the third resort, its brakes squeaking when it halted beside where she and Hook stood near the dirt bike in the cover of a stand of trees.

After restraining Kate from storming the bungalows, Hook had called his friend Ton who'd appeared ten minutes later, ready to earn a thousand baht for going to the desks of the resorts and speaking to the Thai clerks, pretending that he was looking for a *farang* who had booked his taxi.

Kate had acknowledged the value of the plan, but—despite all her years of training—had found it almost impossible to wait for the man to do his rounds to the bungalows.

Ton leaned out the window. "*Khun* Harry," he said and beckoned Hook closer.

Kate, standing at Hook's shoulder, expected Ton to report what he had from the first two resorts: that nobody fitting the descriptions of Morse and Suzie had been seen.

But this time there was more urgency in the man's voice. "I think the people there," the taxi driver said, jerking a thumb over his shoulder, "them are lying."

"Why?" Hook said.

"Them tell me resort closed for renovation. But I see light in one bungalow."

Hook got the driver to explain where the occupied hut was situated. When Ton had done this, Harry thanked him, handed over the money, and the taxi bumped away into the night, a trail of dust obscuring its red taillights.

"Let's go," Hook said.

Kate shook her head. "No, you wait here." She handed him the snub-nose. "You back me up."

"With this peashooter?"

"Let me do this, Harry, please," Kate said, and without waiting for a reply, she cut into the jungle, using the moon to navigate by.

She stepped over fallen branches and spikes of bamboo, crossed a stream that stank of human shit and found herself at the perimeter of the resort, looking at ten wooden bungalows built around an empty swimming pool. The front desk, in a thatched open-sided structure, was far to her left, and she could hear tinny laughter from a Thai television game show and the low chatter of the night staff.

She caught a gleam of light from the bungalow farthest from her, built almost in the jungle.

Kate moved through the undergrowth until she stood behind the bungalow, which rested on low concrete legs. The small bathroom window, set high in the wooden wall, glowed with the light of a green incandescent bulb. She broke from the cover of the foliage, crossed to the window and saw that it was free of glass, merely a rectangle cut into the wood, covered with filthy mesh, dead moths and bugs trapped in the net like specimens.

She heard only the nocturnal insects, the distant drone of a motor-cycle and the muted garble of the TV show the desk staff was watching.

Keeping close to the timber wall, holding the sawed-off, Kate moved to the side of the bungalow. It was windowless, an air conditioner mounted to the wall, the fan spinning within its housing, the motor giving off a low whine.

The bungalow *was* occupied and Kate was certain now that her child was inside.

She could sense her pull, drawing her like the moon draws the ocean, and just as irresistibly. Kate had to fight the urge to rush the door. She had to forget she was a mother, had to find the zone where time slowed, where she entered the flow state and her concentration narrowed and all doubt left her and she did what she did without thought or emotion.

But she could not.

Her heart hammered at her chest. Her throat was tight. Sweat dripped from her hair, and the bandage on her left hand itched. She was terrified.

Kate fought her body for control and lost. Cursing herself silently, she sucked air so thick she could taste it and then she walked slowly toward the front porch, conscious of the sound of her shoes on the grass and the gravel, an undammed surge of adrenaline giving her the shakes. She had to clench her jaw to stop her teeth from chattering.

Useless fucking bitch.

Reaching the front of the bungalow she pressed herself to the wood, holding the Remington against her chest, and inched herself forward until she stood outside one of the pair of windows that flanked the door, pinkish light coming from behind the closed curtains.

She listened again.

No sound.

She put her face close to the glass and peered in through a chink where the curtain didn't quite meet the window frame.

Morse, dressed only in a pair of boxers, sat on the bed, smoking.

There was no sign of Suzie.

Kate inched her way up the two steps onto the balcony. The wood creaked. She stopped, sweat pooling under her arms and breaking in trickles from her hairline. She wiped her face with the back of her arm and moved forward, reaching the door.

She waited. Listening.

After drying the sweat off her left hand on her shirt, conscious of the bandage and the lost finger, she took hold of the door handle and turned it slowly.

Locked.

She stepped back and raised her right foot, sending all her weight into her leg, her shoe striking the timber beside the lock, the plywood splintering and the door swinging inward.

Kate ran into the room, leveling the Remington at Morse who was still seated on the bed, staring at her impassively, smoke curling from his lips as he exhaled.

She scanned the hut. A cane chair. A bar fridge. A wooden closet standing near the bathroom door.

"Where is she?" Kate said in a voice she barely recognized. "Where's Suzie?"

The pale man said nothing and, keeping the sawed-off pointed at him, she moved toward the closet. Eyes still on Morse she reached out a hand and opened the door, hearing the hinges creak and then hearing something else.

She took her eyes away from the tall man, but kept the weapon extended, and looked down and saw Suzie lying on the floor of the closet, trussed, gagged, her eyes wide with terror.

Kate's training was washed away by a flood of relief.

Her child was alive.

Too late she heard a sound behind her and she spun as a figure in a gaping nightgown flew at her from the bathroom, a figure with a man's bony chest and a woman's painted face, long black hair streaming.

Kate saw the gleam of a short blade and she fired. She saw blood bloom on the almost-female face then felt a sharp pain as the knife took her in the chest. She knew it was bad when all strength left her and the Remington slipped from her grasp and she folded in on herself, the room tilting wildly, and suddenly she was lying on the wooden floor, looking at up Suzie who screamed soundlessly into her gag.

Kate had to fight to keep her eyes open, to stop invisible hands from dragging her down into the gathering darkness, and when she tried to speak to her child, to tell her that everything would be all right, no words came, only a flow of thick, hot blood.

EIGHTY-ONE

Nadja kneeled behind the giant Mercedes-Benz, feeding a length of garden hose into its tailpipe. When the hose was shoved in as deep as it would go, she lifted a cloth from the cement floor of the garage and stuffed it into the gap between the hose and the pipe, so no carbon monoxide would escape.

Nadja gave the hose a last tug to see that it was securely wedged in the tailpipe and then she squatted for a moment with her back against the huge chrome bumper, watching Janey Burke use old issues of the *Washington Post* to close the crack between the bottom of the roller door and the concrete slab. When she was done with that, the diminutive redhead sealed the one small window with duct tape.

Nadja walked the hose toward the rear door of the car and dangled it through the open side window. She slid in beside Lucien who sat slumped on the leather seat, breathing shallowly, and closed the door. Holding the hose with one hand, she activated the electric window with the other, and the glass rose, lifting the green and black hose with it, trapping the rubber against the doorframe. Closing the window all the way would put a crimp the hose, so she stuffed a towel into the gap between the glass and the metal.

She slid from the car, closed the rear door, and got in behind the wheel, leaving the driver's door agape. Starting the Mercedes-Benz, she listened to the beat of the obsessively maintained engine, feeling the steady rhythm coming up through the floorboards and the constant and reassuring vibration of the steering wheel beneath her gloved fingertips.

As Nadja quit the car, she caught a whiff of the warm gas wafting through the mouth of the pipe that dangled just by her husband's left cheek, pure, unfiltered carbon monoxide filling his lungs.

She took a last look at Lucien slumped in the rear of his silly old car, then she beckoned Janey and the two women left the garage and entered the kitchen, shutting the door behind them.

EIGHTY-TWO

When Hook heard the gunshot, a loud smack that had the screaming birds boiling from the trees, he jumped aboard the Yamaha, kick-started it—the noise be damned—and took off at such speed that the rear wheel slid on the loose gravel and he almost lost control. He fought the bike and tamed it and hurtled down the bumpy track toward the bungalows.

Hook swung off the pathway toward the empty pool, skirted it, the tires nibbling at the cracked tiles, ramped a hump in the grass, and landed heavily, cursing, bringing the bike to a sliding halt, chewing dust.

He heard a flat slap and something buzzed past his ear, shattering the window of the hut behind him, and Dudley Morse burst from a bungalow, caught in the rectangle of pinkish light that fell through the open doorway. Hook could see that the tall man had Suzie, bound and gagged, slung over his shoulder.

Morse fired again, missed, and ran for a path that led into the trees which separated the bungalows from a small beach.

Hook spun the accelerator of the Yamaha and surged after Morse, trees and bushes flying at him in the yellow eye of the bike.

He cleared the trees and spotted Morse sprinting for the beach, a muddy little cove that attracted few tourists, unlike its more glamorous sibling on the far side of the cliff.

Too late Hook saw a shelf of rock in his path and he hauled up the handlebars of the bike like a steeplechase jockey at a jump. For a moment he thought he was going to make it, but the rear tire clipped the boulders and he was unseated from the Yamaha, airborne, in free fall for a split second before he hit the rocks, his wind smashed out of him.

Hook fought for breath and hauled himself to his knees in time to see Morse dragging a kayak from the sand to the water. The man threw the child across the tapering hull, pushed the craft out and jumped aboard, his long arms windmilling the double-bladed paddle.

Hook gained his feet and, clutching his ribs, staggered onto the beach, the gibbous moon casting a broken reflection in the black, rippling ocean.

When Morse hit the low breakers, the kayak started to yaw and Suzie slid from the prow into the water. Morse circled back but the child was gone. He corrected his course and made for the cliff and the next beach.

Hook, oblivious to the pain in his ribcage, ran from the sand into the ocean, splashing, gasping, floundering. When the water was deep enough, he threw himself into a clumsy crawl, each stroke a spear to his side, and when he reached the spot where the girl went down he dived.

He saw nothing.

Came up for air.

Dived again, his hands churning empty water.

His lungs bursting, he shot to the surface, sobbing for breath, and then he went under again, forcing himself deeper, and in the moonlight that pierced the clear water he spotted a dark shape. As he plunged toward it, he saw that it was Suzie, her bound feet scraping the silty seabed, her one arm free, hand pointing upward, her hair washing away from her head like kelp.

Hook grabbed her and churned to the surface, sucking air, treading water, shouting her name, the child limp in his arms.

He towed her to the beach, dragged her from the ocean, and lay her face down on the sand, pumping her back, saying her name over and over like some primitive incantation. Water jetted from her mouth and she spat and gasped, and he hugged her to him and cradled her while she cried and spoke words he did not understand.

Hook untied her and carried her back across the beach and over the rocks, past where his broken bike lay like a felled beast and along the path through the trees.

He stopped a moment when he had the bungalows in his sight, expecting police, but the resort was eerily quiet, even the babbling TV stilled, and he suspected that the Thai staff, like the frightened birds, had fled into the night.

Approaching the bungalow Morse had occupied, Hook set the girl down on the grass. She clutched at his sodden shirtfront with hands made viselike by raw terror.

"It's okay," he said, gently prying her fingers apart, "I'll be right back."

Dripping, he walked toward the bungalow, climbed the steps, and stood in the doorway.

Kate lay on the floor between the bed and the open closet, a dark pool of blood fanning out from her body. He didn't need to touch her to know she was dead, but he entered the room, stepping over another body of indeterminate gender (he glimpsed a bloody, rouged face cratered with acne scars) and he knelt beside Kate, touched her throat, and looked into her empty eyes.

Green eyes. Like his.

All she got from me, he thought, her eyes. And a taste for deceit and subterfuge.

Hook covered her with the sheet from the bed and left the bungalow. He walked over to the child, who sat hugging her drenched knees.

He crouched beside her and wrapped her in his arms, trying to still her shaking body.

"Is Mommy dead?" Suzie said.

"Yes," he said, "she is."

The girl buried her face in his chest and sobbed, and he lifted her and carried her away.

EIGHTY-THREE

Nadja was in her en suite, running a bath, the mirror already steamed up. She stripped off her clothes and stood naked, the black ankle monitor an obscenity on her pale body.

She found a pair of scissors in the cabinet behind the mirror and placed her right sole on the rim of the bathtub and was about to cut through the strap of the monitor when she stopped herself. What if it sent out some kind of a distress signal that brought thuggish surveillance personnel to her doorstep?

No, too risky. She could live one more night with the thing on her ankle.

The bath was ready, so she lowered herself into it, and as she slowly washed her body with the buttermilk soap she favored, it was as if she were sloughing off the decades she'd spent in Lucien Benway's claustrophobic orbit.

After she and Janey had left Lucien in the idling car and returned to the kitchen, the small woman had kneeled and retrieved from the tiles the plastic bag they'd used to smother him, shoving it into her pocket.

She'd pointed at the broken glass and mess of alcohol on the floor. "Let me clean that up."

"No," Nadja had said. "You go now."

They'd stood looking at each other, suddenly awkward, two women who, had they met in other circumstances, would have raised one another's hackles.

"Thank you," Janey had said.

"No, thank *you*."

They'd laughed and embraced for an awkward moment and then Janey, limber as a gymnast, had left through the kitchen window, dropping into a walled alley hidden from the front of the house. She'd scaled the wall and melted into the night, invisible to the dregs of the press contingent.

Nadja had found a dustpan and a brush and swept up the broken glass, depositing it into the trash. She'd mopped up the scotch and rinsed the cloth at the sink. Peeling the orange gloves from her hands, she'd balled them up and dropped them in the garbage can.

Then she'd come upstairs and drawn her bath.

The bath that was cooling now, as she lay submerged, feeling very sleepy.

She rose from the bathtub, dried herself and dressed in a chaste pair of flannel pajamas.

In her room Nadja slid beneath the freshly starched lavender-scented sheets of her bed and, as soon as her head touched her pillow, she fell into a deep, dreamless sleep.

EIGHTY-FOUR

When Janey Burke finally arrived home (so buzzed by what she and Nadja Benway had done that she'd walked aimlessly around her Foggy Bottom neighborhood for she didn't know how long) she was amazed—and more than a little appalled—when she realized that she was hungry.

No, fuck hungry, make that *ravenous*.

A case of the munchies way more intense even than when she and David had smoked weed and binge-watched the hoary old sitcoms (*Three's Company, Family Ties, Cheers*) that he'd downloaded from BitTorrent, stuffing their faces and choking as they'd rolled on the bed, helpless with laughter.

But the refrigerator—the massive silver Maytag that David had bought with his first paycheck from the *Post*—was empty, save for leftover mac and cheese that had sprouted a three-day beard.

David, big, gluttonous, tactile David, had been the food buyer. Thumping into the apartment laden with shopping bags each night, in a state of high excitement because he'd discovered a new Korean takeout or an Afghani food store or a Cantonese bakery tucked away in Chinatown, he'd foist stinky kimchi, skewers of seekh kabab, and sickly sweet mooncakes upon her, licking his big fingers and making ecstatic grunts of appreciation.

Janey found a box of Cheerios in the kitchen closet and poured some into a bowl with milk. She took the bowl through to the bedroom and pulled her shoes off, sitting cross-legged on the bed and staring at the dead TV. When she lifted a spoon of the cereal to her lips, she lost her appetite and deposited the bowl on the bedside table.

She'd just killed a man.

Well, technically, she was the accomplice in the murder of a man.

That may not be right, either, because Lucien Benway may not be dead yet. He may still be slumped unconscious in the rear of his gross old Mercedes-Benz limo, inhaling the carbon monoxide from its huge engine.

"No catalytic converter, darling," Nadja Benway had said when they'd first discussed the plan in her kitchen. "I googled it."

"I don't know what the fuck you're talking about," Janey had said.

Nadja had waved her cigarette dismissively in that uniquely European way, explaining that new cars had a gadget that eliminated almost all the carbon monoxide from their exhaust emissions. But the Mercedes-Benz had never been modified, obsessive little Lucien keeping it identical to when it had rolled off the production line in Stuttgart in 1968.

But that was splitting hairs.

If he wasn't already dead, he soon would be.

So, what did Janey feel?

Nothing.

Kinda empty.

Not guilty, no. Fuck that.

But sad. She felt sad.

And then she allowed herself, for the first time since she'd seen David lying dead at the morgue, to feel utterly bereft.

Janey got up from the bed and crossed to the closet. She freed all of David's shirts and jackets from their hangers, tossing the clothes onto the bed. Delving into the drawers and getting armloads of his underwear and socks and sweaters and jeans, she added them to the pile.

She went through to the bathroom and there she struck the mother lode when she upended the laundry basket and separated his soiled things from hers, taking the dirty sweats and underwear and socks, adding them to the mound on the bed like seasoning to a meal.

Then she climbed up and submerged herself in her dead husband's clothes.

God, there it was: his smell. That indefinable scent that was David. Traces of food and weed and the cheap roll-on deodorant he insisted on wearing—the smell of *him*. Of his sweat. Of his skin. Of his hair and his beard. His big, hairy man-animal muskiness pervaded the fabric.

She started to weep and then to cry and then to wail, and things reached fucking epic Old Testament proportions when she howled and tore at his clothes until her fingernails bled and she babbled incoherently, snot bungeeing from her mouth and nostrils until she exhausted herself and fell asleep clutching a particularly ripe pair of skivvies to her face, the knowledge that she would never again be loved by him a huge black wave that dragged her into a bottomless ocean of sleep.

EIGHTY-FIVE

Hook sat in the speedboat with his back to the hull, his arm around the silent child. Twin Mercury outboards thundered behind them, sending the boat speeding across the black water of the Andaman Sea.

JP was seated at the wheel in the cockpit, staring through the windshield into the night. Behind him, Kate's body, wrapped in the sheet from the bungalow, lay hidden from the eyes of the girl by a stack of scuba tanks, life jackets, and cooler boxes.

When Hook had walked Suzie away from the resort, he'd called JP and begged for his help. While they waited for the Frenchman, Hook and Suzie had hunkered down in the trees and he'd held the child, who'd shivered and cried without cease.

By the time JP had arrived in the gaudily painted truck he used to transport tourists on diving expeditions, Suzie's shakes had subsided and she'd fallen into a semicatatonic state. They'd left her sleeping on the front seat of the truck while they'd entered the resort bungalow—JP's face white beneath his tan when he'd seen Kate lying dead. He'd muttered something in French, whether a fragment of a Catholic death rite or a cursing out of a cruel, interventionist god, Hook would never know.

In silence they'd wrapped Kate's body and carried it out and laid it on the flatbed.

JP had then taken Hook up to his wooden house, where he'd packed everything that could identify him, and then they'd driven the jungle-fringed back roads to the small harbor where JP's boat was berthed. The pier was deserted at night and, unseen, they'd carried Kate aboard the speedboat and set off for open water.

The child was asleep again and Hook unthreaded his arm and lifted his laptop from the deck. He carried it to the side and dumped it. Followed by his cell phone.

He walked to the cockpit and stood beside JP, whose face was lit by the amber glow of the instruments.

"Are we far enough out?" Hook asked.

"Almost. Give me maybe two minutes then we'll reach the tides that will carry her away from shore, out toward India."

Hook walked back to the child and stood with the hot wind in his hair, tired deep into his bones. The boat slowed as the outboards throttled back, the silence oppressive when JP cut the engines and the craft drifted on the swell.

Hook didn't move, just stood with his hands in his pockets, staring down at the water like it had something to tell him.

JP rose from behind the wheel.

"Okay?" he said.

"Yes."

The Frenchman moved aside the diving gear and the sheet was revealed, white in the moonlight.

He bent and grasped Kate's feet. Hook joined him and took her head and they carried her to the rear, resting her on the gunwale.

"Do you want to say something?" JP asked.

Hook shook his head. "I wouldn't know what to say."

JP looked at him and shrugged. "On three."

They pitched Kate over the side. When her body splashed into the water it stirred up trails of phosphorescence. It wasn't magical tonight. JP had weighted the body and it sank quickly.

The Frenchman took his place behind the wheel, fired up the outboards, and turned the speedboat in a lazy arc until he was traveling parallel with the mainland, the lanterns of a line of shrimp boats strung like glow worms near the shore.

JP was taking Hook and the girl two hours up the coast, where he would put them ashore and an overnight bus would carry them to Bangkok and their uncertain futures.

Hook sat beside Suzie and put his arm around her. The rumble of the outboards and the motion of the boat dragged him toward sleep, but when he dozed, he saw bodies and blood, so he woke and stared out across the ocean to the curve of the horizon, a dark meniscus against the sky, and felt a rush of vertigo so powerful that it had him clutching at his seat, suddenly aware that only gravity and a fragile envelope of air shielded him from the immensity of space.

EIGHTY-SIX

It was raining in Bangkok. A deluge, sheets of gray water plunging from the low, heavy clouds that shrouded the supertowers, drains overflowing, streets underwater, the early morning traffic gridlocked.

Hook and Suzie sat in the back of a crawling taxi, the driver tapping the wheel and muttering in Thai. Maybe he was praying to the garish Buddhist talismans that littered his dashboard.

Hook wiped condensation from the rain-blurred window and looked out at a city he'd once known all too well. He hadn't been back in the years since he'd abandoned his suicide by bargirl and booze but little had changed: squat buildings in need of paint sandwiched between soaring glass high-rises, the golden spires of temples prodding the soggy sky, black electric wires like thick strings of licorice dangling between poles at the roadside, and, even in the rain, the all-pervasive smell of street food wafting in from the sidewalk stalls.

Suzie sat staring at nothing, her hands in her lap, as immobile as a statue. He put his arm around her shoulder and tried to draw her to him but she was rigid, and when he looked at her he saw that her jaw was clenched.

She had spoken only in monosyllables since Hook had brought her back to life on the beach the night before, and he wondered if her child's mind was capable of hating him for returning her to a world of immeasurable pain and grief.

On impulse he freed a banknote from his pocket and shoved it at the driver.

Ignoring the man's protests, he opened the door and stood up into the flood, instantly soaked by water as warm as a tepid shower. He reached into the car—his bruised ribs bitching—slung their one backpack over his shoulder, and grabbed the child, lifting her out into the torrent, holding her to him as he weaved through the cars, their wipers mewling and ticking as they flailed at the rain, avoiding the bikes that zipped like wasps between the stalled vehicles, their riders swaddled in pink plastic ponchos, and found the covered sidewalk.

Suzie was spitting water, her hair plastered to her forehead, her eyes wide. He set the girl down on the sidewalk and crouched beside her.

"You okay?"

She nodded.

He stood and took her hand and led her into an alley crammed with tiny stores, most of them selling dirt-cheap knockoffs of Western designer brands.

"Why don't you find some clothes you like?" he said.

"Girl stuff?"

"Yeah, girl stuff."

She didn't crack a smile but she nodded, and he followed her through the maze of stores, where she selected or spurned garments with the practiced eye of a Bloomingdale's fashion buyer.

Watching her while she was being fawned over by two very made-up Thai shopgirls who chirped like caged birds, Hook bought a burner phone.

When she'd filled two bags with clothes, Suzie looked across at him and nodded. "I'm done," she said.

On their way back to the street, they passed a noodle bar and Hook pushed the door open, ushering the child into the frigid interior.

He waved a hand at the waiter and ordered steamy noodle broth for them both. When the man left, Hook pointed toward the restrooms.

"You want to go and change into some new clothes?"

Suzie nodded.

"Need me to come along?"

She shook her head and slid from the booth, carrying one of the bags of clothes.

Suzie returned a few minutes later wearing jeans embroidered with butterflies and flowers, a brightly patterned shirt, and pink high-top sneakers. With her short hair and huge eyes she looked beautiful and vulnerable and he had to resist the impulse to hug her.

She sat facing him. "I put the boy clothes in the bag. Is that okay?"

"Yeah," he said. "We'll dump them."

"So I'm not going to be a boy again?"

"No, never."

"Where are we going, Grandpa?"

"We'll stay here in Bangkok while I fix things, then we'll see."

The steaming noodles arrived and Suzie took a sip, set down her spoon and didn't lift it again, her eyes on the teeming sidewalk. Hook was hungry and, feeling somehow ashamed, emptied his bowl.

"Eat some more," he said.

She shook her head and looked up at him. "Grandpa?"

"Yes."

"Do you believe in heaven?"

"Yes, I believe in heaven," he said, even though he did not. He was more of a hell man.

"Do you think Mommy's there?"

He found a smile and said, "Yes, she's there. She's definitely in heaven."

Suzie stared at him and then subsided into silence again, looking out at the street.

Hook, a man who had traded in lies for most of his life, was having his first brush with real innocence and he found it disquieting.

The rain stopped with the suddenness of the tropics, the sun already blasting through clouds that evaporated like cotton candy.

Hook left money on the table and stood. The child followed and they went out onto the sidewalk. Pedestrians were shedding raincoats and furling their umbrellas, and stall holders were removing plastic covers from their tables of clothes and trinkets.

The traffic was moving again, in the sluggish way of Bangkok.

Hook flagged down a cab and gave the driver the address of a hotel, a huge, impersonal monolith in Pratunam. It was a favorite destination of package tourists, fleets of giant buses seething and hissing as they disgorged rumpled travelers outside the lobby. A middle-aged *farang* and a child would raise no eyebrows.

Hook checked in using a fake passport that he'd held onto from his operational days. It was good enough to fool desk clerks, but he'd need something better to travel on.

They took the elevator up to their tenth floor room. Two double beds side by side. A giant TV. A view over the sprawling city.

Suzie lay down on the bed farthest from the window, curled into a ball, and fell asleep.

Hook showered away the last few nightmare days, inspected his ribs—a mottled yellow-blue—and dressed in fresh clothes. He sat a while on the bed by the window and watched the child sleep, her face almost peaceful in repose, only the spasming of her fingers hinting at her distress.

Hook left the room and went up to the business center on the top floor of the hotel. It sported a couple of elderly desktop computers and a printer. The place was deserted in the age of tablets and smartphones.

He took a seat and googled Suzie's grandparents, the parents of her dead father. The only family Suzie had left, other than Hook, and he didn't count. A dubiously dry alcoholic. A man on the run from himself. He was not parent material.

Hook would get Suzie to the Houranis. That would be his mission. He would leave her where she would be safe and loved.

That's what he told himself, anyway, as he tapped at the keyboard.

It didn't take him long to find them.

Omar Hourani had died of a heart attack weeks after his son was blown to pieces in Pakistan and Fatima Hourani had lost a lengthy battle with cancer three months ago.

Hook closed his eyes and ran a hand through his hair.

Jesus.

He erased Google's search history and left the business center. As he walked back toward the bank of elevators, he passed a cocktail bar, dim and inviting, the only direct light falling on the bottles behind the bar, like a shrine.

A woman with long black hair, sitting alone on a stool and drinking a cocktail, looked up at him and smiled. That smile breathed life into something he'd thought long dead and Hook hesitated for only a moment before he walked into the bar.

He returned the woman's smile and got as far as ordering a Cutty Sark when he glimpsed his reflection behind the booze bottles and he fled for the elevators, jabbing at the button like a Vegas slots junkie. The car arrived and he stepped inside, confronted by a tribe of Harry Hooks in the mirrored interior. Turning his back, he stood watching the green lights that charted his descent.

EIGHTY-SEVEN

Congressman Antoine Mosley, a gym bag slung over one massive shoulder, entered his office in the Longworth Building and found his chief of staff, Tommy Poster, pacing the carpet, muttering into his cell phone, scratching at a bald head so cratered and grooved it looked like he wore his brain on the outside.

Mosley had showered at the Capitol gym after his morning weight workout—he could bench-press three hundred pounds—and came in feeling like a fuckin warrior god, ready to drop-kick ass over the Potomac.

He famously lived in his office—the *New York Times* had photographed him inflating an air mattress beside his desk—and had built a makeshift kitchen in a small windowless room on the opposite side of the corridor, outfitted with a plug-in cooker and crammed with a supply of peanut butter, creatine shakes, and whey protein energy drinks.

"I'm not a creature of DC," he'd told the reporter from the *Times*, "and every morning when I wake up on the floor of my office I am reminded that my home is not here, it's back in my district with my people. The people who sent me to Washington to do their work."

And it was nobody's damn business how many nights a week he spent in the Chevy Chase apartment of a pneumatic lobbyist his grandmother would've described as "high yellow."

Poster ended the call and leaned against a tufted leather club chair and stared at Mosley. He raised his left hand, fingers clawed and said, "Fan," simultaneously raising his right hand and holding it in opposition to his left as he said, "Shit."

Then he mashed his hands together.

Mosley lowered his backside onto the corner of his wooden desk and said, "You gonna stand there and be all fuckin mysterious and performance-arty or are you gonna tell me wassup?"

Poster lifted his iPad from the chair and swiped at the face.

Mosley held up a paw like a peckerwood cop at a roadblock. "Now don't you go all fuckin YouTubey on me. Brief me, motherfucker. Brief me."

Poster crossed his arms and said, "Lucien Benway was found dead at his Georgetown town house this morning. He'd gassed himself in his car."

"Jesus."

"There's more."

"Of course there is," Mosley said, all street gone from his voice, sounding like what he was: an Ivy League lawyer with things on his mind.

"The black box from AirStar Flight 2605 has been found."

"Interesting timing."

"Yes."

"And?"

"Pilot error. There was a failure of the onboard computer. The copilot took over the controls and put the plane into a stall from which it never recovered. The investigation is ongoing and there'll still be an official report, but ..." Poster shrugged.

"I've been played like a cheap banjo?"

"Yes. Your enemies are already making a lot of noise. There's talk of you witch-hunting an innocent man to his death."

"Lucien Benway could never be described as innocent."

"In general terms, no. But as far as AirStar Flight 2605 goes ..." Poster raised his palms to the ceiling. "Anyway, you're being accused of trying to discredit the administration with baseless and inaccurate assertions."

"And my friends? What are they saying?"

"What friends?" Poster shook his pitted head. "I hear from the Speaker's office that he'll be addressing the press within the hour and he'll say you acted unilaterally and in your own interests rather than the party's. He's already called your accusations," Poster consulted his iPad, "'A farrago of nonsense contradicted by inconvenient facts and simple common sense.'"

"Well, at least he didn't call it an imbroglio," Mosley said with an empty laugh. "Okay, so we've got a fight on our hands?"

"Yes. The media is all over me for a statement from you. I'm suggesting we 'no comment' them for now."

"Have you ever heard me use those two words?"

"Not consecutively, no."

"Don't be a smart-ass."

"Then what do you want me to tell them, sir?"

Mosley sat up straight, swelled his barrel chest and said, "You tell them no *motherfuckin* comment."

EIGHTY-EIGHT

Another taxi. Another traffic jam. This time on Wireless Road in Bangkok's swish Lumpini district, home to embassies and the opulent shopping precincts that were evidence of booming Thailand's Rising Tiger economy.

Hook sat in the back of the cab beside the kid, sweating in the afternoon heat that overwhelmed the air conditioner, dying for a smoke, a drink—Jesus, anything to get him through the next few minutes.

"Where are we going, Grandpa?" Suzie asked.

"We'll be there soon," he said, deflecting.

She looked at him and, heartbreakingly, took his hand, and he knew just how Judas must've felt.

Hook didn't have it in him to withdraw his hand but he couldn't meet her eyes and looked out the window as the taxi trundled past a ridiculous mall—all towering *campanili* and soaring *belvederi*—built to realize some Asian developer's Italianate wet dream.

When Hook had returned to the hotel room from the business center he'd found the girl still sleeping. He'd opened the refrigerator and, looking past the chorus line of little booze bottles that had winked and waved at him, lifted out a can of Coke and cracked the tab, feeling the fizzy bubbles on his face as he'd taken a sip.

Hook sat at the desk and used the remote to switch on the TV, keeping the volume low. He surfed until he got CNN and watched in amazement as a reporter stood outside Lucien Benway's house and spoke of the little troll's death. A death that was being called a suicide, though Hook couldn't see it. The reporter called Lucien an innocent man, which made Hook laugh.

He had a sudden flash of Dudley Morse, unbound from his creator, adrift on an ice floe, sailing to his end like Frankenstein's monster.

A White House spokesman, a youngish man with a sharp haircut and a Harvard accent, appeared on the screen.

"Even in this era of conspiracy theorists," he said in the voice of privilege, "accidents *do* happen. And it was an accident that caused the crash of AirStar Flight 2605. A tragic accident, but still an accident, that claimed the lives of one hundred and seventy-one people, including Kate Swift and her daughter, Susan."

Hook killed the tube and sat watching the child sleep. He was watching her but seeing her mother, and an image came to him, an image from some fantastical parallel reality: his toddler daughter running in the snow, wearing a jumpsuit of a red so deep that when her little legs faltered and she fell, she looked like a bloodstain, and he saw his younger self lifting her against a Kodachrome-blue sky as she giggled through a beard of snowflakes.

Hook rose from the chair and hurried to the window, letting the hard sunlight burn away all remnants of the absurd daydream and when he felt tears in his eyes, he told himself they came from the glare, not from self-pity, but he knew he had to act.

Fast.

He returned to the desk, found a sheaf of hotel stationary and a pen and he wrote everything he could about who the child was and who her mother had been and folded the pages and sealed them in a yellow envelope.

Then he'd dumped out the contents of the backpack and filled it with the new clothes he'd bought for the child earlier.

Hook had shaken her awake and said, "Come on, kiddo. Let's go do some sightseeing."

If she'd wondered why they were taking the backpack, she hadn't asked.

The taxi pulled up outside the sprawling wedding cake that was the US Embassy, the boom at the gate manned by Thai cops and a contingent of Marines in their khaki shirts and black-and-white peaked caps.

Hook had been there many times in his operational days, his last visit more than a decade ago to placate the ambassador who had been embarrassed when it was leaked that Lucien Benway—without troubling the Thai government for their permission—had set up a so-called black site in the country's northern province of Udon Thani to torture an al-Qaeda nabob who'd been renditioned from Malaysia.

The highlight of the meeting had been when Hook had to explain to the ambassador—those were more innocent times—that waterboarding wasn't a form of aquatic recreation, but was, rather, one of Benway's "enhanced interrogation techniques."

Glory days.

Hook opened the door and stepped out into the heat, carrying the backpack with him. He gestured for Suzie to follow.

She stood looking up at Hook as he slung the pack from her shoulders, removed the yellow envelope from his shirt pocket, handed it to her and pointed to the stairs leading to the consular and American citizen services office.

"You take this letter and you go up those stairs and you tell the people inside who you are and you give it to them, okay?"

"Aren't you coming with me, Grandpa?"

His voice was missing in action so he just shook his head and then turned and climbed back into the taxi, slamming the door.

The child ran to the cab and slapped the closed window, crying, calling his name.

"Go," Hook said to the driver. The man's dark eyes regarded him in the rearview. "Go! Get me the fuck out of here!"

The taxi accelerated and Hook looked back and saw Suzie sprinting after the car, shouting his name, and then she stopped running and her cries faded and when the cab changed lanes she was lost from view.

EIGHTY-NINE

When Nadja Benway, wheeling a small Louis Vuitton suitcase, approached the front door of the town house, a towering young man with buzzed hair, his muscular body fighting to free itself from his dark suit, stood in her way, thick hands clasped before him.

"Please step aside," she said.

"I'm afraid I can't, ma'am," he said.

"Do you want me to scream?" she asked, looking past him at the baying media who were being held in check by the chunky man's cookie-cutter cousins.

These men had invaded her house within minutes of her calling 911 to report the death of Lucien, flashing badges that identified them as agents of the FBI and the Department of Homeland Security.

She'd sat at the kitchen table, still in her dressing gown and pajamas—the ankle monitor covered by the flannel pants—doing her finest impersonation of a grieving widow and told of how she'd come down in the morning to look for her husband. When she'd seen his coat hanging in the hall but no sign of him she'd looked in the garage, where she'd found him slumped dead in the rear of the car, its engine still idling.

At this she'd produced honest-to-god tears and had to wipe her eyes and blow her nose on a paper towel.

Once their questions were done, they let her go to her room upstairs where she stood at her closet and weighed her options.

She made her selection and laid her clothes out on the bedspread: a crème silk blouse with long sleeves, a very plain black skirt, and a charcoal cashmere cardigan. A pair of burgundy penny loafers, the leather newly buffed, stood by the bed.

It was time to remove the ankle monitor.

Nadja lifted her foot onto the vanity stool and took a pair of scissors to the band, amazed at how easily the blades carved through the rubber. She tossed the ugly thing into the trash, unconcerned about what the spooks would make of it when they scoured her bedroom, as they undoubtedly would.

After she dressed, she sat at her mirror and arranged her hair in a chignon and applied only a little lipstick and just a hint of Samsara behind her ears and on her pulse points. She checked her hands—the ring finger tellingly bare—to see that the muted sage nail varnish hadn't suffered damage during last night's high jinks.

Satisfied with her appearance, she looked up the number of *Vanity Fair* magazine in New York, dialed it on her cell phone, and asked to speak to the editor.

A bored-sounding woman asked who was calling.

When Nadja identified herself, the woman sounded a lot less bored and told her she'd get him out of a meeting.

Nadja sat smoking while she waited, listening the men tearing Lucien's office apart. It had taken time and effort for them to penetrate the door.

Earlier, Nadja had considered which of the media to talk to. Certainly, she could have commanded any one of the hacks downstairs to do her bidding if she'd chosen, but she knew it was time to be strategic. Time to secure her future.

She was beautiful.

She was mysterious.

She was the very recent widow of a deliciously Machiavellian little toad.

She was *made* for *Vanity Fair*.

"Mrs. Benway," the editor said in his smooth, unplaceable accent. "May we express our condolences? We've just heard the news."

"Thank you," she said. "And please, call me Nadja."

"So, Nadja, you must have quite a story …"

"What do they say? Stories happen only to people who can tell them."

He chuckled before saying, "Forgive me for being indelicate, Nadja, but you haven't yet spoken to anyone else in the media, have you?"

"No, my dear, my pearls are reserved for a very high class of swine."

He had the good grace to laugh and then handed her over to a lackey who took care of her flight details to New York and a reservation at Soho House.

She ended the call and sat on the bed, seeing her life spooling out ahead of her.

The *Vanity Fair* piece would inevitably lead to a book deal, and the television appearances she would make to publicize her memoir would ensure a profitable future of minor celebrity.

This was, after all, only her due.

She'd earned it.

Nadja had carried the Louis Vuitton down to the kitchen, removed her charcoal of the peasant girl from the wall and zipped it away in the suitcase that held just a few of her things. There wasn't much she wanted. Most of it would only serve to remind her of her lost years with Lucien.

She'd walked to the door where she now stood and looked up into the eyes of the hefty young man and said, "I mean it. If you don't let me pass I shall scream."

"Let her go," a voice said, and she saw a blunt-faced man with lifeless white hair standing in the doorway to the living room.

The thug stepped aside and Nadja walked out into the biting cold, a low gray sky perched like a lid atop the cluster of row houses, to her waiting cab. She welcomed the catcalls of the media with their thrusting microphones and bursting flashbulbs and whirring video cameras, knowing that rather than robbing her of something, they were *giving* to her, adding to her notoriety, adding to her cachet.

Adding to her bankability.

NINETY

In the taxi, fleeing the child, a cold hand reached in from nowhere and took hold of Hook's heart and squeezed it until he couldn't breathe, until he could barely find the air to lean forward and say to the driver, "Stop. Stop the car."

Fighting the door open, he threw money at the man, stepping out into a wall of heat and gasoline fumes that almost knocked him to the blacktop, dodging cars and bikes as he ran in a lurching lope back toward the embassy, his lungs aflame, his bruised ribs screaming, sweat stinging his eyes, certain that Suzie would be gone. But he found her sitting on the sidewalk, crying, still clutching the yellow envelope, a Thai policeman and a couple of passersby standing over her.

Hook, sweating, drinking thick air, lifted the girl, hugging her to him as he found enough breath to smooth things over with the cop. He waved down another cab and bundled her inside. Suzie didn't look at him as they drove away, just sat hunched and crying, crying for what he had done, sure, but crying too from way more fear and sorrow than a kid her age should have ever had to know.

He patted his pockets for a tissue but came up empty and she wiped her nose on her sleeve and turned her face away from him and closed her eyes and fell asleep—or at least, pretended to.

It was suddenly gloomy and it started to rain softly, car headlights reflected in the wet streets, and the traffic was as slow as mud.

Hook sat hypnotized by the patter of the rain, the hiss of the AC and snatches of Thai pop music wafting in from adjacent cars, and only when a barefoot old monk in saffron robes begging alms from the pedestrians overtook the taxi did he realize they weren't moving at all.

That was okay. He had nowhere to go.

As he watched vivid bursts of neon blooming across the *Blade Runner* skyline, Hook tried to conjure a plan.

A way forward.

He could not, and a rush of panic took him low.

Then, when he closed his eyes and tried to calm himself, he saw a face, the pink, closely barbered face of the one man who could grant Kate Swift's wish for her child, and as Hook opened his eyes, blinking, a string of numerals coiled from somewhere deep in his memory and took the form of a long-forgotten telephone number.

Mistrustful of the provenance of the number—and doubting its currency—Hook punched it into his cell phone and listened to a purr that went unanswered for an eternity before he heard a flat Midwestern voice say, "Yes?"

"This is Harry Hook."

A beat and then the Plumber said, "Harry, it's been a long time."

"Yes."

"Where are you?"

"I'm in Bangkok," Hook said.

"The hottest city in the world, or so I'm told."

"I have Kate Swift's daughter with me. Susan."

There was a longer pause. "And what of Kate?" the Plumber asked.

"That's for another conversation."

"What do you want, Harry?"

"We want a lot of things."

The Plumber sighed. "Yes, I'll bet you do."

"First of all, we want to come home."

"Do you now?"

"Yes."

"So it's a happy ending you're writing then, Harry?"

"Well, we're American. Happy endings are our national belief."

The Plumber chuckled, a dry sound like rice being sieved, and they talked for a few more minutes before Hook ended the call.

He looked at the child beside him and reached out a tentative hand, his fingertips touching her upturned palm. When his granddaughter's fingers tightened on his and she opened her eyes and stared at him, Hook thought about fate and the laws of chance and how everything that can happen will happen.

THE END